PoppyHarp

PoppyHarp

Simon Avery

BLACK
SHUCK
BOOKS

First published in Great Britain in 2024 by
Black Shuck Books
Kent, UK

Set in Caslon by WHITEspace
www.white-space.uk

Cover and interior layout © WHITEspace, 2024

978-1-917173-03-2

For Chris and Joel
'By the time you look again, it's become a memory.'
I miss you both.

Once upon a time, not so very long ago, in a lonely old house in the countryside, there was a little girl called Imogen.

Every day she climbed upstairs to the top of the house.

At the top of the house was an attic, and in that attic was a doll's house.

And in that doll's house lived a great many things.

Old things, lost things, forgotten things.

One of those things was Florian. He was a rabbit who wore a rather grand top hat and a waistcoat.

There was magic in that doll's house. Every time Imogen sat down in the lonely attic to play, she said, 'Take me Elsewhere!', and the house grew tall and grand around her.

Then Florian would take Imogen by the hand and whisk her away on a great many adventures, leaving a trail of buttons so that they could find their way home every day.

This is the story of their adventures…

Prologue

Summer 1973

With the benefit of hindsight, I see that PoppyHarp was as much a part of Oliver's life as he was Malcolm's, perhaps even before the two men met. Indeed, I like to think that PoppyHarp was there in the shadows when Oliver and his daughter, Imogen, arrived at my children's home in the summer of 1973. I was seven at the time. I'd been placed in the care home after my mother had died; a brain hemorrhage while she was buying perfume in Boots. She was dead before the ambulance arrived. I'd sat at her side, bewildered and weeping inconsolably, clutching her hand until someone pulled us apart. After that I was immediately at the mercy of the system. I had no relatives who would care for me. My father had never been in the picture; he'd abandoned my mother soon after she discovered she was pregnant. A social worker with a well-clipped beard and a bright pullover arrived a few days after my mother had died. He had a terse manner; he was ill-equipped to deal with kids, probably only about 21 himself. He seemed much older at the time. I was a quiet, slightly withdrawn child, so losing my mother and the stability of my home, the familiarity of my bedroom, the kitchen table where I did my homework, only exacerbated my reticence around people.

The home was a faded Georgian townhouse in a state of eternal disrepair. Margaret and Anneka, the two women who ran it, had worked all their lives in the system. They were part of the cohort of war widows and those left unmarried by the shortage of men following the Second World War who had found employment and residence by taking up jobs in children's homes. The system was changing by the early seventies, and would eventually be open to all kinds of abuse, but Margaret and Anneka were resolutely part of the old guard. They took all of us lost and troubled children in and administered to each of us without a moment of impatience or a cross word.

For the first couple of weeks in the home I reluctantly took part in group activities and went to school as if nothing had happened, but spent most of my time in the bedroom I shared with another young boy called Jason. The only familiar things I had left were my books. I read them and re-read them. I didn't sleep much. At night I stared up at the dusty ceiling, listening to the broken tap dripping into the sink beside my bed, and to Jason, crying in his sleep. He had lost both of his parents in a car accident. I wanted to comfort him somehow, but I was grieving too, and I had no idea how to navigate my way through it all, either together or alone. I had photos of my mother stuck to the wall beside my bed but I found it difficult to look at them for too long. It felt like something fundamental had left my life, and that void would never be filled again.

And then one day Oliver and Imogen Frayling arrived. Jason came hurrying upstairs that afternoon, breathless with excitement. "Noah," he said, his errant fringe falling in his eyes. "They're here! Imogen and Florian and all of the others. They're *right here!*"

I'd watched the first couple of episodes of *The Adventure of Imogen and Florian* from my mother's bed while she was still alive. She'd had a portable black and white TV in her room. You had to get out of bed to twist the aerial in order to retrieve the wayward TV signal. But that show, it was imbued with a curious magic. Imogen was a little girl who would go upstairs into the attic of her rambling, sepia-tinted home to play with a doll's house. A faded old rabbit called Florian would take her by the hand and she would shrink down and go on adventures in the doll's house with him. The animals were animated by stop-motion photography. Oliver Frayling had created the show single-handedly before selling it to the BBC. He was the writer and the narrator and had spent a year on the painstaking process of filming the twelve episodes. It hadn't exactly set the television firmament alight, but to a certain kind of child there was something deeply appealing about the world he had created; a kind of ramshackle charm, threaded with a gently surreal melancholy. It exerted a curious pull of nostalgia when I watched it, for something that was already long gone by the time it appeared.

I'd continued to watch the show at the home; some of the other children had gradually joined me but they later claimed that Florian, a partly taxidermied rabbit with dirty white gloves and a threadbare top hat, had given them nightmares. He had a slightly sad, pinched face, with a chisel of dirty teeth in his grey muzzle. The other animals had a similar shop-worn appearance. For me the slightly sinister aspect was part of its charm, but I could see why it had caused so many sleepless nights.

Nonetheless, Margaret and Anneka agreed to Oliver and Imogen Frayling making the home one of the stops on their short tour to promote their show. Oliver didn't immediately fill any of us with confidence, with his National Health spectacles, his long, out of shape pullover, and his prematurely grey hair. He had the uncomfortable stoop of a man who'd been apologetically tall from an early age. Old before his time, although he would have only just turned 30 at that point. In one hand was the holdall filled with the characters from *The Adventures of Imogen and Florian*, and in the other was his daughter, Imogen. She was nine at the time. When I was 24 I would meet her again and we would fall in love. But on that day in 1973 she didn't seem to fit in this space. She was the girl from the television; it had never occurred to me that she actually existed anywhere else but in that house with those sad old toys. Yet here she was, slightly hesitant but generous with her smiles. She had grey eyes, bitten fingernails and hair tied up into a tight ponytail. She was wearing some faded jeans. I remember that detail quite clearly. I was used to seeing her in a laced Edwardian dress and candy-striped tights. This air of modernity was a disconcerting, yet slightly thrilling modification. She was a *real, living girl*. At the age of seven, I was vaguely aware that *The Adventures of Imogen and Florian* was a children's television programme, but part of me had difficulty adjusting. Losing my mother had taken all of my thoughts and feelings and left my attention diffuse; the show with the little girl and the rabbit had become an almost necessary weekly escape hatch when it was all too much for me. I fled inside it readily. Part of me didn't want it to be *just a show*.

But then Oliver unpacked the holdall and placed the toys onto the dining table while we watched. Here was Antoine, the tatty old rat in a fez, Fizbatch, the

monkey with cymbals, and finally Florian, resplendent
in his waistcoat and top hat. Assembled on the table
in that draughty front room with the shadows of
afternoon creeping into the high ceilings, they looked
even more sad and careworn than they did on the
television. Being here robbed them of their magic
somehow; I remember that notion creeping up on me
that day, the sense that this little enchantment was
being taken from me too, and all that was left was a
slightly diffident man with nothing but lifeless toys
and a daughter whom he treated very much like an
employee. We all stood staring at Oliver for a while.
He seemed deeply reluctant but I assume he'd already
done this sort of thing before. The BBC had probably
encouraged him to tour the schools and children's
homes to drum up interest in his show. But Oliver was
not a man with the wherewithal to regard children
as children. He simply spoke to them as adults and
then grew impatient if you didn't keep up. It wasn't his
fault. He'd somehow missed that essential component
of fatherhood while he was away in his cowshed,
making puppets and stories and bringing them, frame
by painstaking frame, to life.

Jason, the boy I shared a room with, made the
cardinal error of finally giving in to temptation and
reached out across the table to touch Florian.

"Don't *touch* it!" Oliver snapped. He stepped
forward, about to snatch Jason's hand away, and then
thought better of it at the last moment. Margaret
and Anneka bristled briefly but held their tongues.
"They're *delicate*," he said gently to Jason. "Delicate.
I'll let you touch them later, with supervision."

Jason's face clouded and tears brimmed in his eyes.
He turned away before anyone could see. Someone

else took his place while he fled to a corner to cry. It wasn't anything new to me. I listened to him weeping every night, whimpering for his lost parents. He didn't grasp that I felt the same as he did, but I didn't have it in me to cry. Now we were familiar enough with each other, he often stood next to my bed and asked if he could get in beside me. I'd lift up the sheets and move over to accommodate him, eventually whispering made-up stories until he fell asleep again.

Oliver talked about the show for a while. He had some index cards that he referred to every now and then. He'd keep shuffling them with his shaking hands, talking quickly to no one in particular. I sat down next to Imogen, glancing nervously at her from the corner of my eye. She seemed much older than me, although there were only two years difference. She seemed quite content to sit and talk to the younger children with a kindness and an assuredness and that her father lacked. "What's your name?" she asked me while Oliver spoke to the children.

"Noah," I said to my hands.

"Do you like them?" she said, indicating Florian and Antoine and Fizbatch.

"Yes, I do."

"Do you watch it?" she said. "Our show?"

"Yes."

"What's your favourite thing about it?"

"I don't really know."

"There must be *something*. *One* thing. Go on, tell me."

I was embarrassed to say it, but when I glanced at her, she leaned forward and smiled to encourage me. "I like that you're not scared," I said. "I didn't realise you had a dad. I just thought you were alone. I thought you were brave, shrinking down and going on adventures in the dolls' house."

"Do you think you would be that brave if you had been in my place?"

"I don't know." I paused and glanced across at Jason, sitting alone, wiping at his eyes. "I don't feel very brave."

"I bet you are," Imogen said. She smiled at me. "I think you all must be very brave indeed."

I nodded, unconvinced.

"What do you like to do here?" she asked. "I imagine you must get up to all sorts of activities and games."

I shrugged. "Mostly I like to read."

"Oh, me too!" Imogen said, her face lighting up. "Look, I have a book with me." She produced a battered paperback copy of *Alice's Adventures in Wonderland*. "Have you read this?"

There were enticing illustrations inside that book; the promise of a strange world, tilted away from this one. A little girl falling down a rabbit hole, a frantic white rabbit, a grinning cat, a mad hatter and a march hare. I could immediately see the similarities between this book and Oliver's TV show.

"My dad gave it to me when I started to show an interest in reading," Imogen said. "It was his favourite book when he was a child. I think it's mine too."

Sensing he was losing the crowd, Imogen said to her father, "Say the introduction to the show, Dad. I'm sure the boys and girls would love to hear it."

Oliver looked doubtful, but he shuffled the cards and when he found what he was looking for he began. "Once upon a time, not so very long ago, in a lonely old house in the countryside, there was a little girl called Imogen. Every day she climbed upstairs to the top of the house. At the top of the house was an attic, and in that attic was a doll's house. And in that doll's house lived a great many things. *Old* things, *lost* things, *forgotten* things…"

It had the requisite effect. Suddenly there was some of that magical allure conjured out of language and into the room. Like a magic spell. Oliver's voice, when it spoke these familiar words, was a deliciously vertiginous thing: authoritative, house-masterly, and aching with melancholy. Perhaps I'm placing all of these feelings there, after the fact as a product of longing for something of my childhood, fraught though it was. Perhaps it was PoppyHarp's doing. A brittle little enchantment on his behalf to get the children on side.

Oliver finally capitulated afterwards, and allowed the children to sit next to him and look more closely at Florian, Antoine and Fizbatch, the old, lost and forgotten things. He called Jason over and placed Florian on the boy's lap. Jason glanced nervously up at him. "Go on then," Oliver said. Jason ran his fingers over the rabbit's rough fur and his stiff whiskers. "He was a real rabbit once, you know," Oliver said, but none of us really understood that. In our minds he was a real rabbit *now*, although admittedly robbed of some of his magic this afternoon. When we next watched him on television, that enchantment would be wholly restored.

The children took it in turns sitting with Oliver, holding the old toys under his watchful but increasingly avuncular supervision. He'd softened, glancing across at Margaret and Anneka for approbation. I think the gradual realisation of our individual plights brought out the hidden father in him.

Later, when it was my turn, I sat down between Oliver and Imogen and quietly examined each of the toys in turn. I expected that at any moment one of them would blink and notice the time, and hurry away from us like that sleepy rabbit in Imogen's book. I stared at them, placed a finger on Florian's beady eyes, but he didn't blink. He smelled old and musty, like the dog we'd had when my mother was alive. Her name was Molly. I had no idea what had happened to her after I'd been moved to the home. I missed that dog almost as much as my mother sometimes. Often, I dreamed of them both and woke in the night, feeling that keen sense of loss all over again. So I tried to stay awake as much as I could. Even now, fifty years and change later, I still have trouble sleeping.

"Noah likes to read," Imogen said to her father, as if by way of introduction.

"That's very good," Oliver said. "Books have been one of the great pleasures of my life, Noah. Without them I wouldn't have ever begun to write myself."

"What do you write?" I asked.

"Well, I wrote *The Adventures of Imogen and Florian*." Oliver glanced uncertainly at his daughter, aware that some of the younger children didn't understand this concept. They had no idea that the man who'd accompanied Imogen and Florian today was also the creator of this world which took them away from their lives for a while. They may have recognised his voice from the opening narration, but otherwise he meant very little to them. At the age of seven I had only a very faint grasp of the idea that my favourite TV show was in some way *made* by someone, fished from their imaginations onto the page and, in turn, onto the screen.

"I like the stories best," I said. "They're like dreams. It's like *anything* can happen."

Oliver smiled, visibly moved. It was the plainest of compliments, but coming from a child it seemed to mean much more to him. This was why he'd created the show in the first place. "Do you think *you* would like to write stories one day?" he asked.

"I don't know," I said. "Sometimes I make them up to make Jason feel better." I lowered my voice so that no one else would hear. "Sometimes he cries in bed, so I tell him stories to help him go to sleep."

"Poor Jason," Imogen said, glancing across at him. He was playing with some of the other children now on the other side of the room, the earlier drama forgotten.

"The thing with writing is that you don't need many materials to do it. Just a pen and some paper," Oliver said. "And your imagination, of course. The thing is, time flies by when you make stories up, Noah. And you can get lost in them if they're good enough. Like this one—" He gestured to Imogen's dog-eared copy of *Alice's Adventures in Wonderland*. "I first read it when I was your age. I must have read it hundreds of times since then."

"What should I write?" I asked him.

He puffed out his cheeks. He'd initial diffidence was long forgotten at this point. "Absolutely *anything*, Noah. They always say 'write what you know'. You could write about your life here with the other children, for instance, but then you could discover a magical rabbit that comes to life, or a secret door behind the wardrobe that leads to Elsewhere. *Anything* you want could happen."

We talked for another half an hour like that. I think it dawned on Oliver that what he said to a child at that crucial age could matter an enormous amount; it could change their direction and shed light in an otherwise darkened world. And for me at least, it did.

They left at five that afternoon. They seemed to take the light with them. Soon it was evening and we were returned to our routines. School the next day. Another night of listening to Jason cry himself to sleep. But after dinner, I found some paper and a pen and went upstairs to my room. I intended to get started on writing down some of the stories I'd made up for Jason. I was quietly surprised to find Imogen's copy of *Alice's Adventures in Wonderland* on my bedside table.

Inside Oliver had written:

Dear Noah,

This is for you. I promised I'd buy Imogen a new copy!

I hope you enjoy Alice's adventures as much as Imogen and I do. We hope you make up your own worlds too. Sometimes it starts with a trail of buttons, and before you know it, you're Elsewhere!

Regards,
Oliver

Part One

Old Things,
Lost Things,
Forgotten Things

One

"Noah?" she said. "Oh, my God, it *is* you."

I looked up from the pile of books on the table, my fountain pen poised over the page. After an hour of continually scratching out my name, I was, if I'm being honest, a little bit on autopilot. This had been the shape of my days for almost six months now. A multitude of strangers with smiling faces, their bodies trembling with anticipation. They would shake my hand and thrust their well-worn books at me, tell me *their* stories. I cared, but part of me was still thinking about Abigail Walker, and I hadn't written anything of substance for almost a year. I wanted to give every one of these people a little of my time but I was *so* tired.

And then there she was. "Imogen," I said, before I was certain it was actually her. I felt like I was falling backwards. A sudden, sweet vertigo.

It's jarring, holding the memory of someone in your head from a different time, and then seeing the reality of how the years have accumulated, taking them away from that person and turning them into someone who only vaguely resembles that memory. I only had to look in the mirror to be reminded of *that* particular fact. Imogen's long grey hair was tied up in a bun. Spectacles on the bridge of her nose. Those gentle grey eyes. A face that I'd lost myself to all those years ago. It felt like a lifetime's distance from me.

I did the maths. She was Imogen at 55. But in my memory, she was Imogen at nine when I'd first met her, and at 26 when I'd loved her.

I dropped my pen and stood, hurried around the table to embrace her. At that point the line had dwindled to six or seven people, each of them clutching copies of the new paperback, some tatty copies of the old ones. I had a good crowd; they seemed prepared to indulge me in this brief distraction.

I walked into Imogen's arms like a starving man at a feast. Her smell was a time machine. By the time I finally relinquished her I was already stranded twenty-nine years in the past.

I was 24 when I met Imogen for the second time. She was two years older than me. It took a week or so for me to realise that the woman I was falling in love with was Oliver Frayling's daughter, whom I'd first met when I was seven. We didn't talk about that. Imogen didn't want to speak about her father at all; over the years there had been a rift. Her parents had separated, and she barely spoke to her father. I quickly learned not to bring up my memory of that day when they'd visited the children's home, as sweet and treasured as it was for me.

Imogen had rented a flat in Worcester that she'd filled with second-hand furniture, frayed Persian rugs, old records and books. A *lot* of books. Imogen had a short fuse then; quick to lust and temper, usually in that order. She was smarter than me, harboured strong opinions on everything; loved to argue the point into submission. She was rarely wrong. We listened to music, we talked about books, we fucked and we fought, repeated the process. We went to a couple of music festivals that first summer in her battered old Mini Cooper. Sometimes one of the front wheels would fall off without warning. She never got it looked at. It added an unnecessary sense of peril to every journey we took. I suppose I never really got to know Imogen; at that age I barely understood myself. It took us a couple of years to grasp that there were aspects of our personalities that, when combined, were combustible. It made the late-night conversations fascinating and the sex unforgettable, but it wasn't enough. In those two years we broke up a couple of times and then drifted back to each other, attracted by something that we couldn't quite define at the time. We were aware that we loved each other, but we knew it couldn't last. Not then.

Although Imogen knew of my writing career, she was unaware that I was selling enough books to merit readings to sold-out theatres and tours across the UK and the US. And here I was in Foyles in London, on the same weekend she'd managed to get away for a rare break from the particular stresses of her life. I wondered what it meant, if anything, this little moment of kismet. We'd wandered so far from each other. Later I discovered that she'd texted a friend on the train home after meeting me. The friend had asked how I looked after all this time. *Just three words will do*, she'd texted. It was a little game they had. After a moment's reflection, Imogen had responded: *Beard. Grey. Sad.*

Standing near her in the bookshop while strangers stared at us, I was seeing our past replayed in brief, rose-tinted moments: Imogen in a summer dress, her hair bleached by the sun, leaning back on the bonnet of that clapped-out old Mini Cooper, feeling the warm skin of her thighs beneath my palms; arguing in a pub in Stratford-Upon-Avon and driving home in silence; sleeping in the car in a lay-by in Cardiff when we'd gotten too tired to make the journey home; barefoot on a hill in Worcester at midnight, stoned and singing and laughing our arses off; Imogen as a little girl, showing a lonely boy her *Alice in Wonderland* book... I saw us as we were, not as we are. There's a strange alchemy to our memories; they're entirely subjective, built on unstable ground.

After the event, I signed the bookshop's stock and shook some hands with one eye on Imogen, still hardly able to believe my luck. The rep from the publisher finished up and let me go. Imogen couldn't stay long. Her train home was departing in a couple of hours.

I'd noticed the wedding band as soon as I'd set eyes on her. Her husband was in the late stages of Alzheimer's. "I haven't had a day to myself in almost a year," she said. "But that's fine. Life takes you down all kinds of paths and not all of them are lined with roses. I love him *more* now, if that's possible. Nothing else has changed. Even though almost everything has." She smiled, her eyes glassy. She was used to handling the brittle emotions of the situation. "My son and daughter are home for a week and they insisted that I get away to London for a day or two. Just to go shopping, have lunch, and try to forget about things for a few hours. Of course, that's easier said than done."

Imogen had wandered around London, feeling a little bit lost, unsure how to go about being herself. She'd lived with the weight of Jeffrey's dementia for a few years now and it had almost entirely eclipsed her life. She'd forgotten how to live a day without anxiety, without Jeffrey being the front and centre of everything. It felt selfish to be out and about, acting like he'd already gone. A betrayal.

But the rain had chased her indoors finally, and she turned around and there I was, sitting behind a table with the last few people in the queue, each of them clutching various copies of books with my name on them.

And then, there was the author himself: Beard. Grey. Sad.

We found a quiet cafe in Soho, a few minutes' walk away. We smiled at each other over coffee, shocked, self-conscious, wary; all of those things at once. Finding each other a third time in our lives; it felt like more than coincidence. But it couldn't mean anything, not in that moment, as joyous as it was. I could see the pain of her life in the lines of her face. I could feel it in mine too.

"So, you got famous," she said.

"Moderately," I said. "I make enough money so that I can go to a restaurant and not worry about the bill at the end of the meal."

"I've read some of your books," she said. " Some of them are in the school library where I work."

"You teach?"

"Part time now, but yes."

"I tried that for a while, but it didn't really fit me too well."

"Are you married?"

"I was. She was a musician. We're divorced now."

"I'm sorry. Do you have any kids?"

"Just the one. Her name is Lily."

"A daughter? Oh, how lovely. How old?"

"She's eight now. She changed my life completely."

"They're hard work at that age."

"Yeah, I suppose. We discovered that she was on the autistic spectrum a few years ago."

"That must be hard."

"It's a challenge sometimes, but it's OK. She's beautiful."

"So what's it like, this being famous nonsense? Meeting all these fans of yours."

"I don't think it's something you ever get used to. I meet people who just want to say thank you because something I wrote changed them a little bit, or helped the world make sense to them. And then there are people who're couples with children, because they met in a line outside Forbidden Planet or Waterstones, and had a common interest that broke the ice for them." I smiled. "Sometimes they come with tattoos of characters I created and they want me to sign their skin. It's *mad*. Just these tiny, magic human moments."

We talked like that for an hour, playing catch up with our lives, opening up rooms to look inside briefly and pass comment. She told me about her kids, Matthew and Mary, who'd grown up and flown the nest, one of them all the way to Australia. We talked about my ex-wife, Abigail. She had walked out on my daughter and me. One day she packed all of her bags and ran off on tour with her first husband, who was a drummer. He was exuberant, the loudest person in any room, and with a body that looked like it was made of iron. *Nothing* at all like me. Abigail had finally left me a message on the machine, saying she wasn't coming home. No reason. Just a long, strained silence where that reason might be. And then she was gone. I played the message a couple of times, then became aware that I was trying to decode it, find something that wasn't there. I deleted it. I tried not to obsess about it but finally I gave in and tried to call her. She didn't answer the phone, didn't respond to my subsequent texts or emails.

It felt like a nuclear bomb had gone off in my life; it didn't matter how far I travelled, I could see the mushroom cloud everywhere I went, and I assumed the fallout would get me eventually anyway.

"I stopped writing," I said. "I lost interest. If I hadn't had Lily to look after I probably would have fallen apart entirely. After six months I filed for divorce. I was awarded sole custody of Lily. I didn't hear from Abigail again."

"That couldn't have been easy."

"In my dark moments I found myself trying to decide what it was I'd done wrong, where the failings existed in our marriage," I said. "I thought we were OK. So, I kept floundering and every day I locked myself in my office and stared at the blank page and wondered what to do with it. I didn't have writers' block; I don't believe in that. I had *ideas*, I just wasn't interested in any of them. Certainly none of them would have engrossed me enough to last me the length of a novel. So I started this signing tour for the paperback of the last book, tried to prop myself up and smile at everyone who came to the table asking for a signature.

"And then there was you," I said. "Seeing you again has made it all worth it."

It was over before we could get any kind of rhythm going between us. I kept catching glimpses of the woman I'd known in my twenties, processed through the subsequent thirty years. I'm sure she felt the same way. We were looking for a person who looked a little like us, but who didn't really exist anymore. It got to five in the afternoon and she said she had to leave, so we exchanged email addresses and we embraced awkwardly and laughed. And then she was gone. I clung to her smell for as long as I could after she'd left. It made me melancholy, but I tried to tuck all of those feelings back into the drawer marked THE PAST and leave them there.

I finished my coffee, gathered up my things and went back to my life. It was only later that I realised that she hadn't mentioned Oliver at all.

Two

Oliver arrived early for his meeting at the BBC. He was nervous about it, although Malcolm had assured him over the phone that the producers loved his ideas and that this meeting was simply a formality, a way to familiarise themselves with the man they were getting into bed with before he took their money and disappeared back to his cowshed studio in the Malvern Hills to make the show.

The giant coliseum-like structure of BBC Television Centre in Shepherd's Bush was built on a bewildering scale. It was labyrinthine and more like a clubhouse than Oliver had imagined. The futuristic vision of the fifties it had been built upon was already giving way, twenty years later, to a slightly faded grandeur. Production staff and technicians and make-up artists bustled from one place to the next with steely purpose. He glimpsed studios and canteens, people he thought he recognised from the telly; he even glimpsed a rather ramshackle looking Dalek being pushed behind the scenes. Laughter and dry monologues drifted from doorways. It was almost too much to assimilate for a man brought up in the wilds of Herefordshire, generally given to solitude.

In the end, the producers were more interested in getting the meeting over so they could break for lunch. Oliver had filmed the first two minutes of an episode, and screened the print for the department head, senior producer and some of their staff in one of the viewing studios. Those two minutes were silent, so Oliver told the story as it unfolded on screen, creating voices for the characters as they popped into his head. They were delighted with it.

"Yes, that's quite lovely," the department head said. "Absolutely splendid stuff."

"We'll mark it in for eighteen months from now. Have a think about what you might want to do in the future," one of the producers said. "Now, off you go and get on with it." He'd sweated his way through the stiff new shirt that Jenny had bought him for the occasion. But they seemed enamoured by his ideas for *The Adventures of Imogen and Florian*. Afterwards, he'd found a pay phone and called Jenny to tell her the good news. She began to cry when he told her he loved her, and that this was surely the beginning of the rest of their lives.

Malcolm was waiting for him on the staircase in the South Hall, which looked down on the fountain in the central courtyard. He was smoking a Sobranie Black Russian and clutching a tumbler of scotch. There was something different about Malcolm, Oliver thought, something eminently approachable. He was a tall, elegant man. His face was a little too severe to be handsome, but his smile and manner were quite benign. He'd been Oliver's first port of call in his dealings with the BBC over the last couple of years. He always asked after Jenny and Imogen, and often expressed the desire to make the journey to the Malverns to see that cowshed where all the magic happened.

Malcolm tossed his cigarette away. "Well, I think that went *swimmingly*, don't you, Oliver?" he said, grinning broadly.

"Yes, I suppose it did, Malcolm," Oliver said. "I can't thank you enough for what you've done."

"Oh, don't be daft," Malcolm said, slapping him on the back. "This is *playtime*. And we get paid for it!" He laughed. "Now," he said, draining his scotch, "what time is your train? I'm sure we've got enough time to have a drink and toast your fine idea. Wet the baby's head, eh?"

Oliver's train wasn't due for a couple of hours, so he agreed.

That day was the start of things in more than one way. It was a doorway opening onto the promise of another life.

Three

I stayed in touch with Imogen after that meeting in London. We emailed every month or so. Sometimes we talked for a couple of hours after Lily had gone to bed. It was easy. It didn't matter that we'd missed almost thirty years of each other's lives, that we'd married and had children and gone down very different paths. The symptoms of her husband's Alzheimer's had worsened since we'd seen each other, leaving Imogen with no other option but to find a hospice where they were better equipped to care for him. Then, six months later, pneumonia had finally claimed him. I left Lily with family and drove from Brighton to the Malverns to be there for the funeral. We talked briefly, but Imogen was busy with the wake, with relatives from all over the world, coping with the occasion by doing anything and everything. She'd seen it coming from a distance, and she'd already mourned the loss of her husband – the man she remembered, the life they'd shared. His personality had been stolen away from her piecemeal until all she'd been left with was the shell of him. She'd been caring for the ghost of a man for almost a year. She'd already come to terms with letting him go.

I half expected to see Oliver somewhere, but there was no sign of him. I wasn't sure whether he was still alive or not. I meant to ask after him, but something always conspired to get in the way. Now wasn't the time, particularly if Oliver was still a point of contention in Imogen's life.

We made plans for Lily and I to visit her over the winter break. We'd both felt enthused about spending time together to catch up on our lives properly, but when I called her a couple of days prior to our arrival to make some final plans, I thought I'd detected a note of hesitation in her voice. Whatever it was she recovered quickly. Although we were planning on staying at her home, she asked if I would mind spending the first night at the local inn in the town.

"Imogen, is everything OK?" I said.

"Of course it is, Noah" she said. "I'm looking forward to sounds of life in this old house again."

—

The old toys in the shop window caught Lily's eye as we drove down the high street, and she perked up so much I had no other option but to slow down and look for somewhere to park close by.

Lethebury is a small market town in Herefordshire, west of the Malvern Hills. It has a significant number of black and white timber-framed structures along the high street, the most outstanding of which is the Market House, a seventeenth century building, raised on sixteen pillars. Beneath it would usually have been a selection of stalls selling flowers and local meat and gifts, but it had been snowing for a couple of days when we arrived; it had chased everyone indoors, save for a few tenacious tourists wrapped up in anoraks. Several inches of snow had gathered at the roadside and up against the buildings. The roads had gradually become more and more treacherous as the day went on. The cold had turned the back roads to ice, so I was exhausted from the drive and glad to arrive at our destination.

The toys were in a dusty shop window at the edge of the high street. We trudged hand in hand back down the road, bundled up in our hats and scarves and thick winter coats. The snow seemed to float upwards into our faces. The sky was pale, creased with a strange luminosity. You could barely tell whether it was night or day. When the snow got too deep for Lily, I lifted her up into my arms.

We stood in front of the window for a moment, our breath pluming in the air before us, just taking in the strangeness of the display. It wasn't a shop anymore. There was no sign over the window, and beyond the display I could just make out the emptiness of the interior. I put Lily down and she pressed her face to the window, the glass condensating at her proximity.

"The Adventures of... Imogen and Florian," Lily said, struggling with the names.

The title caused a kind of vertigo in me, threatened to tip me all the way over into my childhood. I bent down next to Lily and looked at the card beside the display.

This is a small selection of the original puppets and models created by Lethebury local Oliver Frayling for his children's' TV show from 1973, 'The Adventures of Imogen and Florian'.

"I *loved* this show," I said to Lily. "Back when I was about your age. Look – this rabbit here, that's Florian."

Lily wrinkled her nose at the sight of the old rabbit. "I don't like how he looks, Daddy" she said. "He looks old and sad."

I couldn't disagree. Florian was the same ancient, partly taxidermied rabbit I remembered from my childhood. He was still dressed in the grand waistcoat, dirty white gloves and top hat. His face was still slightly threatening, with the chisel of dirty teeth in his grey muzzle. The years had not been kind to him. He was leaking sawdust. His beady eyes seemed to consider you, even when you looked away from him. I remembered touching his eyes when I was seven, hoping he might blink. Beside him was Antoine, the old rat in a fez, frozen in a posture that could only be described as 'camp', and there was Fizbatch, the monkey with cymbals, his grin so wide you could see all of his rotted teeth. The trail of buttons around them was the detail that sent me toppling headlong into my memories. The three of them had lingered there for almost fifty years, both on the screen, and with Oliver and Imogen in the children's home.

"Can we go inside and look at them?" Lily asked.

It took a moment to stir from my reverie. I leaned on the door but it was locked. I tapped on the glass a couple of times but there was no one inside. I was filled with a strange and inexplicable melancholy at the sight of these sad, neglected models in the shop window. I couldn't put my finger on why exactly. A ghostly sense that the past was closer than I thought; perhaps it was just waiting beyond this window, through that door. I heard the ticking of a great grandfather clock in my memory, the sound of chimes and cogs and springs like a liturgical countdown returning from there to here, from childhood to adulthood.

"Why don't we get settled in our rooms," I suggested to Lily, "then we can come back tomorrow and look at them again, see if there's anyone home." Tomorrow we could go and visit with Imogen, and perhaps it would be time to finally broach the subject of Oliver Frayling.

Lily glanced at the rabbit and the rat and the monkey one last time with a kind of longing that I hadn't seen in her since Abigail left us. I clung to these moments of connection for her; they were hugely important to the parent of a child with autism. We'd had Lily tested when she was three years old, and she was found to be on the lower end of the autistic spectrum. Within five minutes of being in her company you'd gradually become aware of those slightly jarring aspects in her manner: she wouldn't make eye contact, she wouldn't pick up on facial cues, and she rarely smiled or laughed; sometimes she wouldn't even respond to her name.

She often cried in her sleep. Her face belied very little emotion when she was awake. She didn't really respond to affection or direct questions. You had to come at things from an oblique angle, and even then, it was one step forward, two steps back. And then sometimes I'd sit there by the bed in the middle of the night, exhausted with the effort of being a single father, and see the tears rolling down Lily's face. I'd sit forward, reluctant to wake her, touching away the tears with my fingertips. Was she dreaming of her absent mother? Were all the emotions she didn't display waiting for her when she dreamed? I suppose they had to be somewhere; even the painful ones were essential to moving on somehow. So I sat back and let her dream, feeling a bit like a failure as a father. But I tried to keep moving forward.

I took one more look at the toys in the window. There was a gentle note of reassurance wrapped up in all of *The Adventures of Imogen and Florian*'s strangeness; I could sense it, lightly buried in my memory, like the warmth of the hearth in my mother's home in Dorset, where I'd spent my first seven years until her premature death; the comfort of her bed and the eiderdown spread out across it; the little portable black and white television in the corner; the milk warmed on the gas hob and clutched between my fingers in the chipped mug; the smell of my mother on the pillow cases... It was a trail of buttons that led all the way back to me.

Four

Oliver retreated to the cowshed on his property in Herefordshire in the summer of 1972. He constructed his own stop-motion animation table from scaffold poles and bits of bicycle, which had a camera gantry that would slide up and down. He began writing scripts and running tests that resulted in his being able to produce two minutes of film a day. He used a second-hand Bolex camera with a Meccano drive mechanism that had an electrically operated release, and gave an exposure of about 3/4 second for each frame. A particular shot might take an hour or more to set up, light and film, now that he was using large models. Later he would use areas of the family home to shoot in. The models themselves had been sourced from a man he knew in Worcester who specialised in a late 19th century style known as anthropomorphic taxidermy, a Victorian whimsy where mounted animals were dressed as people and displayed as if engaged in human activities. Oliver had been practising his art for several years, but this was stop-motion animation taken to another level.

He was dimly aware that he was neglecting the life he treasured usually above all else. His wife, Jenny, his daughter, Imogen. But this was, he sensed, his moment. He had to seize it with both hands. The money, £200 an episode for a series of twelve shows, had helped with their immediate financial problems, but Oliver had his eye on the long term: provide the BBC with a quality product and they'd surely ask him to continue, either with another series of *The Adventures of Imogen and Florian*, or they'd request something else. He had plenty of ideas rattling around in his brain that he'd happily develop, given half a chance.

Jenny worked in Hereford for an insurance company. It didn't provide much but it was enough to keep them afloat. But her mood swings were becoming more frequent, more pronounced, and Oliver often found it difficult to coax her back to the woman he knew after a day toiling in the cowshed. He wasn't even sure that this gentle coaxing was the correct course of action to choose. Bipolar was not a term that had even been coined back in 1972; manic depression remained a woolly area for a local GP out in the sticks to deal with effectively. Imogen fared a little better as she inadvertently became the de facto star of his little children's show. By the time Oliver had written the scripts, adapted the taxidermied animals, built the doll's house and recorded the finished soundtrack along with all of the music and effects, he realised that he'd run out of time to find an appropriate actress. Imogen didn't mind. She was just happy that her father was paying attention to her after so many months of neglect.

They roamed around their Victorian Gothic rectory during that summer with the models in tow, Imogen in her old pinafore, Oliver turning it into as much of a game as possible for his eight-year-old daughter so that she didn't get too bored. But it was inevitable that she would. The process was laborious. He made do, fudged a little of it later. It was rough around the edges and he was a little embarrassed to show

Malcolm some of it when he finally made his sortie out into the wilds of the Herefordshire countryside to see Oliver.

"It's not good enough, is it?" he said after projecting the first episode on the wall of the cowshed.

"Don't be daft," Malcolm said. "It's bloody *wonderful*." He smiled and said quietly, "I'm *so* proud of you, Oliver."

Oliver didn't know how to respond. It was such a strange thing to say. Sitting beside him, Malcolm looked like a rare butterfly amongst the chaos of the studio. His beautiful pin-stripe suit was already getting dusty from all the old toys and furniture and boxes and notebooks and parts. A sense of discomfort passed briefly between them. Malcolm glanced at him, at an uncharacteristic loss for words. He smiled, placed a hand on Oliver's knee. Oliver looked at the hand for a long moment, feeling slightly disconcerted. It was like seeing an old face in a crowd, or finding something beloved that you'd lost long ago. He couldn't put a name to the sensation.

After a moment, Malcolm withdrew the hand and stood. "I suppose I should be getting back to the smoke," he said. "It's getting late."

Oliver walked him to the station. They conversed, but something had changed and he did not understand it, or perhaps was unwilling to accept that he understood it all too well. It was too much too soon. He stood on the platform long after Malcolm had gone and stared at the empty tracks.

Five

Imogen had booked us into the Sixpence and Stars inn for the first night of our stay in Lethebury. It was a beautiful timber-framed seventeenth century building. It had once been a tannery and part of an old open cattle market. The roaring open fire was more than welcome after so long cooped up in the car, and twenty minutes spent trudging through the snow. We stamped it from our boots and exhaled, drinking in the comfort of the little place.

I gathered Lily up in my arms while I talked to the landlord and by the time we were shown to our room, she was already asleep. I took off her wellingtons and wet coat and laid her on the bed, wrapping a blanket around her. I went and fetched our belongings, which didn't amount to much – a little pink case for Lily and a rucksack for me. I left her to sleep and retired downstairs for a drink, used the pub's Wi-Fi to look up Oliver Frayling and *The Adventures of Imogen and Florian* on my iPad. I'd texted Imogen to tell her we'd arrived safely, but the conversation about her father could wait until we were face to face tomorrow.

I was surprised to find so much information on Frayling and his work. As well as the relatively detailed overview of his career and separate pages on the programmes he'd worked on, there were multiple websites given over to sixties and seventies nostalgia and its associated memorabilia. I'd had no idea how potent certain images, theme tunes and characters were.

I recalled lying in my mother's bed, watching the first episode of *The Adventures of Imogen and Florian*. She had a portable black and white TV whose aerial was pretty unreliable. Perhaps this is why people of my generation have these hazy recollections of the programming of our youth; it was before the technological watershed of the eighties. Nowadays everything is recorded, digitised, archived, available on-demand. In the seventies we had no way of recording the things we watched on TV. As such, I harboured slightly muddled memories of the shows of my youth, although I remembered watching *Programmes for School and Colleges*, *Play School*, *Andy Pandy* and *The Magic Roundabout* while I was in the children's home. But unlike some of those shows, which had found a second life by being discovered and released on DVD, Oliver Frayling's show had been lost, taped over by the BBC, thus ensuring its strange, unverifiable attraction. It could only be vaguely recalled. The old, lost, forgotten things he'd conjured up remained just that. It was, to a writer, deliciously alluring.

After half an hour I discovered that there was one crucial solitary fragment of the show: its opening scene, narrated by Oliver Frayling himself. His voice positively *ached* with melancholy. I heard him speaking the opening narration in the children's home, and something changed in the room, as if the air was suddenly charged with that indefinable magic that the show had.

Once upon a time, not so very long ago, in a lonely old house in the countryside there was a little girl called Imogen. She was nine years old, dressed up in an old

Edwardian pinafore and striped tights, just like a sepia-tinted Alice.

Every day she climbed upstairs to the top of the house. At the top of the house was an attic, and in that attic was a doll's house. Oliver had utilised his own home as his set. It was his father's house, and his father's before that, a grand old Victorian thing. At the top of the staircase was a huge, stained-glass window, the light illuminating every dancing dust mote as Imogen climbed.

And in that doll's house lived a great many things. Old things, lost things, forgotten things. Beneath the gentle narration was the sound of a great ticking grandfather clock, and a piano being played in a distant room of the house, a pretty but plangent melody that I'd forgotten entirely but knew intimately. There was a gentle poetry to it all.

One of those things was Florian. He was a rabbit who wore a rather grand top hat and a waistcoat. There was magic in that doll's house. Every time Imogen sat down in the lonely attic to play, she said, 'Take me Elsewhere!' and the house grew tall and grand around her.

I read several articles on Frayling which made mention of the crude set-up of his studio, a converted cowshed in his back garden in the wilds of the Malvern Hills, pioneering the idea of externally made shows appearing on the BBC. It was this distance from the trends and pressures of the London studios that allowed Frayling to make such an idiosyncratic show.

And then Florian would take Imogen by the hand and take her on a great many adventures in the doll's house, leaving a trail of buttons so that they could find their way home every day. This is the story of their adventures…

The work was still crude, but there was an undeniable magic to it, despite the quality of the reproduction on YouTube, and despite re-viewing it with the weight of almost fifty years of life in-between. It was hard to credit such potency to the man pictured on his Wikipedia entry. He was exactly as I remembered him – an avuncular-looking, heavy-set man with long grey hair that had receded far from his forehead and curled around his ears. A thick, out of shape pullover and baggy brown corduroy trousers. Overgrown eyebrows and loose jowls, soft dewy eyes squinting from beneath National Health spectacles that had been repaired once too often with masking tape. I could see traces of him in Imogen's face now, in those eyes.

There were other details that piqued my interest – the wilderness of the years since *The Adventures of Imogen and Florian*; the curious side-step of *PoppyHarp*, his Play for Today, transmitted in 1977; his work as a volunteer for the Royal Observer Corps monitoring post in preparation for the event of a nuclear attack on the UK between 1965 and 1991. The most startling fact was undoubtedly that he'd gone missing in 2008, never to be seen again. I couldn't believe that Imogen had failed to mention this since we'd reconnected.

By this time the day was beginning to weigh on me. The drive in tortuous conditions had been wearing. The drink by the fireside and the lazy fall of snowflakes beyond the window were a soporific. For an hour or so, Oliver Frayling had taken me away from my life in much the same way as he had during my fractured childhood. There was still magic there.

Six

(Excerpt from an article in *Cult Times* by Dave Cook, 2001)

THE FORGOTTEN MAN: AN INTERVIEW WITH OLIVER FRAYLING

DAVE COOK: Tell me about the process involved with making *The Adventures of Imogen and Florian*.

OLIVER FRAYLING: It's just a lot of slow, fiddly work, really. It involved me fumbling around in the dark until I managed some rough approximation of what I saw in my head when I wrote it. I knew next to nothing about film-making. Still don't, really. I went and asked for advice from some friends of my wife who made educational films. They told me that as long as I had my own particular vision and could commit myself to bringing the story to life, then I'd probably be able to make something worthy. They also told me the four most important things anyone needs to know about film-making.

DC: Which are?

OF: You know, for the life of me, I can't remember! (Laughs)

DC: So, there you are in that cowshed of yours...

OF: Oh, yes, I would sit in that bloody shed for months on end. But it was absorbing work. I lost myself in the process and wouldn't even notice a day passing, and then wonder if my family had missed me.

DC: And had they?

OF: Yes, of course they did. It ruined my marriage I suppose. And coloured my relationship with Imogen.

DC: But you also made much of *The Adventures of Imogen and Florian* in your house, with your daughter.

OF: Yes, it was nice to involve her in some way, although the novelty wore off for her quite quickly, as I recall! It amounted to months of work, probably almost a year to produce twelve episodes.

DC: And you narrated the show as well.

OF: Well, I'd written the thing so I thought I may as well tell the story too. In fact it happened by accident when I realised that I had to provide something for the chaps at the BBC when I screened the rough footage for them. There wasn't really enough money to even entertain the notion of employing an actor to do the voice-over.

DC: As a result of the 'wiping policy' at the BBC in the sixties and seventies, none of the episodes of *The Adventures of Imogen and Florian* survive in the archive, do they?

OF: That's what I've been led to believe. By the early seventies, television companies couldn't justify the expense required to store all those cans of film in large warehouses. It became a fire hazard too. So they decided that any film over three years old which was deemed to be of little or no historical value would be destroyed. It wasn't just my little show, though. Episodes of *Steptoe and Son*, *Hancock's Half Hour*, *Dad's Army*, *Doctor Who*... They were just purged from the archives. It's incredible to think of now.

DC: In this digital age, many of the children's shows of the seventies have been rediscovered and repackaged on DVD for a new generation. Do you wish something remained of *The Adventures of Imogen and Florian* to ensure its cultural significance?

OF: I don't really think about it to be honest. It seems like such a long time ago. Apart from making *PoppyHarp*, I left the television industry behind almost thirty years ago.

DC: What led you to making *PoppyHarp*, your Play for Today, in 1976? (Play for Today was a BBC television anthology drama series which ran from 1970 to 1984. The plays covered all genres, from historical pieces, fantasies, biopics, and occasionally science fiction. Notable contributors included Dennis Potter, Stephen Poliakoff, Alan Bleasdale, Mike Leigh and Lindsey Anderson.)

OF: A variety of factors that came to a head in my personal life around that time, I suppose. The response to *The Adventures of Imogen and Florian* was less than enthusiastic, which, after investing so much time and effort into it, was quite dispiriting and I became quite depressed about it. A friend of mine in the industry who had advanced up the ladder within the BBC pulled a few strings and asked if I had any interest in producing something more adult in nature, and *PoppyHarp* came out of that. That particular time in my life, the circumstances surrounding its creation are all really still quite personal to me.

DC: How would you like to be remembered?

OF: Oh, bloody hell, I don't really have any need to be preserved in aspic. Although I remember all of the people in my life who meant something to me, all it causes is a yearning for something that's long past. I often feel overwhelmed by wanting a certain moment back, or to exist in it, rather than my current circumstances. But you can't go back, can you? Can't mend what's broken. So you just keep buggering on, as Churchill would say.

Seven

I was woken from a fitful sleep by a scrabbling sound in the room.

I jerked awake in the chair beside the bed, my hand reaching out for Lily. She was still asleep, the tears drying on her cheeks. It was jarring. Even with the curtains closed, the room was filled with the luminous quality of snow on the ground outside, and a pale night sky filled with the promise of more.

I was still only half-awake. Despite my exhaustion, I wasn't sleeping well. I'd got used to Abigail's absence on the other side of the bed, but my mind wouldn't stop pulling at all the loose threads. Whenever I did fall into a fitful sleep it was filled with dreams of longing for what was lost in my life, now forever in my rear-view mirror. Often, that sense of irresolution left no space for grief or relief, no place to rest and reflect. It was a question mark that chipped away at my self-belief. I was always glad for the eventual faint glimmers of light creeping around the drawn curtains each morning, grateful for Lily waking, the tears long dried on her face.

And then it would be another day, and I would rise to face it.

But we were still in the early hours of the morning. I reached across to my phone on the bedside cabinet and woke it: 4.16 am. The scrabbling sound resumed and I rose to locate it, creeping forward in a crouch. I thought it might be a rat. I fumbled with my phone and switched on the torch, began to sweep it across the floor.

Lily rolled over in the bed but didn't wake.

Something shifted at the periphery of my vision, something low, scurrying across the pale carpet in strange jerking motions. The movement seemed to jar something in the wiring in my head. We're socially conditioned from childhood to be sensitive to something moving from the corner of our eye, like a spider which moves in a manner that feels odd to us. This was not that. The dark shape was large, roughly the size of a small cat, but its movements were curious, and it took me a moment in my sleep-addled state to realise what it was that disturbed me about it: it was as if I were blinking slowly, missing frames of visual information. The object was moving as it would in a stop-motion piece of animation.

My joints stiffened involuntarily in something like fear. For a moment I thought I wouldn't be able to move, but my concern for my child took precedence over everything. I scrambled onto my hands and knees and swept the beam of light from my phone across the carpet, waiting for whatever it was to move again. There wasn't much space for it to escape. The room was locked, the en-suite door closed. The only place it could go was beneath the bed. I glanced at Lily again but she still hadn't stirred. Her face was creased with what seemed to me like apprehension, as if reacting to what was happening in the room.

And then I saw him. It was Florian. Of *course* it was Florian. He stumbled in quick jerking steps from the other side of the bed towards the wardrobe. He looked exactly as he did in the window, in the recesses of my memory: the worn top hat, the embroidered waistcoat, and the dirty white gloves. I experienced that imbalance again that suggested that the next stop was my childhood, or else the nut-house. I let out a breath that sounded more like the cry of a lunatic. It caught Florian's attention. He froze in the middle of the floor as if he was caught in a spotlight. He was leaving a trail of buttons behind him. He stared at me with those empty beady eyes. It resembled the unfocused gaze of a blind man. I felt a curious shift from fear to a rapt, child-like wonder. It was *Florian*. He was *alive*!

Lily woke then. I took my eyes off Florian for a moment and saw my little girl appear at the foot of the bed. She glanced at me and then across at the rabbit. I saw her eyes visibly widen in delight. The same rapt, childish delight that had stopped me in my tracks.

Florian sniffed, and his mouth opened, revealing those dirty, jagged teeth. His tongue moved, as if he was swallowing. I imagined Oliver Frayling filming this from some god-like position above us, moving Florian's head, then clicking the mechanism on the Bolex camera, getting the 3/4 second exposure, and then moving Florian again, one tiny increment at a time.

"Daddy, is that… is it *Florian*?" Lily asked.

"Yes," I said, at a loss for words. This wasn't in the parent's instruction manual as far as I knew. We were in uncharted territory. I was trying not to swear, but *fuck me*, the situation called for it.

The old rabbit moved then, those missing frames of life causing some kind of cognitive dissonance as my eye captured the image and my brain attempted to process what it was missing. Again, there was no template for this in the real world. I reached for Lily's hand, either to reassure her or, more likely, myself. Around us the real world creaked on: the radiators sighing in the dead of night, the sound of a dog barking outside, a car hissing past though the snow-filled streets of Lethebury... The strange alchemy dissipated as Florian reached the side of the wardrobe and then promptly disappeared behind it. Frames seemed to be missing from the film. There was a moment where I realised that I was holding my breath. Finally, I exhaled.

But Lily wasn't ready to let Florian go. "Behind the wardrobe!" she cried. "Behind the *wardrobe*. See where he went, Daddy. *See where he went!*"

There was a meltdown on the way, I could sense it. Another symptom of children with various forms of autism. Sometimes it comes from nowhere, often in public places, an explosion of distressing proportions. All you can do is hold them and talk to them, find some way to reassure them. But I could do something about this, and I did. I dropped my phone on the bed and switched on the light. The gap between the wardrobe and the wall amounted to no more than an inch, and Florian was far wider than that. But we were evidently through the looking-glass here, people. With some effort I pushed the wardrobe away from the wall, making a space sufficient for us to see where the rabbit had gone.

There was no sign of Florian. It was as if he'd evaporated into the air. Lily jumped off the bed and crawled down beside me with my phone. The flashlight was still on. She shone it behind the wardrobe. "Daddy, look!" she said.

There was a door.

It was solid oak with an arched head, no more than six inches high. Something about it caused that giddiness again; a stray memory of an episode of *The Adventures of Imogen and Florian* featured just such a door. It was also, of course, the kind of door that Alice would have had to down a potion to fit through. Much of Oliver Frayling's world was clearly influenced by Lewis Carroll's books. I was speechless. It was Lily, with the tenacity and fearlessness of youth, who scrambled behind the wardrobe and pressed one finger down on the door handle. I reached out for her, but there was no way she could get in there without a struggle. She was too big.

The door swung open. I couldn't see through it; Lily was taking up all of the space between the wall and the wardrobe. I still had a hand on one of her bare feet in expectation of the doorway swallowing her whole. She shone the light in and bowed her head to peer inside.

"What can you see?" I whispered.

She didn't say anything for a moment. She simply stared into the doorway, a look of enchantment on her face. Even at her age, and with her learning difficulties, a part of her was dimly aware that this was an extraordinary occurrence. When she lowered her head into the doorway, I took hold of her more firmly, suddenly deeply anxious that she might vanish in the blink of an eye and I would be left abandoned here, with no real way to explain her absence, feeling as if I had dreamed her whole existence. She glanced back at me. "Somewhere else," she said finally. She smiled again; her face illuminated by some light source from within. Ripples of gold and red and yellow, the intimation of moving water. I heard sounds too, or imagined I did. Children's laughter and the ticking of a great clock, the whirr and click of cogs and springs and hidden mechanisms, the distant melancholy sound of a piano being played in a distant room of the building. Of the doll's house.

"I can't get in," she said. She glanced at me with a look of exasperation. "I'm not *small* enough to get all the way *in*."

She tried again, but her shoulders were too wide. She left out a cry of frustration then, and slapped at the wall repeatedly until I had to take her in my arms and hold her there until she was calm again.

Eight

He'd told himself he wouldn't go back to see Malcolm again, but then one day he called, and Oliver was on the train from Worcester to Paddington Station. Here, finally, he could feel his heart lifting away from the baseless fabric of his real life in Lethebury.

He'd wasted a year of his life on *The Adventures of Imogen and Florian*. He'd even agreed to make a short tour of schools and children's homes with Imogen and the puppets. It was a largely dispiriting task; he didn't know what the children wanted. All he could offer were Florian, Antoine and Fizbatch, but they looked like a sorry representation of all that toil. There were a handful of kids who'd grasped who he was and what he'd done, but they were few and far between. He was often glad that Imogen had accompanied him; she had a keen sense of how to entice the children in, even at that tender age.

On more fanciful days he'd allowed himself to imagine that children all over the UK would sit down in front of his little TV show and be enchanted by what he'd dreamed up; that the BBC would call him in twelve months later, sit him down and beg him for more of the same, or something else that he could dream up in that cowshed of his.

But that call had never arrived.

So he'd sat at home and stewed in his own juices, frustrated by the limitations he perceived in *The*

Adventures of Imogen and Florian; the mistakes that there hadn't been time to rectify; the clumsiness of using his own daughter, who barely understood that she was supposed to be acting.

He'd become distant with Jenny and Imogen, given to mood swings, sudden bursts of uncharacteristic anger. They were at odds with each other, unable to understand what was broken and if they should be expected to even attempt to mend those fences. When Oliver recognised these shortcomings in himself, he'd take himself off to the cowshed and stand, slightly lost, amongst all the broken toys and antique furniture, the taxidermy, the books and the boxes filled with random junk he'd collected obsessively, imagining a day when he might use them in one of the episodes. What should he do next? If the one thing that made him happy in life wasn't viable, then what was he left with? Jack it all in and become an insurance man? A door-to-door salesman? A bus conductor?

Just as he was reaching the end of his tether, Malcolm called. It was a dull afternoon in the November of 1974. From the kitchen Oliver could see tumescent clouds erasing the heights of the Worcester Beacon, bearing the promise of another day of rain. The rooms were filled with a sickly yellow glow that seemed to drain the life from the daylight hours.

"Oliver!" Malcolm said. "My dear boy, how are you?"

He didn't want his spirits lifted, but he allowed the briefest flicker of a smile to reach his lips. "I'm alright I suppose, Malcolm."

"And how are Jenny and that little girl of yours?"

"They're fine too, Malcolm. Quite well."

He heard Malcolm falter for a moment. His voice was usually so full of *joi de vivre* that it swept everyone in its orbit up by their bootstraps and out of whatever mood they were in. "Oliver," he began, and he faltered again. "*Look*, I'm sorry I haven't called. I'm *sorry* that your little show didn't make a splash in the way we'd hoped."

Oliver fancied he could detect genuine regret in Malcolm's voice when he said, "I feel like I let you down. I think perhaps I didn't do enough on my end to make it more of a success… I honestly can't express how sorry I am."

"It isn't your fault, Malcolm," Oliver said. He watched a murmuration of starlings framed in the sky beyond the window. A mass of birds, like charcoal, smudging a helix across the sky. "If there are any shortcomings then they are surely mine. It simply wasn't good enough."

"Don't be daft, Oliver. That is absolute *nonsense*. I saw how you toiled on every aspect of that project."

"Well, be that as it may, it doesn't really matter who buggered it up in the end, does it?"

Another pained silence. Perhaps Malcolm wasn't used to this kind of conversation, apportioning blame, admitting to perceived shortcomings. Oliver saw the BBC as some sort of hermetic boy's club where the days were spent slapping each other on the back, getting lightly pissed over lunch and endlessly on the hunt for some *how's-your-father* in a quiet broom cupboard whenever they could get it. Blame was taken care of either behind closed doors or by simply not bothering to pick up the phone to inform you of how you'd failed the Corporation. All too abruptly you were no longer a member of the club and out in the cold.

"I'd really like to see you, if that's at all possible, Oliver," Malcolm said then, and Oliver felt that sensation again, of the world tilting away beneath his feet. He thought again of Malcolm's hand on his knee in the cowshed, but it was still something that he couldn't bring into focus for himself. Everything in his life had been for his family; the perceived onus on providing for them, even when he was well aware that it was Jenny who was keeping them afloat. Thank goodness they had inherited the house, otherwise they would never have kept up with the mortgage repayments. As it was the place was gradually crumbling around their ears. Seeing Malcolm was about securing another job of some kind; the confusion of those other thoughts and feelings were pushed down somewhere deep where no one could see them.

"Of course," he said, without a further moment's thought. "When?"

———

Jenny had wanted to know if it meant that the BBC wanted him to work on something new.

"I've no idea, love," he said, packing his battered old suitcase. He hadn't used it in years. They hadn't been able to afford a holiday since 1968: a week in Skegness. It had rained every day.

"Well, if there's nothing on the table, then why are you rushing off down there?"

"*Nothing on the table*?" he said. "Since when did we start talking like we were running a business?"

"Sometimes I think you've forgotten that it's just that: a business. You didn't spend all those months making that programme for nothing."

"It feels like I did."

"They *paid* you for it. You can't think about who watches it. Surely any work is better than none at all."

"That's why I'm going down there, love. I have to go into the lion's den in order to find out what they want."

After a moment's hesitation, Jenny said, "Will you be staying at Malcolm's?"

Oliver didn't look up. He kept shoving socks into his case. "Yes, that appears to be the plan."

Jenny didn't say anything else. After a moment, he looked up and discovered that she'd already left him to it.

——

He met Malcolm at Paddington Station. He was waiting on a bench on the platform, as immaculate as ever in a pin-stripe suit, a silk scarf draped with artful imprecision around his neck. He swept his hair away from his forehead and came to greet Oliver with open arms. It wasn't what Oliver was used to, but he accepted the brief, rather cosmopolitan exchange with as much grace as he could muster amongst the bustling throngs of people.

"You look well, Oliver," Malcolm said. "*Robust!*" He smiled broadly. "It's a pleasure to see you again."

Oliver smiled, feeling stiff and ill at ease. "You too, Malcolm." Part of him wanted to get on with business and cut this short. If Malcolm hurried it along, perhaps he wouldn't have to stay the night. He was beginning to have misgivings about the whole affair.

"Look," Malcolm said, "I hope that it's not too much of an inconvenience but something has come up that I really can't avoid…"

"At the BBC?" Oliver asked. As much as he'd convinced both himself and Jenny that he disliked the place, there was an undeniable thrill to being within those hallowed walls. The life that it contained, the focused industry, the alluring promise of a familiar household face around every corner.

"No, I'm afraid not, old chap. This is more of a personal matter. Julian, a friend of mine is having some difficulties with a mutual acquaintance. It's a frightful business. Have you heard of Kenneth Bliss?"

"*The* Kenneth Bliss?"

"One and the same, yes. Old Kenny is hunkered down at Julian's pad in Pembroke Gardens, saying that he's considering ending it all. Julian thinks if I show my face, it'll improve the situation somewhat."

"I can come back another time…"

"I won't hear of it, Oliver!" Malcolm said, guiding him away from the platform and into the station concourse. "Kenneth's a *frightful* drama queen. It seems like he threatens suicide on a weekly basis. It'll only take a couple of hours and then we'll discuss business as planned."

They caught the tube. It only took ten minutes from Paddington to Kensington. On the way, the two men sat, their knees touching. Oliver could smell Malcolm's aftershave, an enticing scent quite unlike anything he'd smelt before. It was ever so slightly intoxicating. "How do you know Kenneth Bliss?" he asked, before the silence grew uncomfortable. Oliver was aware of Bliss from those 'Keep On…' movies which ran on wet Sunday afternoons on the TV; humour in the British comic tradition of the music hall and saucy seaside postcards. Smutty innuendo that faintly embarrassed Oliver if truth be told, but he enjoyed the well practiced farce and pratfalls. And everyone knew Kenneth Bliss: those nasal, whining, cockney inflections, the flaring nostrils, the fussy nature, and his camp but biting wit. Oliver couldn't imagine the actor being part of his day. He seemed much larger than a damp November afternoon in London could contain.

"He's been in the studios at the Beeb for the last few days recording 'Christmas at Cold Comfort Farm' for the Morning Story, which they'll broadcast on Christmas Eve." Malcolm pulled a pained face. "I've known him for a few years. Mutual acquaintances and all that. We all move in the same little circles in London, I'm afraid. All very incestuous…"

Oliver wondered after those little circles. The notion made him faintly anxious. Part of him wished he was in his bunker on the hill, sitting quietly in that little room with the instruments primed, waiting for someone to push the button in Russia.

Malcolm's friend Julian lived in Pembroke Gardens, part of a complex of small studio houses in Kensington, built in the 1890s by Charles Frederick Kearly. It had been the centre of creativity for a brace of London artists for almost a century. "You get all sorts around here," Malcolm said as they made their way to Julian's door. "And not just artists. Ballet dancers, architects, photographers… *all sorts.*"

Large wrought iron gates led to a Queen Anne-style gatehouse. Beyond a red brick archway the courtyard garden was a sanctuary of calm, only slightly diminished by the saturated qualities of winter. But the clamour of London faded gradually until all Oliver could hear was the sound of birdsong. The garden was enclosed by two terraces of six units and a boundary wall. Huge canted windows allowed the necessary light required for the artists.

It occurred to Oliver just before the door was opened that Malcolm's friend Julian must in fact be Julian Grayson, the painter and photographer. He recalled reading about him in the Sunday paper one weekend. He split his time between London and California, socialising with people like Andy Warhol and Christopher Isherwood. He'd become a figurehead to the burgeoning gay rights movement in the late sixties. Many of his paintings featured naked young men beside swimming pools, or else beautifully abstract portraits of ordinary people whom he met on the street. Jenny said they were filthy. She'd thrown the paper away. After she had gone to bed, Oliver had fished it out of the bin and looked at the pictures again, perplexed at his feelings about them. What struck him about the work was the *restlessness* of it.

And then he was there at the door, a slightly overweight young man in grubby tank-top, baggy trousers held up with brightly coloured braces. Bleached blonde hair. Circular tortoiseshell spectacles, sliding down the bridge of his nose. A half-smoked cigarette perched between his lips. Covered in paint.

"*Alright*, our Malcolm," he said finally in flat Northern tones. "You're a sight for sore eyes. Kenny's inside. I'm afraid the daft bugger is doing my head in now."

He stepped aside to let them in. Julian wiped his hand and then held it out to Oliver. "Who's your friend, then, Malcolm?"

"This is Oliver Frayling," Malcolm said, his hand on Oliver's back, seeming to brandish him proudly.

"He's an animator. Stop-motion. He made a children's show for us. He's really quite brilliant."

Oliver coloured. No one had ever been so effusive in their praise of him before. Even Jenny, who had been tirelessly supportive of what they both perceived as a hobby turned business opportunity, often seem nonplussed by the results of his labours. She'd sat down to watch the first couple of episodes of his show when they'd been transmitted, but had managed to find other things to do that prohibited her watching the remainder of the series.

"Thank you, Malcolm," he said. He felt a sudden surge of emotion that he had to sit on top of; he didn't want to scare off the famous people with tears.

"Is this that *Imogen and Florian* chap you keep banging on about?" Julian said.

Hearing the name of his show on Julian Grayson's lips seemed to unseat Oliver from the world for a moment. He had no idea how far it had reached. Indeed, the only people he'd met who'd seen it were a handful of kind people with children in Lethebury, and the kids he'd met on the tour of schools and homes.

"I saw a couple of them," Julian said, stubbing out his cigarette and leading them into the studio. "I thought they were inspired. *Bloody* inspired, actually. Lovely and surreal. Just my sort of bag!" He put a hand on Oliver's shoulder and said, "I'd like to pick your brain about them later. I'd love to hear about your techniques. Malcolm says you work in a converted cowshed?" He laughed. It sounded like a braying donkey. "*Bloody* marvellous!"

Oliver felt that urge to escape diminishing somewhat. Praise engendered a craving for more of the same. It seemed to entice him from the lifelong compulsion to hide himself away in the dark of a cowshed or an underground bunker, and into the light and colour of Julian's studio. It was a high-ceilinged room with a galleried landing. Canvases lined the walls, and a work bench was covered in curled-over paint tubes and a multitude of brushes in jars. There were hundreds of black and white photographs strewn across its surface. They seemed to be family photos. He caught a glimpse of Julian in some of them, his clothes garish, his hair and glasses a little too outrageous for his surroundings.

In the centre of the room was a large canvas on an easel. A work in progress. An old couple, quite clearly Julian's parents, the subject. There was an unfinished, speculative quality to it, a variety of styles clashing, vying for attention. Oliver studied it, stepping back to better understand it. He felt a boldness dawning on him. Was this all it took? A little approval to bolster his self-esteem? But it was more than that, and there was still some hesitation about what the rest of the weekend would hold, a reserve that he suspected these men didn't have much time for.

Kenneth Bliss was sitting upstairs in the galleried landing, which doubled as both a bedroom and a sitting room for guests. His posture was stiff and angled away from the interlopers. Oliver wondered what was wrong with the man. Neatly combed hair, Brylcreemed into a severe side-parting, a freshly-pressed white shirt and baggy cardigan, a pair of grey flannel trousers. Bony knees pressed together. He wouldn't as much as look at them when Julian led them upstairs to make them tea. He'd sent an assistant out for cake from the high street.

"Kenneth!" Malcolm said with slightly exaggerated enthusiasm. "And how are we today?"

Bliss pulled a face, sniffed, still turned away from them. "Oh, wouldn't you like to bloody-well know, Malcolm."

Malcolm sat down beside him and pulled up a chair for Oliver. "Now come on, Kenneth, I'd like you to meet someone and we can have a positively wonderful afternoon chewing the fat." He squeezed one of Bliss's bony thighs. "You can tell him some of your stories."

"I'm not in the *mood* for telling stories today," Bliss said, folding his arms. "Look at me." He pulled the shirt away from his body. "I've lost two and half stone in the last six months due to worry. Pretty soon there'll be bugger-all left of me."

"Stop bloody complaining," Julian said, placing cups of tea on the table in front of them. "Excuse the magazines," he said to Oliver, dropping them on the floor so they fanned out across the paint-spattered surface. Oliver glanced at them and then quickly away. *Hung Heavy, Taste of Beefcake, Leatherstuds…* "There's a bookshop in Earl's Court got raided by the police the other day," Julian said. "They tried to confiscate their stock. Said it was all pornographic. I went down there to protest, but it didn't do much good…"

Oliver kept glancing at them while they sat talking that afternoon. At some point Julian fished one out and showed him a feature that *Playguy* had published on him and a friend. He leafed through the pages and Oliver glanced around, unsure how to react. It felt as if they were each of them trying to test the water with him. It made him anxious all over again. Julian sat down beside him and showed him the pictures.

Blown-up Polaroids of Julian and his friend, posing in a bathroom in Paris, both of them stark naked, a sheen of oil glazing their flesh. "Look," Julian said. "The light we used gave the effect of a painting by Caravaggio. You see?"

Oliver did. He chanced a glance at Malcolm, but he was deep in conversation with Kenneth Bliss. He allowed himself to look at the photos with an impassive eye, but something in his gut responded instead. His skin was prickling with embarrassment. Oliver didn't wish to offend Julian, even if it was further from his experience of people than he had ever known. Discussing the light and artistic sensibilities of naked men in a bathroom! This was the myth of how they'd acted in the swinging sixties in London. It seemed absurd to be conversing with the kind of people Jenny, and much of the population of Lethebury, would be appalled by. A supposed den of iniquity.

But as the afternoon wore on, he felt more and more at home around them. Bliss's icy exterior began to melt, and he started to tell stories about working with Joe Orton, Peter Cook and Dudley Moore, Richard Burton. They were surely heavily embroidered but he was quite the raconteur. Despite constant protestations to the contrary he adored being the centre of attention.

"*Keep On Camping*," he said after a moment's pause. "I was lovely and young in that one. Very *trim*, you know," he said, stretching out one leg, showing them his profile and sucking in his cheeks. "It's one of the few I can bear to watch. We had a just barely decent script to work with for a change..."

They discussed painting and poetry, old films; Malcolm told them stories about life at the BBC. It grew dark outside and, at some point, guests began to arrive at Julian's door; Oliver was being introduced to men and women whose names he forgot almost immediately. They milled around both upstairs and down in the studio. At some point he found himself sharing a bottle of brandy with Julian while they stood in front of the unfinished painting of his parents.

"It's defeating me, this one," Julian admitted. "I've started it so many bloody times and scrapped it again and again. No technique seems to do the trick."

Oliver mulled over the photos of Julian's parents on the bench. There was a picture of Julian's father as a handsome young man on a beach, bare-chested and sporting a quiff and thick black framed glasses. His mother in a flowery-print dress in another. She was holding the hem of her skirt up above the waves rolling in around her knees. Laughing. Carefree. Beautiful.

"Perhaps you're trying to portray them as they were in all these photos," Oliver said. "There are so many years to choose from here. I think you need to find just one or two that really say everything about them and focus on that." He smiled. "And then put the rest of them away until you're finished."

Julian nodded, drained his glass. "I suppose you might be right. I've agonised over it for months."

"You can't bring them back to life," Oliver said. "With the best will in the world."

Julian nodded again and Oliver realised he had tears in his eyes. He placed a hand on the man's back.

"Sorry, Oliver. I barely know you."

"That's quite alright."

"I don't know," Julian said, glancing around at the people in the studio with a look of mild horror.

It was as if he'd only just noticed that they'd arrived. "Sometimes you get distracted and you look away from something that's always been there. And by the time you look again, it's become a memory."

———

Oliver made a call to Jenny later that evening. He found a quiet spot with the phone wire stretched as far as it would go and told her he was fine, that the day was going well. He was a little merry, if truth be told. He tried to keep it from his voice, but Jenny knew him too well.

"Are you at a *party*?" she said.

"More of a gathering."

"At that Malcolm's?"

He noted the tone of disapproval in her voice when she said his name. "No, we're at an artist's place in Kensington. Kenneth Bliss is here."

"Kenneth Bliss? *The* Kenneth Bliss?"

"Yes, you know, from those *Keep On...* films."

"Isn't he, you know, queer?"

"Well, you know, that hasn't come up as such."

Silence.

"Jenny?"

"Will you still be home tomorrow afternoon?"

"Of course."

Afterwards he felt the wind had been taken out of his sails by the exchange. When he returned to where Malcolm and Kenneth were sitting, he felt as if he was intruding on a private moment, but Malcolm smiled at him and patted his hand.

"I keep having dreams about a lad I met back when I was seventeen," Bliss was saying. "Perfectly innocent afternoon in its way. One of those endless summers. You never remember it raining in your past, do you? Just summers. We collected blackberries. Then we sat on the beach and talked. He took his shirt off. I kept mine on. I was too ashamed of my body to do the same. He was beautiful. So *piss-elegant* in his way. All cheek-bones and wrists. Tanned hairless skin. I wanted to be the centre of his world forever." Bliss smiled, his eyes somewhere in the distance, away from the heat of all these people and their mindless chatter. "It was just a kiss. That was all it was. A sweet, sweet kiss... I never saw him again, even though I went back to that place every afternoon for a week." His eyes refocused and he glanced at Malcolm, at Oliver. His face was hard, his voice brittle. "I found out he'd been hit by a postal van not two hours after we'd kissed. Died later that night in hospital. I overheard my mother talking about it. She said his name and I had to run away to the beach. I wept for hours. All gone, gone, *gone*."

"Oh, Kenneth..." Malcolm said, taking Bliss's hand.

"I keep my countenance but inside I'm screaming. The casual cruelty of the world. All those creative, beautiful people, trodden underfoot, while the barbarians march on..."

They sat in silence for a moment, allowing Bliss his quiet reverie.

"*Oh*, what am I *like*?" Bliss said then, his voice curling around the words, a smile spilling around his lips. "I mean, *really*?" He laughed but the sound of it was still so brittle that Oliver wanted only to be away from him, to allow him his grief. "And now, here I am, doing voice over work for fucking *toothpaste commercials*. No one wants a limp-wristed old queen like me anymore, do they, Oliver?"

"Actually, they might," Malcolm said then. "Oliver here is going to make a Play for Today for the Beeb, and I'm sure if you ask nicely, he'll find a part for you."

"A Play for Today?" Oliver said.

"I'm sorry, I've been meaning to tell you all bloody day, but well, *this* happened. What do you think?"

"How did you get them to agree to that?"

"I get to tell *them* what to agree to these days, Oliver. I'm Head of Commissioning for Arts now. We have a slot opened up for a writer/director and we need to fill it, pronto. I threw your name into the hat at the last production meeting."

"But I have no experience in that kind of thing."

"Oh, come on, Oliver, you're *overqualified* if anything. I have some thoughts about what we might be able to collaborate on. Something a bit more *adult* in nature for a Play for Today, of course. But I think you might be able to incorporate some of the stop-motion animation in it too. It'll make it unique."

Oliver didn't know how to respond. It felt like a delicious gift and a burden of great magnitude, all at once. He felt panicked and elated.

"Say you'll at least consider it, eh?" Malcolm said, squeezing his hand. "If only for Kenny's sake." He leaned forward to whisper in his ear. "You don't have to cast the daft old bugger in it if you don't want to…"

The lights went out at that moment, and a theatrical gasp filled the air, then laughter.

"Another bloody power cut," Kenneth hissed in the dark. "This bastard government…" Even after Heath had been ousted in the February 1974 election, the country's generating supply was still precarious. Power cut off without warning. Oliver was used to it out in the country. You just put some logs on the fire and got some blankets and waited it out. No one seemed overly concerned here either. The conversations continued and the drink still flowed, even if the music had stopped. Someone found a radio and turned it on. Malcolm was still holding Oliver's hand, his head bowed close enough for them to touch foreheads. Oliver stiffened, but something about the relative concealment of the dark gallery allowed him to relax his grip on whatever it was he'd been hiding from all day. This close he could smell Malcolm's aftershave, that intoxicating aroma. He felt the other man's cheek against his. Oliver closed his eyes. "I don't know…" he began, and then faltered. His heart was pounding. "I don't understand this…"

"I know you don't," Malcolm said. He sighed in Oliver's ear. "But it's alright."

They remained like that for a while, their faces touching, their fingers entwined. In the dark. Oliver felt the changes. One little step at a time.

Part Two

Life,
Happening Elsewhere

One

I wondered if, after his nocturnal escapade in our room last night, Florian would still be in the shop window display. The next morning, before we left the inn, I'd sat Lily down to ascertain how she felt about what had happened last night. With her difficulties, Lily was a very different kind of eight-year-old. Compared to her other 21st century counterparts, who documented everything from their breakfast to their bus ride to school on Facebook and Instagram, Lily was very much like a child from a different age. She had no time for phones or iPads; happier with her colouring books and crayons and rudimentary reading books. Her attention was diffuse, hard to corral for long. I couldn't be sure how she'd feel about what had happened, if she'd consider it in the same way she would a dream, or if she'd carry some anxiety about it that might explode in some other situation, later down the line. Context was difficult for her, so I tried to talk it through without denying it had happened, without revealing any of my own misgivings about the event, of which there were, of course, many. After she'd gone back to sleep, I'd gathered up the trail of buttons that Florian had left behind, and then pulled the wardrobe away from the wall again, my heart pounding, but the tiny door was no longer there. I'd sat for the rest of the night, watching, weighing the buttons in my hand, waiting for the old rabbit's return, growing more concerned about my own sanity. I could have chalked it up to a hallucination, but it was clear that Lily had seen it all too.

We pulled on fresh winter clothes and made our way around the back of the pub and into the mounds of fallen snow. In places it almost came up to my knees. I lifted Lily into my arms and we made our way down the street and back to the shop. The sky was pale and filled with the promise of further wintry showers. The streetlights were flickering off for the day, replaced by the lights in shop fronts as their proprietors opened up. I smelled bacon frying and coffee roasting as we tramped down to the storefront. The streets were empty. The only sound was the snow squeaking underfoot.

Florian was in the exact same spot that he had been yesterday. A thin film of dust remained on his shoulders and his top hat. It was almost as if he'd never moved. I stared at him for a while, willing some twitch of that dirty snout. Nothing.

I knocked on the door again while Lily pressed her nose to the glass, face lighting up. There was still no one at home. I crouched down beside my little girl and looked at the display with her.

Lily seemed to harbour no real anxieties about Florian's nighttime wanderings. In fact, it had appeared to have kindled a curiosity in her that I wanted to encourage as much as I could, despite what had happened last night. I'd convinced myself that when she was an adult she'd recall the event in the same way she would a dream. I didn't think it would harm her unduly.

"I know someone we can meet who'll be able to tell you all about Florian," I told her. "We're going to stay with Imogen, who went on all those adventures with him."

She didn't look at me, but I didn't expect her to. She tugged at the bobbles that hung from her woollen hat until locks of her blonde hair escaped. After a moment, she said, "Can I play with him, Daddy? I don't think he's all that scary anymore." She considered Florian and his friends for a moment, biting her lower lip. "I think he looks sad, just sitting there."

"He probably is," I said gently. "He used to have lots of adventures in a big doll's house with Imogen."

"Where's the doll's house?"

"I don't know," I said. "But I'm sure that Imogen will. Maybe she'll show us if we're good."

She glanced at me briefly. "OK," she said after a moment.

———

The school waited for us at the top of a narrow lane. Ancient timber-framed buildings dating back to the 17th century leaned across the cobbles, almost touching in the middle, blotting out the pale morning light. A picture postcard of a lane. The snow was thick; the slight incline meant we had to take our time making our way up there.

The school was closed to the children today due to the inclement weather. It was a small but grand-looking red brick structure, with a large arched foyer and a vaulted ceiling, and stained glass windows that set fire to the pale morning light.

I read somewhere that odour memories get etched into the brain, particularly early smells, which seem to achieve a privileged status in our mind. Memories triggered by smells are more vivid and more emotional than those triggered by sounds, pictures or words. My hippocampus lit up as soon as we entered that school. It was a sensory assault of memories of childhood that more modern schools didn't seem to contain. The uncommon scents of carbolic soap and crayons, blackboard dusters and stale school dinners, sweaty plimsolls and newly sharpened pencils. It was a strange frisson, made up of elation and melancholy and fear. I hadn't enjoyed my school days. After my mother died, I'd found it hard to make friends, even at the children's home, so my childhood was largely spent alone. I spent a lot of time reading *Alice's Adventures in Wonderland* and writing my own short stories after Oliver and Imogen had visited the home. But despite the loneliness there was still that slight yearning for the simplicity of it all: a time before bills and obligations and heartbreak.

Everything was a trigger: Lily's wellington boots squeaking on the parquet floor, the sight of the pegs where the children would hang their duffel coats and bags, the glimpse of tiny wooden desks in one of the classrooms with the chairs on top of them, the crude paintings of houses and parents and trees and pets hanging on the walls... All of it rendered strange and ghostly due to the emptiness of the building.

We finally found Imogen in one of the classrooms. I watched her for a moment, her attention on some documents, the contents of which she was transferring to a computer. Her long, tapered fingers moving quickly over the keyboard. Her long grey hair, tied up in a bun, stray curls hanging around her long pale neck. Spectacles on the bridge of her nose.

Those welcoming grey eyes that I recalled above all else from a lifetime away. She was Imogen at 55; she was Imogen at 26 when I'd loved her; she was Imogen at nine, trying to coax a lonely boy out of his shell; she was Imogen on the TV, travelling Elsewhere with Florian the rabbit. You could get lost forever in the folds of memories within memories. Oliver Frayling would probably have approved of that idea.

She glanced up before I could say her name. She looked past me and at Lily. Her face changed; from a woman behind a desk who I didn't really know, to the woman I did, who'd seen me at my best and my worst. At the height of summer in a field with thousands of others, off our faces and dancing like the world might end if we stopped, and at the end of a day when it wouldn't stop raining and we walked away from the place where her husband was laid to rest. And everything in between. She smiled and she was Imogen. *My* Imogen.

We met in the middle. She took me in her arms and I inhaled her. Another flood of emotions based on a scent forgotten and remembered again. I allowed myself a moment, my chin on her shoulder, one arm around her and the other still gripping Lily's hand. Just a little moment of indulgence, and then it was over. After we relinquished each other, Imogen crouched down to child's height. "And you must be Lily," she said. "Well, aren't you the little heartbreaker. I've heard all about you from your dad."

Lily chanced a glance at me for reassurance and I squeezed her hand to tell her it was OK. "Hello," she said, turning away, her face nestled into my coat, a shy smile on her face.

"This is Imogen," I said.

"*The* Imogen?" Lily said from behind the safety of my coat. She stared at the woman in front of her, trying to fit the idea of who she had been versus who she was now into her head. It was a good, hard stare.

Imogen glanced up at me quizzically.

"We saw the display in the window in town," I said. "Florian and his friends. They made quite the impact on Lily."

Imogen nodded. "Well, the apple doesn't fall far from the tree, does it? I suppose we have to talk about him," she said. "About the old man." She smiled. "I suppose it's about time."

———

Imogen took us to a cafe at the corner of the cobbled lane. The street was busier now. All the shops were open and there was a steady stream of traffic making its way through the town. Huge mounds of shovelled snow heaped at the roadside.

It was a tiny place, set out like a boutique for the tourists, no one else in there. The windows were steamed up. We stamped the snow from our boots and I unbuttoned Lily's coat and loosened her scarf, removed her hat. Her fine blonde hair stood up, filled with static electricity. I left her at a table by the window with Imogen and ordered some food, two coffees and a hot chocolate for Lily. While I waited, I watched Imogen speaking quietly to Lily, smoothing her hair down with a palm, engaging her with what seemed like relative ease. I considered her for a moment, still trapped somewhere between here and *there*.

"How have you been?" I asked Imogen when I sat down.

"It's a bit of a rollercoaster, I suppose,' she said. "Up and down. I don't think I was prepared for how quiet the house is now. It seems huge. And empty. I've been trying to decide whether to decorate for Christmas. It seems a bit silly now there's just me."

I closed my hand over Imogen's.

"I have friends here," she said. "It's a nice community. It was Mum and Dad's community. You can feel them pulling for you when things like that happen." She smiled to prove to me that it was OK. "The kids stayed for a month to help me through it."

"How did they cope with it?"

"Better than me," Imogen said. "I think you get to an age where you can accept your kids being able to take over and deal with things that you can't. Matthew lives in Australia now. He's a psychotherapist. Two kids of his own. Mary is an education consultant in Cambridge."

Our food arrived and we ate in a companionable silence. I cut up Lily's food for her, encouraged her to eat a little more than she wanted. My food went cold. It usually did these days. Outside it had begun to snow again. It gathered quickly at the windows. I saw people trudging past, collars turned up, their breath pluming behind them.

"When can I see the doll's house?" Lily asked after we'd eaten.

"The doll's house?" Imogen said.

"That window display with the toys is the first thing we saw when we arrived in town," I explained. "Lily has become fond of Florian. I explained that my oldest friend went on adventures with him when she was a little girl."

Imogen nodded. "Dad's little folly for the Beeb."

"We hardly ever talked about it when we were together."

She smiled a smile I remembered well. A subtle delaying tactic that only attractive people can pull off successfully. After some deliberation she said, "When I was younger, I didn't *want* to talk about it."

"We were together for two years, Imogen. I think we spoke about it once."

"I think you always loved that show more than I did."

"I didn't really see the wizard behind the curtain like you did."

"Just a glimpse."

"I never forgot him taking an interest in me, encouraging me to write."

"Giving you my copy of *Alice in Wonderland*..."

"He said he'd buy you a new copy!"

"He forgot. Mum bought me one eventually."

"I still have it."

"I don't doubt it."

"I didn't have much at that home. It felt like treasure to me."

"That whole time wasn't very good for my family," Imogen said. "Dad's career with the BBC didn't really amount to much, but it was a bone he couldn't let go of for years. It broke the family up eventually."

Imogen looked at Lily, who'd resorted to her crayons and sketchbook. "Don't you find Florian a little bit scary?"

Lily shook her head, her hand curled around the crayon. She had been trying to draw the old rabbit from memory in the corner of her colouring book. She'd remembered the top hat and the hard square of rotten teeth in his muzzle. The little doorway at the edge of the paper was ajar. I wondered what Lily had seen. Something about what was beyond that door, above all else, filled me with dread for something that hadn't yet happened.

"Not anymore," Lily said. "We saw him last night. He was in our room but he escaped through this door…" Lily pointed to her drawing.

I fumbled for a way to explain it away but then I noticed that the colour had drained from Imogen's face. A hand had risen to cover her mouth in shock.

"Imogen?" I said.

But I could see it in her expression. It explained her last-minute reticence about us coming here.

She'd seen Florian too.

Two

"That's very good, Kenneth, but could you go through it again and this time can you just speak it naturally… don't *act it*, in fact, just try to let go of all that *acting* stuff. Say it as if you were *thinking* it for the first time."

"Yes, Oliver, of course. You are, after all, in charge."

And so it went. Kenneth Bliss was frequently brilliant, but almost insufferable to work with. They were filming on location in the little town of Great Malvern and its environs. Oliver had harboured real misgivings about his ability to turn the script he and Malcolm had worked on into something of worth. On the first day with the crew, they had all turned towards Oliver expectantly and he'd wanted to turn and run for the hills. Luckily Malcolm had insisted he be there for the duration of the shoot to help Oliver over the nerves and expectations he felt he'd never be able to meet.

It was certainly a far cry from working alone in his cowshed with his taxidermied animals and toys and his Bolex camera. He'd only really had to direct Imogen then, and she was only doing what her father told her, in exchange for small rewards.

After the initial proposal for the idea had been approved by the BBC, Oliver had started taking the train down to London every Friday afternoon to work on the script at Malcolm's place in Pimlico. After the hours of hard work, with one of them at the typewriter and the other pacing backwards and forwards, smoking endless cigarettes, brewing countless pots of coffee, Malcolm would spirit them away in a cab to dine with Kenneth or Julian, or to a party somewhere in Kensington in a room filled with famous faces. It was a dizzying and eye-opening time. It was a different world where drink flowed freely, and the morals of a life lived in rural Worcestershire seemed to have no harbour.

The seed of the idea for *PoppyHarp* belonged to Malcolm. He'd confided to Oliver that he'd had an imaginary friend who'd helped him through what he regarded as an 'awkward' childhood. But PoppyHarp had arrived during the onset of his adolescence, as a kind of sexual awakening. "It was like the sound of a note moving from dissonance to consonance, to resolution," he said. "And then my ears popped. Pop! Just like that. And there he was in my bedroom. PoppyHarp."

Malcolm talked about PoppyHarp at the end of the night, when he was tired or tipsy. Strange stories about an imaginary friend that seemed tangled up in his anxieties about his burgeoning sexuality in a small Northern town. Sometimes he referred to him as if he was entirely real, even now. He often wondered what had become of PoppyHarp, how his life had turned out. It was the seed of an idea that turned into the script they collaborated on.

After some weeks of reticence, there had been other factors to contend with that refused to be deferred. It came to a head one evening, which had been filled with black cabs and parties and excellent wine, but then it was over and they were back at Malcolm's flat in Pimlico. Malcolm lowered the lights and put a record on the gramophone. All of the windows were open, the first warm days of summer at the door. They slipped off their shoes and unbuttoned their shirts, fell onto the couch, exhausted, a little bit squiffy. The heat was triggering something else inside Oliver, something that sprang from the musk of their bodies and the delayed sense of whatever it was growing between them. He'd refrained from responding to Malcolm's attentions for as long as he could. Malcolm had accepted these rejections with quiet grace and patience.

Oliver hadn't slept with Jenny in six months. She'd surely sensed the change in him; turning away from him every night until he came to bed later and later. Finally he had made a bed up in one of the spare rooms and sat, reading in the small hours, wondering what had become of his life. He felt a keen sense of having already betrayed her, although any infelicity at that time existed solely in their over-active imaginations. Jenny's mood swings were becoming more pronounced, more unpredictable: from breathless exuberance to barely being able to get out of bed in the morning. They didn't argue. Neither of them seemed to want to acknowledge what it was that had come between them, but they both knew what it was. It was 1976. A different time. Homosexuality might have been legalised in 1967 in Britain, but this was Lethebury, a little town in the middle of the Malverns. Everyone knew everyone else; gossip spread like wildfire. Oliver didn't know how he felt about these elements of his life himself; events seemed to be forcing his hand. He'd always hated to be rushed into anything. Perhaps that was why he had hoped *The Adventures of Imogen and*

Florian would be a success; that way he could have hidden himself away in the cowshed for a few more years. They might have been able to muddle their way through their marriage somehow, despite its failings.

But then that evening on the couch Malcolm said something he didn't catch. Oliver had leaned forward and asked what he'd said, and Malcolm had kissed him. A speculative kiss; nothing more, nothing less. Oliver could smell that dizzying aftershave of Malcolm's mixed with the musk of a day in a hot office and a night at a party in Kensington. Sweat and tobacco and alcohol.

"I don't know how to do any of this," Oliver whispered. He pressed his forehead to Malcolm's and closed his eyes. All he could see was Jenny, there in the house with Imogen at her side. Manic, when he'd left her this morning. Baking pies and organising their receipts and bills into boxes so they could find everything when they needed them. She wouldn't meet his eyes, wouldn't acknowledge his readiness to leave. Imogen hadn't kissed him goodbye. His daughter, once so full of life, with so many questions and an endless thirst for adventure, had grown quiet and deeply suspicious of his absences too; she simply avoided interaction with him as much as she could now, which upset him more than anything else. He could accept Jenny's coldness, he had earned that, but Imogen? He couldn't abide the thought of alienating his only child. He wanted to sit her down and explain what was going on in his life, in her life. But how could she begin to understand what was happening when he barely grasped it himself? That closeness they'd had on their little tour of the children's homes seemed so very long ago now.

"Just let yourself go, Oliver," Malcolm said. "*Abandon* yourself. Forget about everything else. Just for tonight."

Oliver kissed him back finally and raised a hand to Malcolm's face. After a moment's hesitation, he ran his fingers through Malcolm's fine blond hair. He'd wanted to do that for weeks. To touch him. One touch led to another until their hands were entwined and they were kissing in the darkness with the sound of London traffic drifting into the apartment. One door being opened that led to another door, and another, deeper into a house he didn't know the dimensions of. But Malcolm coaxed him through with gentle encouragement. It felt like a controlled explosion in his life. Over the next few days and weeks, he came to realise that there were shards of that explosion in everything. Some of them shone like diamonds, some of them were sharp to the touch. He tried to conceal them as well as he could.

It was the beginning and the end of something.

After several weekends they had the script hammered out between them, and the synopsis had passed muster with the faceless fellows upstairs at Broadcasting House. Malcolm had somehow managed to convince them to approve Oliver as the director, and within a few weeks they were sent 110 miles up the M1 to Pebble Mill studios in Birmingham. Malcolm had requested it as their base of operations. No one asked what they were up to so far away from London and consequently, edgier fare could be produced. Here in the Midlands they would be allowed to make the play the way they wanted without any unnecessary distractions. Here was a place for expression of the individual, dissident or questioning voice. *The Times* and the *Daily Mail* had expressed reservations about the Play for Today series having left-wing concerns and bias, saying it was all alienated youths and institutionalised pensioners. Malcolm suggested *PoppyHarp* would only lend fire to these views. They were following, he insisted, in the trailblazing footsteps of *The Naked Civil Servant*, which had aired last December on ATV.

Oliver had misgivings about the whole affair. He was still, despite his growing feelings for Malcolm, deeply entrenched in his conservative upbringing, and harboured a natural reticence of being the centre of attention. But Malcolm was pushing him every day, insisting upon hidden depths to his skills and identity. He was deeply resistant to the idea of directing the play, but Malcolm wouldn't hear of such qualms. He was happier than Oliver had ever seen him, and Malcolm made sure that Oliver knew it was because of him. At that point, Oliver realised that he was caught between hurting the only three people he'd ever really loved in his adult life: Jenny, Imogen and, now, Malcolm.

BBC Internal Circulating Memo
(PRIVATE AND CONFIDENTIAL)

SUBJECT: Play for Today synopsis
13 February 1976

<u>PoppyHarp: a play by Oliver Frayling and
Malcolm Church. (Synopsis)</u>

After his mother dies, an ageing comedian
returns to his childhood home in the
wildness of the Malvern Hills to put her
affairs in order. He spends his days lost
in the memories of his youth and coming
to terms with a life spent denying who he
is. One day a curious man arrives at his
mother's door claiming to be PoppyHarp, his
imaginary childhood friend.

PoppyHarp will not go away. Once
remembered, he is impossible to forget.
And PoppyHarp has spent the intervening
years living a life unfettered by Phillip's
self-imposed restrictions, leading to an
inevitable conflict between the two men.

<u>In this Play for Today, Oliver Frayling and
Malcolm Church examine the notion of an
individual determined to live life on his
own terms, unrestrained by a society in the
midst of change.</u>

It had, of course, been Malcolm's idea to cast Kenneth Bliss as the ageing comedian in *PoppyHarp*. During the writing process, Oliver had quickly accepted the idea of Bliss as the old man with stifled homosexual proclivities. He was also aware that this process was a way to articulate what he couldn't fully accept about the changes in his life. Malcolm was cajoling him away from old habits of restraint, towards vistas he could scarcely imagine. He was doubtful that the life he lived at weekends in London could be the basis of a change of circumstances. It was an endless parade of brilliant faces, being swept from parties to meetings, forever caught in oddly intense conversations with strangers. He considered himself a simple man, with simple tastes. He could accept change incrementally, but London would be a step too far. It wasn't who he was.

Bliss proved to be difficult for much of the shoot. Every day, trying to get what they required of him was like drawing blood from a stone. Oliver could see all too clearly why his career had faltered in recent years. He was difficult, pig-headed, a bit of a know-it-all. After the first week of filming, they all had dinner in one of the old hotels in Great Malvern. All the windows were open. It was the summer of 1976, and they were in the grip of a heat wave of absurd proportions, the hottest summer in the UK since records began. Heath and forest fires broke out in parts of southern England. Massive swarms of seven-spotted ladybirds descended across the country. Widespread water-rationing was implemented due to the severe drought. Oliver woke up sweating, got out of the bath sweating, went to bed sweating. It was an intolerable way to work. Bliss spent the meal baiting Malcolm, because he knew him better than he did Oliver. The actor was a cowardly man at heart, bitterly unhappy with all aspects of the production. He couldn't seem to grasp that someone else's vision of how to do something could be superior to his.

"You're rejecting all of my ideas, all of my decisions," he kept saying. "You just don't trust my *instincts*."

"Don't be daft. Of course I trust your instincts, Kenny."

"But that's just it, Malcolm. You *don't*. I've been doing this for *decades* now. *Countless* films. No bugger complained before now."

"Oh, I'm sure they did, Kenneth."

"Fuck off, Malcolm."

"You'll just have to trust us," Malcolm said, placing his hand on Oliver's shoulder. "You'll see. Sometimes you have to take a chance every now and then. Let yourself be exposed. Vulnerable."

"Yes, I *know*, Malcolm. You're trying to divest me of all the artifice you think I've built up over the years. Taking away all of my lovely little ticks, all the voices and mannerisms." Bliss thumped his fists on the table to ensure everyone was aware of his displeasure. "Surely if you hired me, then that is what the audience will expect to see."

"This is different material to what you're used to, Kenneth," Oliver put in tentatively. "I appreciate your misgivings, but I promise that if you trust me I will not in any way humiliate you or misrepresent you."

"I appreciate that, Oliver. It's not that I fear the message of the play. God knows I've dealt with the stigma of—" He lowered his voice, but it was so theatrically trained that it carried across the room. "—*homosexuality* for much of my life." He sat back and pressed a napkin to his perspiring forehead. "I should probably have done that season in Skegness with Richard Briers instead."

"Millions of people will see this play, Kenny," Malcolm said. "You can't say that about a season at the end of the pier in Skeggy, now can you?"

"The very nature of these things is that they are ephemeral, Malcolm. Who will remember an obscure little play fifty years from now? Here today, gone tomorrow."

"No, people will remember this one, Kenny. This will be one for the ages. I *guarantee* it." He squeezed Oliver's hand beneath the table. Oliver was mortified that one of the crew might notice the little intimacy. "Think about *Nuts in May*, *Two Sundays*, *Penda's Fen*. Wonderful plays with real substance."

Bliss flared his nostrils and then rose, stalked away. He went outside to smoke alone, pale and theatrically distraught. They left him to it.

———

Although they had hired a young actor to play PoppyHarp, Malcolm had insisted that Oliver use some of the techniques he'd perfected on *The Adventures of Imogen and Florian*. The actor would be filmed using the stop motion technique Oliver had perfected with Florian and the cast of other toys and taxidermied animals. It was a time-consuming process that none of the crew were prepared for, much less Kenneth Bliss. After a day of filming in the almost stifling heat of the old farmhouse they'd used for filming, Bliss was almost apoplectic at the length of time it took to complete the pain-staking method of filming the young man moving across a room. Even when Malcolm insisted he see a rough cut of the finished procedure, he remained unmoved. It left Oliver rattled, uncertain about continuing with what seemed like something far too experimental and unconventional for an adult play.

Oliver steeled himself for the next day, wondering if the technique could be simplified, if the result was another day of Bliss over-reacting. But Bliss arrived in high-spirits, eager to begin. He didn't even break stride when Oliver set to work on what proved to be eight hours of piecemeal recording, process over performance. Kenneth joked with the crew and fluttered around Rupert, the young actor playing PoppyHarp. He looked like a love-sick teenager. Oliver couldn't complain. If he worked hard, they could get the lion's share of technical shots in the can by the end of the day. Then they could concentrate on the character stuff.

After they broke for lunch, Oliver found Malcolm in one of the caravans the BBC had supplied for make-up and catering. He was smiling. "How are you finding Kenny today?" he said brightly.

"Much better," Oliver admitted. "He hasn't complained once. The crew think he was body-snatched in the night."

"Splendid."

Oliver stared at Malcolm, at the sly smile on his face. "What did you *do*, Malcolm?"

"What makes you think I did anything?"

"I know that look by now."

"Oh, *do* you, now?" Malcolm rose and stood close to Oliver. There wasn't much room in the caravan. They were almost touching. Oliver could feel Malcolm's breath on his face. His mouth was inches away from his. Suddenly his breath was shallow, his heart racing.

"Not *here*, Malcolm," he said finally and stepped away, bumping his hip on a table in his haste. "Anyone could walk in."

Save for one day off when they had gone hiking in the hills, Oliver had insisted that they restrain themselves while they filmed out here in the Malverns. No funny business while Oliver tried to get this right.

"It's Rupert," Malcolm said.

"What about him?"

Rupert, the young man they'd cast after seeing several actors for the role, was conducting himself admirably in what was his first real serious role. He'd been made up to look slightly artificial. He was, after all, playing an imaginary friend. Oliver had brought in an old ventriloquists' dummy he'd found in a box in his cowshed for the makeup artist to draw inspiration from. PoppyHarp was a figure divested of inhibitions; the same inhibitions that had destabilised the comedian's whole life.

"I made a small addendum to Rupert's contract," Malcolm said, sitting back down. He poured himself a cup of tea then sat back, pinching the crease back into place on his trousers.

"What kind of addendum?"

"Actually, nothing was written down. It was more a gentlemen's agreement, I suppose." He lit a cigarette, leaned back. "It's his first real acting job, and luckily he was more than willing to go the extra mile to prove to me how serious he is about his career."

"You didn't…"

"Me? Don't be daft, Oliver! What do you take me for?"

"So, Kenneth…"

"A little extra-curricular acting on Rupert's part. It's costing me a bit more out of my own pocket, but I'd say it's worth it if today is anything to go by."

"What exactly have you asked him to do, Malcolm?"

Malcolm shrugged. "A spot of flirting in the hotel. Asking Kenneth to help him run his lines in his hotel room. And to just take it from there."

"Christ, Malcolm. I don't know how I feel about this."

"You don't have to feel *anything* about it. This is for your benefit."

"It seems a bit harsh, getting Kenneth's hopes up like that."

Malcolm snorted. "Trust me, Kenny can cope with it. He's no stranger to causal trade, and he's had the parasite infections to prove it. Listen, I didn't get to where I am today without learning which weapons to deploy to make strategic advancements."

"But it's immoral, leading him up the garden path like that."

"Look, Oliver. As it is, you get to piddle around all day to your heart's content, getting the stop-motion work in the bag, and Kenny's enjoying the attentions of our Rupert for a few weeks. Everyone's a winner."

———

It got the requisite performance out of Bliss. Rupert kept his mood sufficiently ebullient all the way to the end of filming, attending to the actor's every mood swing with what Oliver considered the patience of a saint. As they dug into the character work and Bliss realised that this was essentially a one-man show, he marshalled his attention to the script and gave Oliver and Malcolm exactly what they suspected he was capable of giving: a subtle and measured performance.

"He's fucking heart-breaking," Malcolm said when they considered the rushes.

Oliver nodded. He wasn't willing to admit to anything until the play was finished. But he suspected that *PoppyHarp* was not the failure he'd expected it to be. For the first couple of weeks his attention seemed too diffuse; there were too many people involved, too many aspects that could not be overseen with any degree of efficacy. But with the play complete and all of the disparate parts in the process of being stitched together by an editor at Pebble Mill, he kept catching glimpses of it: the product he'd seen in his mind's eye while he and Malcolm wrote it. It seemed impossible that they might get all the way to the other side with something so promising.

"It's a one-man show," Malcolm said. "I knew the old queen had it in him."

By the end of summer, they had a final cut of the play that ran to 87 minutes. Malcolm invited a few close friends to a screening room at Broadcasting House after the bigwigs upstairs had seen and agreed to it. Malcolm had stayed cool as a cucumber while Oliver sweated his way through another new shirt.

A large crowd arrived to Malcolm's little screening party. By now they were all familiar faces to Oliver, and he greeted them with varying degrees of warmth. He genuinely enjoyed seeing Julian and some of his friends, but there were always two or three colleagues of Malcolm's who left him cold. They were either beaming fake smiles or else sniffing for blood in the water. They didn't know how to approach Oliver. He was an outsider, but he'd produced something that was causing the appropriate buzz in their little circles, and he was *with* Malcolm. To all intents and purposes, he was 'out' in London, whatever that meant. It made him uncomfortable, knowing that Jenny and Imogen were at home in Lethebury, going about their lives without him, beginning by now to accept his absences. It was almost as if he'd already left them. But that was far from what he wanted. It was still a relief to go back home, even if Jenny was cold with him and Imogen distant. Imogen had to cope with her mother's failing mental health alone now. Every time he returned his little girl seemed a little older than before. Dealing with Jenny's mood swings was making her grow up too fast. It should be his responsibility to shoulder, not hers. Soon she'd be a teenager, filled with resentment for her father and his shortcomings.

The screening went well. Kenneth made the most of the adulation that night, even though he was grieving the loss of Rupert, who'd promptly disappeared into the city as soon as filming was over. He was strangely pragmatic about the whole affair. At some point the work on *PoppyHarp* had begun to engage him for the first time in years. He and Oliver had sat one evening on one of the final days of the shoot, talking more freely now that they knew and respected each other's talents; that in many ways, they were on the same page.

"I suspect I've left it far too late to make anything of my life now," Bliss said, but there was no trace of self-pity in his voice, none of those nasal inflections that he'd fallen upon almost subconsciously in the past to avoid ridicule or to raise a cheap laugh. "I identify myself in *exceptionally* shallow terms, Oliver. I always have. There's a struggle to break through all those self-imposed lies and become your own true, significant, contradicting, difficult, bloody-minded self."

"At least you're aware of these things, Kenneth," Oliver said. "I'm not sure I could say that about myself. These days I feel even less sure about who I am."

"You know, Oliver," Kenneth said with a gentle smile, "you only *think* that you don't. You believe you'll hurt people by admitting it, but it's crueller to let these things go on and let resentment grow. Someone will *always* be hurt. The trick is learning how best to minimise that anguish. Leaving now is better than leaving later."

They didn't really have time to speak at the screening party, but Bliss found a moment to cast a slightly wounded smile across the room at Oliver before leaving early.

The party went on a little too long, moving downstairs to the BBC bar. Oliver decided to get back home to Jenny. He'd made a decision after months of cogitating on it. The truth of things was that he now loved both Jenny and Malcolm equally, but for very different reasons. He had no real evidence that there was a future here in London with Malcolm. Indeed, he didn't think he was cut out for this city anyway. Everything moved too fast for his liking, and people seldom offered anything without expecting something in return. Lethebury's sedate pace had always been more suited to his demeanour. He'd broached the subject with Malcolm frequently of late, but he didn't want to even suggest some kind of shoddy part-time romance with him. That was short-changing both of them. Perhaps there was some kind of compromise, but he was damned if he knew what that was. Malcolm seemed content the way things were. He had his own friends, and a network of contacts in London; his days were mapped out for him with the BBC. Moving away would have been out of the question.

But it couldn't continue. Jenny was in a wretched state. The doctor had finally referred her to a specialist in Birmingham, who confirmed that she was suffering from manic depression and prescribed some extremely strong medication for her. After that she spent her days numb. She couldn't work like that, so they were struggling to make ends meet. They didn't talk anymore. Imogen's schoolwork began to deteriorate. She was concerned about her mother, angry at her father's absences. Oliver had no idea how Jenny was explaining the situation; he couldn't face the job, so he avoided it, aware how cowardly that made him. He'd decided to rectify the situation by throwing himself wholeheartedly at making things right again.

He left the party and caught a taxi to Paddington station, managed to get an evening train back to Hereford. He watched the day fade away across the fields, and the closer he came to home, the more sure Oliver was about his decision. It was the only real option that he could really consider. Jenny just had to see that he'd left that part of his life behind; he'd had his dalliance with London and all the associated fripperies, and now here he was, ready to make a go of it, if she'd have him back. It seemed like the only sensible option. He bought some flowers from the station in Hereford and caught the bus home to Lethebury.

The house was dark when he arrived home. Even if Jenny had gone to bed, she would leave at least one or two lights on for Imogen, who was afraid of the dark.

Oliver stepped off the bus, gripped with a sudden panic. He ran down the lane and into the drive, the flowers crushed in his fist. He wrestled the keys from his pocket and into the lock, stumbled into the hall, calling her name.

Nothing.

He found the note on the mantelpiece. It was brief and to the point.

I'm leaving you, it said. And, indeed, she had.

Three

"So, Oliver went missing about twelve years ago?" I said.

"2009," Imogen said. "It has to be seven years before you can make a claim for a 'declaration of presumed death' from the High Court."

Imogen had offered to drive us out to Oliver's house in her Land Rover. It was in the valley, about a mile away. She had some chores to get through there anyway, so Lily could see some of the toys and models and, most importantly, the doll house from *The Adventures of Imogen and Florian*. We'd quietly decided not to talk about the rabbit yet, not when Lily could listen in. But I could see it in Imogen's face: a mixture of consternation and relief at the mention of seeing Florian in our room last night. She'd suspected she was going quietly mad; this proved that she was not.

"You don't think he's still alive?"

Imogen shrugged. "Despite all of our differences I'd like to believe that he just ran away, to be happy with someone. I can't allow myself to think he committed suicide. That he died alone…" She sighed. "It caused quite the stir at the time. He turned Lethebury into a bit of a circus for a couple of weeks."

"I must have missed the news reports," I said. "It was probably when I was in America with Abigail. I didn't think Oliver was that famous."

"Oh, he wasn't." We left the town behind and Imogen turned off down a narrow road that wound all the way down into the snow-covered valley. As we breasted a rise, there was the vale, spread out below us, the fields and the forests and the farmhouses buried in snow. A strange realm of transformed country.

"He'd been going off for quite some time, and not coming back for days on end. When Jeffrey and I confronted him about it he told me to – and I quote – 'Not make such a fucking song and dance about things.' So I just let him get on with it. You couldn't really talk to Dad about anything so I suppose I just stopped trying. But I kept going to check on him. I couldn't help it. And the kids wanted to see their granddad. They would have been about ten or eleven at the time. It was difficult to explain why he acted the way he did.

"But then one day became a week or more and he hadn't been back at all, so I started to get concerned. There was no note, of course. But I had to get the police involved at that point. And by the time search parties were being organised, the local news crews turned up. Once they discovered that Dad had made TV shows for the BBC, that seemed to make his disappearance *much* more fascinating somehow. The police and the town scoured the area for at least a week. Searches being organised up hill and down dale for days on end." She shrugged. "Of course, they didn't find him. He'd been a Royal Observer Corps volunteer since the sixties. Do you remember them?"

I'd heard of them, but my knowledge of their activities didn't stretch too far.

"They were supposed to have been on the front line in the event of a nuclear attack on the UK when the Cold War was still going on." She smiled. "It seems incredible to imagine now. There was a *bunker*. It had a ladder down to a couple of rooms that the volunteers would go and hide in and measure the level of fallout and what not. Well, after the bunkers were all decommissioned, Dad bought the land it was on with whatever savings he had. I think everyone fully expected him to be down there after he went missing." She shrugged again. "But he wasn't. I'll show you it later."

"Was there a will?"

Imogen nodded. "It took a while to get to that point. Without a body, the inquest has to rely on evidence provided by the police investigation and whether the senior officers believe that the person is dead. Once we were through all that red tape, I was granted probate, and I could get on with Dad's assets, such as they were. I'd made a start on it but then Jeffrey's health deteriorated and it all had to take a back seat. Dad's house in the valley has been left to deteriorate in the meantime. It's only in the last month or so that I've had the energy to get back to it."

"What are you going to do with the house?"

"Once I've removed the things that are of worth, I'll have it done up and then put it on the market."

"And then what? Will you move away from here?" We'd passed the home she'd made with Jeffrey for almost twenty years on the way to Oliver's. An immaculate barn conversion, on a hill overlooking the town, surrounded by acres of land.

"There are all these memories here in Lethebury," she said. "Good *and* bad, I suppose. I grew up here, I moved away, then, when I came back in 1996, I met Jeffrey and started teaching at the school. We had Matthew and Mary, we raised them here. You couldn't ask for a much better environment to bring children up in." She smiled. "But you know, it feels like everything is tinged with this *sadness* now. It can't be helped but there it is. When I remember seeing Jeffrey reading the morning paper in the conservatory on a Sunday morning, I also see him hunched in that same chair, looking at me with that awful expression of bewilderment and alarm. Knowing in his more lucid moments that it would only take him further and further away from me, and there was nothing to be done about it, and that, of the two of us, I would have to shoulder the burden of that fact alone.

"That's too much to bear every time I walk in the room. *Too* much."

"There's still plenty of time, Imogen," I said. "More than enough time to start again. It doesn't have to be difficult."

She linked her fingers with mine, then just as quickly relinquished them to change gear. "That almost sounds like an offer, Noah," she said, flashing me a puckish smile that I remembered all too well.

—

Oliver's house was a grand old Victorian Gothic pile. It seemed to loom large in the valley somehow, like Wuthering Heights or Manderley. I remembered the facade well from the opening shot of *The Adventures of Imogen and Florian*. It was surrounded by rolling hills and fields, little knots of woodland and rushing streams. When we got out of the car, all you could hear was the crunch of untouched snow underfoot and sweet, clear birdsong from the trees. The air was bitterly cold; it kept trying to creep inside your collar and up your sleeves; anywhere it could to chill your bones. The sun ran a shallow arc across the sky.

I unbuckled Lily from the backseat and carried her through the drifts of snow to the front door with Imogen, who was fumbling through a large set of keys she'd lifted from her handbag. We stood waiting in the stillness, Lily's hands on my shoulders, peering around at the sudden rush of arresting sights and sounds. Our breath plumed around us like ghostly vapour.

"Is this where the doll's house is, Daddy?" she said. She looked engaged again. It was thrilling for me to see that little spark of something that had been missing from my little girl all these years.

"It's inside, sweetheart." I squeezed Lily tightly in my arms.

We kicked the snow off our boots and stepped inside the hallway, a large open space with chequered tiles and an imposing staircase with a galleried landing. There were bills and circulars and other assorted detritus piled up behind the door. There was no electricity. Imogen had brought a torch for when the light fled from the afternoon. There was a dusty stillness to the house. I heard the sonorous ticking of a grandfather clock, and it was another of those senses reawakened by a vivid memory, that of the opening titles of *The Adventures of Imogen and Florian*. I was half expecting to hear that mournful piano playing a familiar melody in a distant room. Our footsteps sounded vast and lonely in the emptiness as Imogen led us upstairs. Disturbed dust drifted in the beams of pale light from the window on the landing. The house was frozen. Most of the narrow rooms that we passed on the way to the attic had been stripped of furniture. All that remained was the wallpaper, relics of the 50s and the 70s; some threadbare rugs on the bare wooden floorboards; nails on walls and the outline of pictures where the wallpaper hadn't been faded by the sun; boxes piled up and marked VASES, BLANKETS, PHOTOGRAPHS, BOOKS.

By the time we reached the narrow staircase up to the attic, I was seeing Imogen as a little girl superimposed over Imogen as a 55-year-old. I'd almost fooled myself that I could hear the piano playing, that the colour was bleeding from my eyes. But that was just my imagination, unboxing that grainy YouTube footage, restoring it to the front of my mind. That the girl from my childhood was also a woman who had lit up my life like fireworks was still a strange and bewildering notion to me.

The doll's house was larger than I'd expected it to be. It was set on a table in the centre of the floor. There were some boxes nearby, labelled DAD'S STUFF. I set Lily down so she could investigate. She walked around it, tentatively reaching out to touch, then glanced across at Imogen for permission.

"It's OK, sweetheart," Imogen said. "Open it up if you want."

She was still uncertain. I crouched down beside Lily and said, "Go on, it's fine."

She pulled the facade away to reveal the interior. There was a strange, delirious feeling to seeing inside. *And in that doll's house lived a great many things. Old things, lost things, forgotten things...* I remembered the wallpaper and the little pieces of furniture and the toys within. Although Florian, Antoine and Fizbatch were sitting in a window on the high street, other characters remained. Several taxidermied mice wearing bowler hats and spectacles, some frogs in the wigs you'd see on solicitors in court, another rabbit in a bonnet and an apron. They all rang a distant bell in the back of my mind; each of them in turn having an adventure with Imogen as Florian led her into the secret rooms and corridors, a veritable labyrinth of subterranean vaults; doors leading to rooms with trapdoors, secret passages. It took on huge, fractured, dreamlike conditions in my head.

"Florian comes back here at night," Lily told me with an alarming measure of conviction. "He travels through the doors like the one behind the wardrobe." She touched each of the characters, as if cataloguing them. "*Magic* doors."

"Is this what you saw through the door last night?" I asked.

She considered this for a moment, recalling scrambling behind the wardrobe and peering through a door she was disappointed she couldn't fit through. "The attic was different. There was lots of stuff everywhere and everyone was here, waiting for him. There were butterflies in cases and a rocking horse and chairs and mirrors."

"It used to look like that," Imogen said. "Before I cleared it all out. That was how it was arranged for *The Adventures of Imogen and Florian*."

"I saw it," Lily said. "Last night. Through the door."

"Did you see the video on YouTube? Is that what you remember?" Imogen asked. She sat beside Lily, and stroked her hair.

"I haven't had the chance to show her that yet," I said.

"Oh," Imogen said.

"But look – Florian's been here," Lily said, pointing at something on the floorboards behind the doll's house.

There was a trail of buttons leading from the house to one of the attic walls.

Four

They had, quite naturally, expected balmy Mediterranean sunshine, but when they arrived in Monaco they were greeted by a sullen sky and rain spitting in their faces. Oliver trailed his luggage (a new case, along with a sharp new suit, which Malcolm had bought him) towards Birdy's house. It was hard not to be overawed by the occasion, but Oliver was, at heart, a practical man. He wondered what point there was to a house that one only lived in a couple of months a year. What a frivolous waste of good property.

Birdy's chateau was crumbling in places, but nonetheless proved quite a captivating rose-coloured building, standing proudly on the bay of Roquebrune-Cap-Martin, between Monaco and Menton, sufficiently removed from the clamour of the casinos and resorts of Monte Carlo.

They'd noticed very little during the frantic cab ride from the airport. Kenneth was wedged between Malcolm and Oliver, complaining loudly and interminably about absolutely *everything*, as was his wont. Malcolm berated him several times, but it only seemed to quell him for a couple of minutes. Oliver held his tongue; he'd harboured severe misgivings about this entire sojourn ever since the idea was floated – by Bliss himself – a month ago. He'd come off a successful run of George Bernard Shaw's *Captain Brassbound's Conversion* with the American movie star, Birdy Irving. Despite Kenneth getting pissed at the press reception, making an enemy of the lead actor, and constantly berating Irving for not learning her lines, the two performers had forged a sweet, if occasionally fractious, friendship. On free evenings they'd ventured out to see other productions in the West End, Irving's disguises so ridiculously elaborate that she only drew attention to herself, if anything. She lacked, Bliss insisted in private, any kind of stage technique, which made her unable to sustain comedic moments. Nonetheless he grew to adore this slight, fine-boned woman, with her flinty disposition and her retinue of fussing assistants in tow. Together they made a sport of giving them the slip and escaping into the smoke and clamour of London, where everything was exotic and new for her, and the source of an endless parade of anecdotes for him. Bliss insisted that Irving was the best person he'd ever met who also happened to be an international star. Malcolm suggested to Oliver that it was entirely about his ego; secretly it was all Bliss had ever really dreamed of: to be more than he suspected he was in his reflective moments (of which there were many). The flashbulbs popping as they left the stage door every evening seemed to suggest that finally he was living the life he'd always yearned after. The play had been greeted with hostility by the press, but it ran for half a year, ending in the February of 1978, breaking all records for a limited season in London.

Before Kenneth fled the theatre on the final night, Birdy had insisted that he visit her in Monaco. She was returning to Hollywood, where she was contracted to shoot a low budget picture for Sidney Lumet. After that there was nothing on the horizon, so she was returning to her home in the South of France. She'd suggested Bliss bring whomever he wished to accompany him. "There's absolutely *masses* of space, darling," she said, wiping the last of her make-up from her face. "We have parties there that seem to go on for days. We even have a private beach if you have the urge to sunbathe *au naturel*."

"Christ," Bliss said, sourly. "I couldn't think of anything more appalling – lying there with me meat and two veg hanging out." He pouted. "It doesn't bear thinking about."

Birdy laughed, although Bliss suspected she barely understood a word he said.

Bliss didn't have to convince Malcolm when he'd suggested the vacation the following night at his flat in Pimlico. It was an entirely different proposition trying to persuade Oliver to accompany them.

"What the devil would *I* do in Monte Carlo?" he said, aware that he was already digging his heels in before he could see the whole picture.

"We can go to the casinos," Malcolm offered. "I'll buy you a new suit. How's that? You'll look grand. We can pretend to be James Bond. Kenny can be Moneypenny, if he plays his cards right. I'll buy him something pretty too."

"Gambling?" Oliver sniffed. "Surely we'll just end up wasting money."

"That's sort of the point, I think." Malcolm puffed out his cheeks. "*Sunbathing*, then. Just lie there and get a nice tan."

"I'm not much for lying in the sun, Malcolm," Oliver said. "I'd just be bored."

"Oh, *do* come on, Oliver," Malcolm said, wilting theatrically against him. "It's the south of bloody

France! You can be yourself there, or anyone you want for that matter." He took Oliver's hand. "It'd be our first holiday together. You wouldn't have to feel... well, I don't know—"

"Repressed is the word you're groping for," Bliss said.

"*Kenneth*," Malcolm said, his expression darkening.

"No, it's quite all right, Malcolm," Oliver said. "Kenneth has a point, doesn't he?"

"I just think, well, Jenny's been gone for a couple of years now. She's moved on. Surely there's no reason to hide your true nature anymore." He smiled. "Well, *is* there?"

Oliver glanced at Malcolm, and then away through the window, where the traffic was murmuring and the streetlights were flickering to life. "No, I suppose not."

Birdy wasn't at the chateau when they arrived, so the servants showed them to their rooms, communicating in fractured English. Malcolm and Oliver were offered a large room that overlooked the bay. It was a simple enough affair, with bare white walls and a stone floor. The four-poster bed intimidated Oliver. He'd not seen grandeur the like of this before, and he stood, surveying the room, feeling as out of place as he'd expected. Malcolm had no such qualms. He sat on the bed and bounced his behind on the mattress. "Quite firm," he said. He'd chosen a crisp white shirt, loose cotton trousers and white plimsolls to arrive in. No socks, which seemed to annoy Oliver for some strange reason. But Malcolm already seemed to complement the location. He looked, Oliver thought, quite handsome and utterly cosmopolitan. Beside him, he felt like the dowdy relation in the shirt Jenny had bought him for that interview at the BBC in

1972, and a pair of corduroy trousers that were some years past their best. "Come and sit down," Malcolm said, patting the space beside him.

Oliver hesitated for a moment and then reminded himself that this whole holiday was an exercise in abandoning his old self, his tired methods of dealing with situations that he felt discomfort in. He had less confidence than Malcolm that he'd succeed. "We have to unpack," he said.

"Oh *bugger* that, Oliver, come on, sit here, next to me."

Oliver stopped prevaricating and sat next to Malcolm.

"Thank you for doing this," Malcolm said after a moment.

"That's quite alright."

"No, I mean this is *important*, Oliver. This isn't just a holiday, is it? This is about you. What you're doing here is a huge step. I know it makes you uncomfortable."

"I suppose sometimes I need a kick up the arse to change," Oliver said. "If Jenny hadn't insisted, I don't think I'd ever have contacted the BBC about my show."

"Well, good on Jenny for that," Malcolm said. "If you hadn't come to Broadcasting House, we'd never have met, and my life would have been the poorer for it."

"Thank you for saying that, Malcolm."

Malcolm laughed.

"You don't believe me when I say these things, do you? You think it's just hot air, but it *isn't*." Malcolm sighed. "When I'm with you, I'm a happier man than I've ever been." He squeezed Oliver's thigh. "Come on," he said, "we should be getting downstairs for lunch. Kenny's probably already berating the servants for being too French."

———

By the time they'd unpacked and joined Kenneth on the covered terrace, the heavens had opened. Out in the bay a cluster of yachts and fishing boats rocked in the wind. The sweep of land containing the coastal resorts was almost totally obscured by the inclement weather.

"Well, this is *fucking* marvellous, isn't it?" Bliss said sourly. "I might as well be in Margate."

"Oh, do give over, Kenny," Malcolm said, reaching across the table laden with cold cuts and sandwiches. "We've only just arrived. The weather will buck up if you stop walking around with a face like a slapped arse. Have some champagne for God's sake."

The rain was different here, Oliver thought. The light, even in this foul weather, changed its aspect. It dripped from the lemon and eucalyptus trees, transformed by its location. But he suspected that perhaps he'd put that characteristic there himself, quickly overwhelmed by this fleeting promise of a better life. This was not *his* life, however, and he couldn't keep some bitterness from seeping through whenever he was faced with what others seemed to come by so easily.

After *PoppyHarp* had been completed in that ridiculously hot summer of 1976, Oliver had returned to Lethebury and waited for it to be transmitted by the BBC. There had been a strange weightless feeling to that lull. Jenny's departure had taken the edge off the euphoria of it all, and he'd nearly forgotten about it by the time Malcolm had called one day to tell him *PoppyHarp* was going to finally air in the spring of 1977. He'd felt an initial thrill and then, later that evening, a panic had gripped him. He suddenly didn't want it to be free in the world. It was too naked and provocative a statement. When he'd written it with Malcolm in London their crowd of friends had called it brave and prescient, but now the nation would see his name on the credits and understand something about him that he barely grasped himself. Lethebury was not London; people were, on the whole, deeply provincial in their views out here. He'd felt sure it would isolate him further from the town; many of them already looked down their nose at him, preferring to side with Jenny, irrespective of the facts.

But what he hadn't anticipated was the overwhelming tide of indifference toward *PoppyHarp* when it was shown. Kenneth had ultimately been correct: *here today, gone tomorrow.* Jenny had apparently made a point of not watching it, and it seemed that much of the town had followed suit. If Oliver hadn't heard from Malcolm the day after, it would have felt like it had never happened. All of that work for nothing.

There had been a handful of reviews in the national papers. '...*an otherwise exceptional performance by Kenneth Bliss is marred by a disjointed and frequently silly script,*' from *The Guardian* was the best notice they received.

Part of Oliver was relieved that it had vanished without trace. Perhaps he'd rushed into all of it too quickly, allowed himself to be swayed by Malcolm's persuasive powers. But here he was, still being cajoled into situations he wasn't entirely comfortable in, which challenged him to be something he still suspected he was not. He had a growing sense of being unmoored from his own life. Kenneth and Malcolm both knew their place in the world. They had discernible talents which meant that their careers had been defined years ago, and they were more or less able to navigate the uncertain waters of show business. Julian too had his gift for art; he'd moved last year to upstate New York, insisting that the light was better there, the gay community more amenable, more accepting. Birdy's invitation had been extended to him, but he was too busy to accompany them on the vacation.

"Birdy won't be here until tomorrow," Bliss told them. "At least that's what I assume the servants are saying. I had to mime wiping my arse in order to get toilet paper from them."

"Stop being so fucking English," Malcolm said, a note of exasperation in his voice. "Will she be alone?"

"Do you mean is that frightful boor of a husband accompanying her? He might be, unfortunately."

"Hudson Powell?" Oliver said. Although he was well aware of Birdy Irving's career, he was more familiar with her husband's work. He had made the kind of films that were endlessly repeated on the TV on Sunday afternoons. Oliver was rather partial to the ensemble war movies he'd made with Michael Caine, Robert Duvall and Donald Sutherland. Suicide missions into enemy territory, escaping impossible odds. Jenny used to silently retreat to the kitchen to sew, leaving him to watch them alone. Powell was a fiery Welshman with a drinking problem, and prone to outbursts of violence, according to the press. There were intimations of infidelity in the marriage, constant rumours of an imminent split. Oliver couldn't imagine coming face to face with him. He was larger than life. But this whole situation, he supposed, was larger than his life had ever been.

"He's a bit of a shit," Bliss said, as quietly as he could, which wasn't very quiet at all. Oliver glanced at the servants at the end of the table, but none of them seemed to register the sleight upon one of their employers. "He came to see the play one night, absolutely *steaming* drunk. We could all see him from the stage. He was sitting front and centre in the stalls with a bottle of vodka between his legs. When Birdy came onstage, he shouted, 'That's my fucking *woman* up there! What a fine piece of tail she is!' It rattled her, but she did her level best to ignore him. Even when she had to deliver a monologue and he staggered forward and tried to put his hand up her dress."

"Bloody hell," Malcolm said. "He sounds like an absolute delight."

"Security dragged him away eventually. We found him asleep in Birdy's dressing room. He'd pissed in the corner and fallen down with his trousers around his ankles." Bliss snorted. "He was a *proper* sight and no mistake. Enormous cock though."

"Oh, well, everything is forgiven then," Malcolm said, laughing.

"According to Birdy they're going through a sort of trial separation, but it's mostly on her part. Powell hasn't agreed to anything. He doesn't want a divorce, but he's quite happy sowing his wild oats with every wild-eyed starlet that gets swept up in his wake."

"Well I hope he doesn't turn up then," Malcolm said. "I imagine we'll have to make ourselves scarce if they end up having it out. He's a big man; I'm not sure

I'd want to be caught in the middle of their domestic strife."

"It's not Powell you have to worry about," Bliss said. "It's Birdy." He shook his head. "*Trust me.*"

———

When Oliver woke beside Malcolm the next morning, he lay in bed for a while, unwilling to open the shutters in case all that greeted him was further poor weather. He had no idea what time it was. He'd taken off his watch after coming to bed and couldn't find it on the bedside table. They'd all been a bit squiffy by the time they retired last night. There was, after all, little to do but drink and eat with the host absent. There were no other sounds in the house so he supposed it was still early. Malcolm lay with his arms flung above his head, his fine blonde hair in artful disarray on the pillow. Oliver felt a tug of feeling towards him, something different to the usual attractions of his personality and profile. He was reluctant to pursue the feeling, to see it for what it was. Everything about this was familiar yet utterly different. How many years had he lain beside Jenny while she tossed and turned, a hand sometimes reaching across to find his for comfort? He'd betrayed her in so many ways. It was a form of flagellation – even now, two years on from her departure – that he was disinclined to relinquish.

Finally, he rose and crept across the room, opening the shutters just a little so he could peer outside. The sight brought an uncharacteristic smile to his face. He left the window and gathered up his clothes, tip-toed to the bathroom down the hall.

He was ready in ten minutes after washing and dressing. His reticence and fretfulness had deserted him momentarily. He felt that weightless feeling of rising before everyone else, and being somewhere that was quite different to his usual surroundings. There was no sign of anyone, not even the servants. Downstairs he crossed the expansive hall and drawing room and let himself out onto the terrace. He stood, allowing his face to be warmed by the sun, quietly awed by the revelation of the beauty of the bay: the grand sweep of coast, the exquisite gradients of colour, the gentle rush of the sea towards the land beneath him. He felt a rush of elation then, to be alone with his appreciation of this place, before Bliss complained about the heat, or Malcolm tried to persuade him to put on his trunks and walk down to the private beach. He was on his holidays, for God's sake! It struck him only then to be grateful for the fact.

He was about to head to the edge of the terrace and pick his way down the goat-track to the cove, intending to enjoy the solitude for as long as he could, when someone said, "Who the *fuck* are you?"

She was seated at the very edge of the terrace, where a riot of pink Bougainvillea climbed the walls. She didn't rise, didn't even seem overly alarmed, but she set down her coffee and put on her small tortoiseshell-framed glasses to properly inspect the interloper.

"I'm Oliver, Oliver Frayling."

"Should that *mean* something to me?"

He smiled at her forthright manner. She could only be one woman. "No, I suppose not. I'm one of Kenneth's friends. You must be Ms. Irving."

"Well, I suppose I must. If you insist."

He hesitated to approach her. Did you invade the personal territory of Hollywood stars, or would someone wrestle you to the ground if you attempted to shake her hand? "It's a pleasure to meet you."

"Is it?"

He laughed. "Are you always this much work?"

She seemed surprised. She smiled at his impertinence. "Are you the TV producer or the artist?"

"Neither I'm afraid."

"What are you then?"

"I'm not altogether sure. I did make a TV show for children. And a play. They were on the BBC, but no one really saw them."

"That's a sorry state of affairs."

"I'll survive I expect. It wasn't really the life I expected it to be anyway."

"Oh, it rarely is. Even when you're good at what you do and you make a success of your life. It's *seldom* what you expect it to be."

"Is *this* not what you expected?" Oliver glanced around, indicating the property, the weather, the unexpected beauty of it all.

"This is pretty enough, but one gets easily jaded."

"One wouldn't know."

"Trust me," she said. "This… *fame situation*. It's not what it's cracked up to be."

Oliver finally decided to sit down at the table. He listened to the sea rushing in below them while he studied the actress's face. She was certainly a handsome woman, and as bird-like as her nickname suggested. But there were fine lines around her mouth and at the edges of her eyes, a hard crease between her eyebrows that he suspected make-up could not conceal from the camera. There was a fatigue to her demeanour too, a slight tremor in her hands as she lifted the fine china cup to her mouth. These things, combined, suggested a woman who was reaching the final days of her brush with the bright lights. Perhaps she was aware that the final curtain was in sight, and that she would be faced with ever more dispiriting reviews and disparaging remarks until all that was left was the memory of the halcyon days, when the world was still at her feet.

"Are you queer too?" she asked.

The question seemed to unbalance Oliver; it felt like the carpet being pulled from beneath him. He'd been to parties filled with gay men who simply hadn't needed to enquire about his sexual proclivities; it had become quite comfortable not having to expand upon his relationship with Malcolm, and to simply bumble along, never making a decision about it, never drawing a line in the sand. But he was far from home, wasn't he? He was meaningless to this woman; she'd reached a station in life where she didn't have to give a shit about anyone but herself. It was safe, he supposed. Alone with a movie star he could be anyone, he could reinvent himself from this moment on.

"Yes, I am," Oliver said. "I'm with Malcolm, the TV producer."

However seismic it felt to say it aloud for Oliver, it was quickly digested and accepted by Birdy Irving. She nodded, drained her coffee cup and then lit a cigarette. "I don't have a problem with queers," she said. "They're *everywhere* these days. Hollywood is positively *riddled* with them."

The comment agitated him. "Like termites then, are we? Or woodworm?"

She gave Oliver a withering look from behind wreath of smoke from her Gauloise. "Many of my closest friends are homosexuals. I discovered that my long-lost father left his wife at the age of 57 and shacked up with a man who cleaned their pool."

Oliver nodded. He could already tell she was clearly a lonely woman, plagued by the usual doubts and insecurities but amplified by a life in the spotlight. All he wanted was to get away, down to the beach, where he could take off his sandals and feel the fine warm sand beneath his bare feet.

"Darling!"

He hadn't noticed Bliss emerging onto the terrace until he cried out to Birdy. He ran across to the actress and flung his arms around her. She smiled wanly at him but didn't reciprocate in kind. She merely allowed Kenneth to fuss over her, and then insisted he sit down when she'd had her fill of his devotions. Her face clouded theatrically then. Oliver could feel his patience ebbing away. If she'd had a couch to hand, she'd probably have fainted onto it.

"Oh, darling, Birdy! What's the matter?" Kenneth said.

"It's that *bastard* of a husband," Birdy said, stubbing out the cigarette violently, as if she was in the middle of a scene. Oliver suspected she always was, somehow. "He's intending to crash our little soirée after all. His new little *whore* has kicked him out of her apartment in Paris, so he's coming back here with his tail between his legs."

Kenneth closed his hands around Birdy's and began to sympathise with her. Oliver, realising he was now surplus to requirements, took the opportunity to quietly slip away.

———

That evening Birdy vanished for an hour, and then, ensuring that her house guests were assembled below, made her grand entrance down the chateau's wide, sweeping staircase. She'd changed into a cream Chanel suit and heels, her hair bundled up, her eyes hidden behind large sunglasses. Bliss and the servants began to applaud discreetly. Malcolm gave Oliver a private pained expression and joined in. Oliver exhaled loudly. "This is a bloody joke," he hissed to Malcolm. Kenneth gave him a waspish look and increased his applause. The whole sorry affair seemed to last an eternity. Birdy laughed musically when she reached them, removed her sunglasses and shyly batted her eyelashes, demure as a Catholic schoolgirl. She kissed Bliss on both cheeks and then glanced at them all in turn, languorous and slightly insolent, as if they were servants too.

Earlier, Oliver had reluctantly put on his suit and allowed Malcolm to knot his bow tie, to fuss his hair down with Brylcreem. Dressing in Monte Carlo required a consideration beyond the limits of his comprehension. "You look very handsome," Malcolm told Oliver, and kissed him. He didn't feel especially handsome; he only felt out of place in these surroundings and in the company of this woman. But Birdy was adamant that she would enjoy her last night of freedom in the company of men, even if they were, as she kept insisting, all queers. Bliss turned a blind eye to her casual slights, but each successive remark during the course of the day had only infuriated Oliver more. He couldn't understand why Malcolm was acting in such a submissive manner around the woman.

"Are you afraid of her?" Oliver had asked him earlier.

"Of *course* not," Malcolm said. "But these people, they aren't like us. You have to understand that; they're utterly divorced from reality most of the time."

"I just don't understand why you're standing for it."

"After all these years in that boys' club at the BBC, I've just learnt how to pick my battles. Sometimes you have to hold your tongue."

A chauffeur brought the large black limousine around and they all bundled into the back. It took them into Monte Carlo. Seated opposite Oliver, Birdy wore a faint, drifting smile that suggested she'd imbibed or swallowed some pills before she'd left the chateau. It certainly seemed to shave the rough edges off her personality. Oliver watched the curve of the coast appear beside his window as they travelled along the Avenue Princesse Grace. The colour was fading from the day and the light on the sea had turned to scattered diamonds. The huge yachts in the harbour were alive with private parties. Music reached them through the open window. The breeze on Oliver's face was fragrant, exotic, infused with something he had no real compass for. The city was flooded with light. On the busy avenues he caught sight of little pockets of life, curious scenes played out with impossibly glamorous people: a middle-aged man in a blue linen suit with immaculately cut grey hair passed by on a moped; a large old woman, waddling along the street, swamped in furs and walking two little Papillions; a young couple arriving at one of the casinos in a turquoise convertible Bentley...

That night they were swept from a waterside bar to a restaurant where they dined on a terrace overlooking the bay. Oliver sampled a dizzying number of dishes. The champagne flowed freely;

Birdy drank dry martinis. People were invited over: a couple of coarse-sounding American film producers, a long-haired Italian glamour photographer and a demure French woman with a sizeable mole on her cheek. Everyone seemed eager to meet and impress the actress, to touch the hem of her garment. As they moved on to the Casino de Monte Carlo, an increasing number of them attached themselves like limpets. The conversation flowed freely. Oliver quietly took in the sweeping sea of opulence of the casino, deeply aware that his astonishment might come off as seeming uncouth amongst this unfamiliar crowd, whose lives were clearly and definitively carved out. But it was hard not to be amazed by the huge columns, the marble, the chandeliers, the haut-reliefs of nude women, the wall-filling paintings. It was somewhat let down by the jabbering sound of slot machines and the coach loads of tourists, wreathed in tobacco smoke, grimly watching their holiday money dissolve in minutes.

Later they were escorted to a private lounge – reserved, he presumed, for certain high-rollers. There were bodyguards set at the entrances. He hadn't gambled; after watching Malcolm lose what amounted to several hundred pounds on a Baccarat table, he could almost hear Jenny tutting loudly in his ear at such wasteful extravagance. Discomfited by his recklessness, Malcolm put his wallet away and stopped drinking, for fear of losing his shirt.

By the end of the night they were all suitably intoxicated, although Oliver was beginning to sober up. Kenneth had groped a waiter and was loudly professing his love for all and sundry. They were lucky not to get kicked out of the casino. They all sat, stupefied, in the back of the limousine, Bliss already snoring loudly on Malcolm's shoulder. Oliver watched the lights of Monte Carlo glimmering behind him. It had left him cold, ultimately. The excess and the casual wastefulness of the idle rich there. It had no place in his life. He didn't aspire to such hedonism as Malcolm and Kenneth did. It simply wasn't in him.

They seemed like strangers to him in the back of the car. Now, more than ever.

———

They were eating lunch on the terrace the following day when Hudson Powell arrived at the chateau. Birdy had been regaling them with anecdotes about working with Fellini and Chabrol, which meant little to Oliver – he'd never heard of either of them, and the stories were clearly heavily embroidered. He'd learned to tune her voice out while they ate together. She never really addressed any of them directly anyway. She always seemed to be performing to some degree; all she required was an audience of some kind, whether they were a captive one or not.

Oliver was feeling quite content, and surprised to be feeling so. Earlier, despite hangovers, he and Malcolm had risen early and crept through the house, let themselves out across the terrace and followed the goat-track down to the chateau's private inlet, which was already drenched in sunlight. There they had laid down towels and stripped down to their trunks. Malcolm took Oliver's hand and led him across the warm sand to the water's edge. The sea was cool and clear. As the water splashed against their bare skin, it seemed to shock away their hangovers.

The further out they went, the more Oliver felt a gradual, if short-lived, sloughing off of the dusty remnants of England and his life. It was an old suit, threadbare and frayed, and yet he continued to wear it everywhere. But the water gently warmed his body, and a lightness settled upon him. The weight of these past few years diminished enough for him to feel as if he could just exist in this moment. He felt the ground go from beneath his feet, and the water buoyed him up. Malcolm still had his hand and they floated up onto their backs together, stared up at the almost unbearably blue sky. Oliver didn't think he'd ever seen anything so utterly perfect. He closed his eyes and could feel the heat of the morning sun on his eyelids. They'd swum around until they were exhausted, then returned to the shore and lay, panting, dazed on their towels. The constant rhythm of the tide coaxed Oliver to sleep briefly. Later the two men kissed and rolled around until the sand covered their wet bodies. By the time they emerged, flushed and filthy, on the terrace for lunch, Kenneth and Birdy were sipping tea and disdainfully surveying the cold buffet that the servants had laid out. Kenneth pursed his lips and gave them both a knowing sidelong glance. They smiled ruefully at him and went upstairs to clean themselves off and dress for lunch.

Birdy was reaching the end of one of her interminable stories when they heard a commotion from within the house. Something crashed to the ground loudly. A voice, raised in anger, followed.

"What the devil is going on in there?" Malcolm said, first to cross the terrace and enter the shadows of the house. Oliver followed the others inside, through the drawing room and into the wide hallway with its mosaic tiling and sweeping staircase. He was shocked to find Malcolm, his head inexplicably locked in Hudson Powell's arms, being pulled in one direction and then another. Oliver could smell the liquor on his breath, even from a distance. Without thought he crossed the hall and took hold of Malcolm in an effort to wrest him free of Powell's grip. The three of them tussled around the room in what quickly became an absurd scene. Powell, although intoxicated, was more powerful than Oliver and Malcolm combined. His body seemed to have been hewn out of granite. He threw his considerable weight backwards and forwards, until they all crashed into the staircase and lost their grip on each other. Oliver's ears were ringing, his face flushed with embarrassment and exertion. He caught a glimpse of Kenneth and Birdy clutching each other, their mouths open, and then felt the wind go out of him as Powell's weight fell upon him.

"Now see *here!*" he heard Malcolm shouting, and then Powell's lumbering, sweating frame was lifted away from him and sent stumbling across the room. Powell's limbs were heavy and his co-ordination so skewed by the booze that he stumbled and slumped against the front door.

"Are you hurt?" Malcolm asked Oliver, his colour up, hair awry.

"No, I'm alright." Oliver took Malcolm's extended hand and got to his feet. He could see cuts on Malcolm's knees and elbows that would need bathing, but otherwise they were relatively unharmed. Malcolm strode over to Powell, who was rising again, his shirt soaked in sweat and his fists raised.

"What the *devil* do you think you're doing, you stupid bloody fool!"

Malcolm stepped backwards as Powell lunged forward, then swayed back on his heels, shadow boxing and laughing, his face now bright red.

"*Stop* it, now! *Stop it*. This *instant!*" Birdy finally strode between Malcolm and her husband, clapping her hands as if they were children in a school yard. Oliver was momentarily concerned for her welfare: she could have been crushed like a twig if Powell had half a mind.

But the sight of his wife seemed to immediately take the wind out of the man's sails. His fists unclenched immediately and fell to his sides. "Birdy," he half sang in that rich, familiar baritone. "My *sweet* darling wife…" He glanced around at the strangers in the hallway as if seeing them for the first time. "Sweet *Christ*," he said, his voice thunderous and very Welsh, "who the *fuck* are all these people in my home?" he said.

"*My* home," Birdy said firmly.

Powell stared down into his wife's eyes, looking momentarily chastened.

Birdy called out to one of the servants, demanding a cafetière of strong coffee, to be served on the terrace. Oliver heard footsteps hurrying away. "Come with me, you silly fool," Birdy said, and took some of her husband's not inconsiderable weight and led him out onto the terrace, leaving Oliver, Malcolm and Kenneth standing in the hall.

"I must say," Kenneth said, smiling, "this is *much* better than Margate. *And* I get to watch men wrestling without having to pay for the privilege."

"What do we do now?" Malcolm asked.

"Make ourselves scarce for a while, I suppose," Kenneth said.

But then they heard Powell's voice rise again from the terrace. "Well, bring the silly buggers in then!" he said. "By all means let me apologise for my behaviour."

They hesitated in the hall, Malcolm still panting from his exertions.

"*Come on*! *Show* yourselves then!"

He'd had fourteen Bloody Marys before his plane from Paris, then downed almost an entire bottle of vodka during the short flight. Powell told them this later, once the coffee had taken the edge off. When they'd sat down at the table on the terrace, his hands were shaking so much that Birdy held the coffee cup for him to sip from. As he bent his head, she ran the fingers of her other hand through his tousled hair. The gesture was so desperately selfless and intimate, so filled with tired devotion, that it briefly refocused Birdy in Oliver's mind. Perhaps he'd been rash in his judgement of the woman. There was still something real, buried beneath the act.

Hudson Powell had one of the great faces. He was not altogether perfectly handsome: his features were not symmetrical enough to be pleasing; his nose had clearly been broken in more than one fight, and then set badly. There was a curious distance in his eyes too that suggested a lifetime of booze and its adverse effects on the brain. There was, similarly to Birdy, a manner of indifference, of a remove from the life normal people lived. There was always, at his station in life, someone else to bring the drinks, serve the meals, make introductions, and chauffeur him from one place to the other.

"One wonders," Bliss said later, "if the poor bugger employs someone to hold his dick when he takes a leak. It is, after all, probably a two-man job."

But after the initial misunderstanding, Powell was effusive in his apologies. Once the tremors had passed, he'd moved around the table, shaking hands and placing a placatory palm on each of their shoulders. Oliver suspected it was more to pacify Birdy than out of any real sense of wrongdoing on Powell's part.

"The heartache and the thousand natural shocks that flesh is heir to…" he said, smiling, as if to underscore the misunderstanding with levity. Oliver didn't grasp the reference or its meaning.

There remained an air of unpredictability in his manner and bearing that made Oliver reluctant to forgive him. Over the course of the afternoon, his patience waned. Powell and Birdy were each other's best friend and worst enemy. For a while the two of them were attentive to the other's every whim, but gradually the cracks began to show. There was the matter of another round of casual adultery that rested in the back of Birdy's mind; Oliver wondered how you could come to accept that kind of thing and remain married to the same person, and then felt a pang of guilt at his own part in betraying Jenny. That remorse shadowed him daily, gave pause to every action that involved Malcolm. But Birdy seemed incapable of letting Powell go, no matter what the papers said about his drunken behaviour and numerous affairs.

And so later, after they'd dispersed to their own private activities, Oliver and Malcolm relaxed in their room, listening to the argument begin between the two actors. It quickly grew to ridiculous proportions, their two voices attempting to rise above the other. There was no escaping it within the chateau, so Malcolm suggested they walk into Roquebrune village and get supper there. Oliver was glad to be away from the toxic atmosphere for a while. The afternoon was giving way to evening when they arrived, the heat turning everything still, as if the world was settling around them, becoming perfect. It was a pretty medieval village, overlooking Cap Martin in one direction and along the coast across Monaco in the other. The streets were narrow, and wound between lovingly restored medieval houses, some of the passages vaulted and covered. They climbed up to the castle and stood staring, breathless, out at the views along the coast as the light began to fade from the day.

Later they found a small brasserie that suited Oliver. The small place was quiet and had no dress code. They ate on a balcony, the top buttons of their shirts undone, looking down at the harbour, at the tourists gradually gathering in similar places for supper. They had rabbit stew and two glasses of wine, spoke quietly to each other, close enough to touch, but resisting the urge.

"I'd like to ask you again about that show," Malcolm said over a dessert of strawberries and Chantilly cream.

"Oh, come on, Malcolm, I thought we'd discussed this…"

"We did, but then you said it was pointless talking about it."

"It's not me, is it? A sit-com…"

"*PoppyHarp* wasn't you either, really, was it? And look how that turned out."

"*PoppyHarp* was a failure, Malcolm."

"I don't consider it a failure, Oliver. It was one of the most rewarding experiences I've ever had working on a show."

"I just mean it wasn't the success we hoped it would be. Look, no one at the BBC is exactly clamouring for me to work on anything, are they?"

"*I* am, Oliver. Isn't that enough?"

"You have a vested interest by now, Malcolm."

Malcolm smiled and squeezed Oliver's knee beneath the table.

"Malcolm…"

"No one *cares*, Oliver. Look – everyone here is enjoying their meal, their holiday. They won't come for us with blazing torches in the night if I squeeze your knee a bit. Come on," Malcolm said, extending his hand across the table. "Loosen up. Hold my hand. Just once, in public."

Oliver looked at his hand and recalled them floating in the sea, not eight hours ago, the load lightened by privacy, the holiday finally loosening his shoulders for a while. Oliver glanced around at the other couples on the balcony, at the waiters weaving through the tables. Finally he shook his head. "I can't, Malcolm. I'm sorry."

Malcolm nodded very slightly and took back his hand, glanced away, down to the sea and the sun sinking below the horizon. Oliver felt it then, a slight withdrawal, almost imperceptible. The moment passed awkwardly.

"Go on, tell me about it then," Oliver said, keen to coax Malcolm back from this retreat. "The sit-com, I mean."

"I thought you weren't interested."

"Sell it to me, then. That's your job, isn't it?"

"Well, we have Sarah Miles coming in next week," Malcolm said finally." Hayley Mills might be in the picture too. It's called *Not This Time, Nanette*. It's about a suburban housewife whose children have flown the nest. Her husband works all hours in the city. Nanette is still in love with him, yet she finds herself dissatisfied with her life. Then she has this chance encounter with a married man. It's essentially a comedy about a woman contemplating adultery."

"I'm not sure what I could possibly bring to that, Malcolm. It just feels like a huge compromise."

"Well, it's about *diversifying*, Oliver. I'd like for you to come on as a staff writer and script supervisor. I'd like you to direct a couple of episodes too. Having that on your CV would open so many doors for you, Oliver. We could start thinking in terms of your career. Doing something like this would be the stepping stone to the kind of material you'd feel more naturally inclined towards."

"I'd have to move to London."

"Well, yes. Look, Oliver, I understood your reticence before, but you know, Jenny has left you now. You must see that there's no going back to what your life was. You've turned a corner. Surely this is the ideal time to embrace change."

"That's an awful lot to ask of me, Malcolm."

"Yes, I'm quite aware of that, Oliver. I know that your background is very... parochial, but that isn't who *you* are. I don't think so, anyway. It doesn't have to define the rest of your life. Don't let it stop you from living it." He extended his hand again, without thinking. "With me."

Oliver stared at Malcolm's hand but he still couldn't bring himself to close his own over it. They stayed like that for a moment, then Malcolm quietly withdrew his hand again. He paid for the bill and they walked back to the chateau in silence.

———

The following morning, Malcolm rose late, but then seemed at pains to demonstrate that the previous evening's conversation had not in any way soured the holiday. Oliver felt sure it was just a brave face, but he had no idea how to salve that particular wound. It felt like Malcolm was continually trying to force his hand. However much he frequently enjoyed his weekends in London with Malcolm and Kenneth, he still had the safety net of returning at the end of it all to Lethebury. Letting go of that felt like leaving the harbour behind and voyaging out into the sea, knowing that he'd never go back. The difference between his old life and the new one was irreconcilable.

In the evening, they played a spirited game of sardines for a couple of hours. But their enthusiasm was soured by Hudson Powell, who came downstairs from calls with his agent and a film producer, angry and already on the way to being drunk. He'd insisted on joining in on the game, then abandoned it midway through, shouting loudly to Birdy that he wouldn't hide in cupboards with a bunch of fags trying to grope his arse. An argument had ensued and everyone had scattered. Malcolm had complained of a headache and gone to bed early. Oliver was left at the end of a warm evening with Kenneth. They'd discovered a beautiful conservatory filled with exotic plants that overlooked the bay, and there they'd sat with the sky darkening around them, talking quietly with a pot of coffee on the table between them.

"I don't think I want to be in anyone's possession," Oliver said, after telling Kenneth about the previous night's conversation. "And that's sometimes how

Malcolm makes me feel. As if he wants to own me, to take all of the things I hold close and strip them away, to reveal the person he thinks I am beneath."

"I wouldn't dismiss it," Kenneth said. "That kind of devotion is not something to be sniffed at. To be *possessed* by someone. How lovely." He sighed."I often long for strong arms around me, Oliver. I'm positively *desperate* for that kind of affection in my life."

"I'm not sure that I am."

"What it is that you want from life then, Oliver?"

"*That's just it*, Kenneth. I don't know. I suppose all I ever wanted from life was to be able to potter around in my shed, making something that children would want to watch."

"But you didn't really want all the other associated… *fripperies*, did you? The BBC and its awful *viewing figures* and all that shit."

"No, I suppose not."

"Well, I suppose you can't expect one thing without the other I'm afraid, Oliver. The same goes for your situation with Malcolm. You can't suppose this casual state of affairs to not grow into something that has significance and permanence, and then treat it with reticence."

"I don't think I take Malcolm's affection lightly, Kenneth."

"I know this is all relatively new to you, Oliver, but every time you reject Malcolm's invitation to live with him in London, you're hurting him every bit as much as you did Jenny when you weren't honest with her."

"So you're saying I'm a coward. Is that it, Kenneth?"

"No, Oliver, of course I'm not. But you are *afraid*. I think, deep down, Malcolm has always suspected that you wouldn't reciprocate his love."

Oliver didn't know how to respond.

"You can't go back to that simpler time, Oliver," Kenneth said. "It's not there now. Jenny has left and taken your little girl with her. She will never trust you again. Either you come to accept this new way of living, or you stay where you are. But if you do that I think you'll be sitting still for the rest of your life. And that, believe you me, is an absolutely *wretched* state of affairs."

———

The next morning, Oliver woke to find Malcolm's side of the bed empty. He lay, relishing the seclusion, the sound of life happening downstairs, out on the terrace, plates and cutlery being laid. They'd all fallen into a familiar pattern of indolence, of expecting to be served their food by Birdy's attentive and largely silent staff, of long days filled with heat and gentle intoxication. This, Oliver supposed, was how the other half lived. It wasn't in him to feel that he was part of that group; his hands were too rough from manual labour, his upbringing too stiff, too structured by work, by the rigid discipline of earning a crust for your family. His life had been in that precarious balance for a while now; it niggled him that it seemed so cut and dried to Malcolm and Kenneth.

After he finally rose and showered, he emerged onto the terrace to find only Kenneth and Birdy, seated beside the pool, drinking cocktails. It was 10 a.m. "Where's Malcolm?" Oliver asked.

"Down on the beach, the last time I looked," Bliss said. He was lying on a sun lounger, looking utterly stiff and English in some well-pressed slacks and a crisp blue shirt, buttoned to the throat. His only concession to the heat that was already gathering was to roll his shirt sleeves up over his bony elbows.

"They went down an hour ago," Birdy said. She was in an all-in-one swimsuit, with a sarong wrapped around her midriff. Huge sunglasses concealed much of her face. Her feet were very small, like a child's. "*God only knows* what they're getting up to down there." She laughed without any trace of mirth, then leaned across to poke Bliss in the side. "Do you know what my husband is getting up to down there? With his Malcolm?" And to Oliver: "He is quite the lovely specimen, isn't he?"

Bliss looked even more discomfited. He glanced up at Oliver. "Hudson's been going on about some film script that he wants someone to see," he said. "Malcolm has a friend who produces movies with Nicolas Roeg. I think he wants an introduction made."

"Ah, they're *schmoozing*," Birdy said. "How wonderful."

Oliver stood at the edge of the terrace to look down the goat-track. He caught a glimpse of Malcolm in the sea. After a moment, he saw Powell wade into view too. They both looked tanned and fit. Oliver felt an unfamiliar knot of tension in his stomach. He wanted to look away, but he couldn't. After a moment, Powell started to wrestle Malcolm, trying to tip him over into the water. Malcolm gave a spirited attempt at resistance, but Powell was a bigger man, with weight and strength on his side. Malcolm sank below the waves and Oliver held his breath for a moment. When Malcolm found his footing again, he was laughing. Oliver couldn't hear him from this distance, just the gulls high above him and the sound of the waves crashing against the shore. Malcolm tried to push Powell down, but the other man was like a brick wall. Powell tossed him aside and Malcolm went under the waves again. This time, when he re-emerged, he took hold of Powell's legs and unbalanced the bigger man, sending him toppling under the water.

"I think they're making their little introductions quite nicely," Birdy said, suddenly beside Oliver. She sighed, drained her cocktail. "Don't you?"

———

That afternoon, Powell insisted they all go out on their yacht. They were driven out to Port Hercule, a marina which sat in a natural deep bay carved out of the sheer cliffs at the foot of Monaco. It was home to a fleet of huge yachts, alongside smaller vessels and cruise ships. It had been used as a deep-water port since Roman times. Now there were high-rises and hotels and the cliff-top palace perched high above on the rock of Monaco.

Malcolm and Powell had emerged from the beach at noon, just in time for lunch. Birdy and Bliss were asleep beside the pool. Oliver had been reading on the terrace, unwilling to give into foolish suspicion, petty jealousy. He allowed them their privacy. He had no real rights of possession over Malcolm; he could do as he wished while they were here, and besides, some harmless horse-play in the sea did not suggest any claim of infidelity, as far as Oliver could see it. But nonetheless, he found himself being short with Malcolm over lunch. Every time he spoke, or laughed, it sent a bright spark of irritation through him. Loyalty, he thought. It meant something, didn't it? Even here.

"Is anything the matter?" Malcolm said in the car on the way to Monaco.

"Nothing," Oliver said. "I'm quite all right."

But Malcolm didn't look convinced. He sat back and stared out of the window, looking pensive.

Bliss and Birdy continued drinking in the car. The actress was moody with everyone at this point, blunt to the point of offensiveness with her husband. Powell sat with his legs wide in the middle of them all. His eyes were dark-ringed with shadows, his intensity shimmering off him like waves of heat. These empty moments seemed to disturb him, robbed him of the impetus he carried with him in all events. He glanced at them in turn with a look of distaste, and eventually through them, as if they were servants. "The boat is magnificent," he said, leaning forward conspiratorially to Oliver, his eyes going momentarily unfocused. "Fucking magnificent. You'll see."

Oliver didn't respond. He only felt even more intensely insignificant beside Powell: his ordinary clothes, his discoloured teeth, his thinning hair. He could scarcely imagine the extravagance of the yacht they were travelling to. As it turned out, it was entirely as he'd expected it to be. He'd seen photographs of the rich and famous, swanning about in places like this; by the time he was following Birdy and Powell down the jetty to their boat, he felt sure someone would intervene and have him thrown out for disturbing the carefully manufactured air of decadence. They boarded the yacht and followed Birdy and Powell as they gave their guests the grand tour. Two servants, the skipper and his crew managed somehow to blend into their surroundings whenever one of them entered a room; Oliver had observed it with mild interest ever since he'd arrived. It was an odd aspect of servitude that he'd never given a great deal of thought to before now. Birdy showed them to an immaculately fitted dining area with wraparound couches, the tables already laid out for lunch. Below that was the main control deck, and a fully fitted kitchen with fridge, sink and gas cooker. Towards the bow was a two-berth cabin with two full size single beds. On the other side of the boat was the master bedroom. Powell flung open the door to show them all. Oliver caught a glimpse of polished wood and wardrobes, an opulent looking circular bed, pictures on the walls, a small bar in one corner. It was another world; Oliver felt he had no real compass for any of it, no way to settle this kind of lifestyle in his mind, to understand how it changed you inside, what the trade-off was when you were elevated to this kind of status.

He wasn't aware that they had left the harbour until they were above decks and he caught sight of the cliff tops receding into the distance. The sea was still as glass, the sky a perfect pure blue. Oliver felt the world diminishing and opening up at the same time. Drained of the noise and urgency of the cities, the cars and the people, the crowded restaurants and the confusion of the days, here on the ocean all that remained was the sway of the water and the sky and the air between. Oliver stood apart from the rest of them and gripped the rail, exhaled, tried to clear his mind of all the obstacles that still seemed in his way. There seemed to be no clear road away from here. He heard the, by now, all too familiar sound of a champagne cork pop, and muted laughter begin.

"Oliver…"

Malcolm was at his side with a glass of champagne for him. Oliver took it and stared out at the sea, at the horizon, the sun shimmering above them.

"I suppose I should be happy," Oliver said. He gestured at it all. "This—" He laughed. "It doesn't happen every day, does it?"

"Apparently," Malcolm offered, "consciously or unconsciously, we are all completely selfish, and as long as we get what we want, we believe everything is all right."

"Is that it? Happiness is getting what we want?"

"I'm quoting someone or other. But yes."

"So unhappiness is not getting what you want."

"Perhaps it's *never* getting what you want. As long as you get what you want every now and then."

"What was all that about this morning?" Oliver said then. "You and Powell frolicking in the sea together?"

"Christ, Oliver, don't tell me you're jealous."

"I'm too old for those games, Malcolm."

"I don't believe we were *frolicking*."

"Birdy says that Powell likes to frolic with men on occasion."

"Well, Birdy would know I suppose."

"Kenneth says he wants something from you."

"I suspect Hudson Powell only romances you if he wants something from you."

"Was that what was happening?" Oliver asked. "Romancing."

"Don't be daft, Oliver. It was just a bit of holiday horse-play. Look—" Malcolm had dropped a bag on the couch when he'd boarded. He slipped a script out and flipped through it. "Powell gave me this screenplay last night before I went to bed. He had it written and he wants to produce and star in it. He's been trying to get Nicolas Roeg interested but Nic won't return his calls. Now, I have a friend, Donald Campbell, who's produced a couple of Nic's pictures. Donald is an Eton boy; he's a bit of a fop to be honest. The total opposite of Hudson, but he wants me to make introductions, get the script to him so as to be a bridge to Roeg."

Oliver glanced at the script. "What sort of film is it?"

"Some kind of gangster crap, but with a bit of sexual fluidity thrown in for good measure. It's about ten years out of date. Sort of like 'Get Carter' mixed in with 'Performance'. A dual role for Powell, so he gets to live out some of his hidden proclivities on screen."

"It doesn't seem all that hidden to me," Oliver said.

"It doesn't have to be out here. People can speculate all they want. The studios and the agents all have ways of repressing things that they don't want the public to get wind of. I've spent enough years in these circles to see the type. He's had to suppress his natural leanings for the whole of his adult life. He comes from this blue-collar background in the south of Wales, from what I gather. One of thirteen kids, for God's sake. The old man spent his entire life down the mines. There's no room for that kind of predilection in that environment. By the time he was free of all that, he'd gotten used to concealing his true nature. So, he married Birdy and found himself in Hollywood's studio system. Covering up who he was inside was paramount to him."

Oliver glanced across at Powell, who was with the skipper on the fly deck, holding forth about some vague, probably embroidered moment in his life. "I was *sick*," he was saying loudly, holding court. "At death's *fucking* door! Wifey down there bought a coffin for me, but it was too bloody small! Birdy said they were going to chop my feet off so they wouldn't have to send it back and buy a bigger one!"

"Birdy knows all about this?" Oliver asked. "His secret life?"

"Yes, of course."

"Why doesn't she divorce him?"

"You know as well as anyone that life isn't always that simple," Malcolm said.

———

The further out to sea they went, the more inebriated Birdy and Powell became. For the first couple of hours, it wasn't overly noticeable. Alcoholism required dedication after enough years at the coal face; it took longer to achieve that sweet spot, and it necessitated a random element for a masculine personality like Powell's; something that turned it into something legendary and anecdotal for posterity. Over lunch he regaled them all with a smattering of these stories, while Birdy stared out to sea, bored at the sound of her husband's voice after all these years. She'd heard it all before, and worse she knew the uncomfortable truth at the heart of all these adventures. And so she drank in a much different way and for entirely different reasons.

"…I went for a beer one afternoon in my local in Paris, where a bunch of ex-pats congregate. And then the next thing I know, I'm waking up in fucking Corsica!" Powell roared. "*Corsica*! I ask you."

Bliss was the only other one of their crowd drinking with any real gusto, but even he seemed deflated by the whole endeavour. He sipped at a brandy and glanced distastefully at Powell. "Don't you ever prefer to be sober?" he said quietly.

"Kenneth…" Malcolm began.

"No, let the old queen ask his question," Powell said. His skin had turned brown over these past few days. His bomb-lit blue eyes seemed to burn with barely suppressed menace. The booze was making him abrasive. "You of *all* people should realise what drink does for a performer." He leaned forward, swilling his own brandy around in the glass, as if he was scrying for secrets in there. "It burns up that stale, lifeless… *empty* feeling one gets when the curtain falls."

"I just go home and have a nice bowel movement, to be honest," Bliss said. He crossed his legs and raised his eyebrows at Malcolm and Oliver. "It's the best one can hope for at my age."

"We should have an arm-wrestling contest," Powell suggested. He refilled his glass, and opened a can of beer, poured it with infinite care and then downed half of it in one. "That'll put the cat among the pigeons."

Malcolm glanced at Oliver, who got up from the table and walked away from them all. He was tired of it now. He stared out at the sliver of land on the horizon, and wondered when it would be over.

"He's a funny bugger, that one, isn't he?"

"He's not one for this kind of thing, Hudson," Malcolm said, glancing after Oliver.

But Powell wasn't finished. "*You*! What the *fuck* is wrong with you, you miserable little shit? You should be thanking me for allowing you to spend time with us. Look! It's the fucking lap of luxury."

Oliver turned. He realised his fists were clenched.

"Ha! The old chap *has* got a bit of fire in his belly after all." Powell roared.

Oliver looked at Malcolm, feeling that fire go out of him immediately. Malcolm wouldn't meet his eyes. Oliver turned away again.

"Fuck it," Powell roared, draining the beer, and rising from the table. "You can't arm wrestle with a bunch of *limp-wristed* faggots anyway."

He turned on his heel and stalked away to the fly-deck, came back and took the rest of the brandy with him.

"My darling husband," Birdy said quietly to herself. "Ever the fucking diplomat."

———

Later, as the boat turned and made its way back to harbour at Monaco, Powell and Malcolm went below decks to discuss the script. Birdy sat with a martini and a pitcher dripping condensation on the table. Oliver and Kenneth sat beside her. She'd become lucid for a while. "My mother," she said, choosing her words carefully, enunciating them, "was French. Smaller than me, even. She was quite beautiful. If I close my eyes, I can remember her in every exquisite detail. We had no money. My father was from Arizona. He was a GI who was stationed in France towards the end of the war. He was wounded and sent to an army headquarters in Paris. My mother met him and fell in love almost immediately. They only had a handful of days together, then he was shipped home. She never saw him again. But a few weeks later she discovered that she was pregnant with me. She tried to get in touch with him and, after some weeks, discovered that he had a wife waiting for him in Arizona.

"We moved to the coast, to Brittany. The rooms of the building we lived in were really quite dark, as I recall. We lived under the roof, like sparrows." She smiled. "My mother told me I was born on a bed of violets. Of course, all French mothers tell their daughters that. There was nothing else I could tell you about those rooms. They contained nothing but my mother and I for fifteen years. We were very cold in winter, save for the days when my mother would bake bread. I can still remember the smell of it." Birdy closed her eyes again, and when she opened them, they were brimming with tears. "She died when I was sixteen. She fell over on the cobbled street that led to our rooms and never got back up again."

Kenneth closed a hand over Birdy's.

"And of course, then there was Hudson."

"You mean you've been with him since you were sixteen?" Oliver said.

"In some way or another, yes. He was on holiday with a woman. He was eight years older than me, quite worldly already. They were recently married. It was their honeymoon."

"Bloody hell, Birdy…" Kenneth said.

"Oh, I never intended to be the scarlet woman, Kenneth, but these things *do* happen. We set eyes upon each other and it was like a lightning bolt. There was nothing that could be done. There was no affair as such. He simply sat down with her that night and said he'd fallen in love with another, and that was the end of it. Hudson has always been a man to act upon his impulses. There's probably a lesson to be learnt about shacking up with a man who'll toss aside his new wife on their honeymoon for another woman…"

"Well, we've all been there, haven't we?" Bliss said, smiling.

"It's unfortunate, but there you are. My life with him is the only real one I know. We flew a month later to New York, where he'd been offered a part in a movie. A small role. It was winter in Manhattan. It was absolutely extraordinary. I close my eyes and…" She screwed up her face, as if it took all of her concentration to revive the memory "…and there it is. The snow falling in Central Park. The endless buildings lit up. The wide avenues and the cars moving in slow motion. He would work during the day and then we would dine in fabulous restaurants in the evening. I was *utterly* in love with him, *utterly* devoted. He told me that just a glance from me would make him physically weak. We fucked almost every night for a year."

"That was when they discovered you, wasn't it?" Kenneth asked. "In New York."

"I visited the set more than once," Birdy said. "One of the producers offered to give me a screen test. A small part in the movie."

"Why do you stay with him?" Oliver asked. "Knowing all that you know. Isn't there a limit to it all? Memories only go so far, surely…"

"I see that you're married," Birdy said after a moment.

Oliver had never removed his wedding band. His finger had swollen beneath it, and he'd found that it was impossible to take off. He rotated it slowly around the skin of his finger sometimes. A nervous action that Malcolm had noticed one evening. "We could have that sawn off, you know," Malcolm had said. "I know a jeweller who'd do it for us."

"Yes," Oliver said to Birdy. "But she left me a couple of years ago."

"Do you miss her?"

"Of course."

"And yet you've changed," Birdy said. "I'm not that smashed. I see that you have feelings for another man. And you're obviously quite conflicted about that. But I think if she called you and said that all was forgiven, then you'd walk over hot coals to have her back."

Oliver looked at the ring. It no longer rotated. He didn't want it removed. It represented solidity, a foundation, a time when everything was quite clear to him.

"I stay because I remember who he was before fame took him away from me," Birdy said. "And I still see that man from time to time."

She smiled sadly. "But not today," she said. "Today he's just a lousy fucking drunk." She leaned across to Oliver. "And if you think that all they're doing below decks is discussing a film, then you're even more deluded than I am."

———

A cab came for Oliver. He sat on his case outside the chateau, watching the sun sink below the horizon. Lights came on inside the house. He heard the clatter of plates and cutlery being laid out on the terrace, the sound of people beginning to arrive. A cork being popped and laughter.

No one knew he was leaving. Oliver had slipped down the stairs and called for the taxi with the handful of French words at his disposal and then stepped outside to wait. Part of Oliver was hoping for Malcolm to emerge and cajole him back inside. To come up with the right words that might change everything for them both. But then the cab arrived and he was out of time. The driver pushed his case into the boot and took him away.

He hadn't gone below decks to see if Birdy was correct. He didn't want to know either way. But he knew then that this life was not his, not really. It had been borrowed. And now it was time to give it back. This holiday had been an exercise in attempting to abandon his old self, to try on a new identity. But it was not so simple as Malcolm buying him a new suit. He could change, but not enough. That was abundantly clear.

Later, as the plane lifted him away from the earth, Oliver held his breath and gripped the seat tightly. His thoughts turned to Malcolm, to the memory of that earlier morning as they'd drifted in the sea, staring up into this sky. As the plane levelled out and a calm came over him he gently but firmly let go of the memory, and he breathed out.

Five

Imogen took us outside to see the cowshed before we left. We followed her downstairs and through to the back of the house. I caught a glimpse of the drawing room, almost entirely empty save for a dusty grand piano beside the French windows. I imagined Oliver seated at it, picking out the melody that played at the beginning of *The Adventures of Imogen and Florian*, and then again to signify that the ending of the show was near and Imogen was about to return to the attic in the real world. A sorrowful tune.

There was nothing else. The rest of the furniture was gone, all the photographs from the mantelpiece, the books from the shelves, the memories from the room.

Beyond the kitchen window, the backyard opened onto a vast vista of the snow-covered Malvern Hills. An unbridled landscape that was darkening at the edges like an old photograph beneath the weight of a flame. The yard was an untidy space, a good acre of land dotted with withered trees and crumbling outbuildings.

"I haven't finished with the fabled cowshed yet," Imogen said, fishing in her pocket for the keys again. "A lot of it was rotted with damp."

"Christ, what a shame. All those things."

"Dad didn't really give much thought to preserving any of it. It just wasn't important to him."

She slid the key into the padlock, then tugged the wooden door away from its warped frame. She had to click the torch on to pick out the contents of the shed. Initially all I could make out were wooden boxes, seemingly filled to the brim with objects. There was a huge table made of scaffold poles and pieces of bicycle, and covered with mechanical junk, the Bolex camera that Oliver had used for *The Adventures of Imogen and Florian*, a few lights on stands. The rest of the workshop was crowded with items that Oliver had accrued over the years: Old Things, Lost Things, Forgotten Things. A huge antique mirror, boxes filled with old photographs from the last century and the century before that, brittle toys and ramshackle furniture, a rocking horse, a chess board, a crate filled with parts for toys: arms, legs, eyes, clothes. Butterflies and beetles in dusty cabinets. Sewing baskets, overflowing with lace and skeins of cotton. Everything was the faint blueprint for a story that Oliver had never been given the opportunity to tell more than once. His cabinet of curiosities.

"I found all of the cans of film for *Imogen and Florian* in here," Imogen said. "*PoppyHarp* too."

"I thought they'd been destroyed by the BBC," I said.

"That's what I assumed too. But they were all here, piled up on the table with a handwritten receipt. He must have bought them back from the BBC with Malcolm's help." Imogen told me about Malcolm then, leaving out the more colourful aspects of their relationship while Lily was around.

"Dad managed to get them converted to VHS in the 90s, so he could see them again in the comfort of his own home. I can put them on for Lily when we get back."

Lily moved around the cowshed, touching things gingerly. Nothing in here was of real interest to her. It was all too damp and dirty and lonely for a child. The toys were covered in cobwebs, and stiff with mould. She stared at it all for a moment and then skipped outside. I told her not to go too far.

"I'm donating the cans of film and all the models and what's left of the toys to the BFI," Imogen said. "I had a chap down from London last month to decide if the cans were the real thing. He seemed ecstatic about it. He said assuming the film was in good condition that the BFI would approve a restoration of it and release it on DVD."

"That must be heartening," I said. "Oliver's show finally getting some recognition."

"I suppose." Imogen glanced around sadly at all the detritus of Oliver's things. "I rather think he'd forgotten about all of this before he vanished. Gave up on it meaning anything. I found a set of journals that he'd kept since the late 60s, right up until 2002."

"Have you read them?" I asked.

"It took a while to bring myself to do it. I brought them home and left them on a table in a back room. I kept flicking through them but I found it difficult to allow myself to feel that close to him after all these years. I couldn't imagine him having the kind of inner life that he might want to commit to a diary."

"It's hard to think of our parents like that," I said. A few years ago, I'd heard from a solicitor dealing with my father's affairs after he'd died. He'd never gotten in touch with me in all those years, and I'd had conflicted enough feelings about the man who'd left my mother pregnant and alone as it was. After he'd died, I'd ended up being the one who had to clear out his house in Dorset. Finding something that was dear to him, that he'd set aside for reasons I might not be able to fathom, was a window onto the man he was. I'd never known him, never spoken to him. I'd thought about him frequently over the years, but I'd been reluctant to pursue tracking him down. Despite my own misgivings, I realised he'd had his own dreams and disappointments, private lusts and foibles and failings that I'd never been privy to, whether we were estranged or not. Similarly, there are many things that I would hope to keep from Lily. Everyone has to keep something that is theirs and theirs alone. You want to keep your children safe from harm, and sometimes that means keeping them from seeing you as you really are.

"I suppose in time they might bring me closer to him," Imogen said. "If I let them. After my mother left him and moved into town, I only saw him for a few days in every month. Mum still loved him – I think – but she felt so betrayed when she found out about Malcolm. And so I spent a lot of my youth thinking of Dad in a certain way, coloured by my mother's feelings and prejudices, which she couldn't keep to herself on a bad day. She had her own struggles with her bipolar that Dad barely addressed. He didn't really understand it. I think he was afraid that he'd caused it in some way – which of course, he hadn't. But he was still culpable. He could have done more. But Dad was just Dad. And ordinarily he was much too close to focus on. Understanding him was like taking a clock to pieces."

"But this business with Malcolm. That can't have been easy for him, can it?"

"No, of course not. In hindsight, at least I could start to understand some of the turmoil he went through with his sexuality. He disappeared into this old cowshed and gradually locked himself away. He never really came back to us. He just cut himself off. We needed him – Mum *really* needed him – but he just wasn't there. Back then the doctors were still just fumbling around in the dark, and she ended up mostly being tranquillised. I had to cope with her mood swings alone from the age of ten. When we moved from here to a flat in town it toughened me up a bit. That was the girl you knew, Noah."

"Oh, yes," I said. "I remember her well. *Spirited.*"

Imogen laughed. "That's putting it mildly."

"I wish you'd told me all of this back then. Maybe it would have changed things."

"I was too young to process all of that, Noah. It wasn't you. It wasn't even me. It was just all too close to the bone then. It was only when I met Jeffrey and had the kids that all those edges got smoothed away. Life does that. *Kids* do that."

I glanced out of the door at Lily playing in the snow. "I suppose they do. You stop focusing on your own bullshit, so they can have the life you didn't have."

"I just couldn't see a reason to go into a day feeling so bloody… I don't know, *combative* I suppose." She smiled. "We had some arguments back then, didn't we?"

"I prefer to think of them as 'heated debates.'"

"Ha! Do you remember that night we ended up having to sleep in a lay-by in Cardiff?"

"Oh, yes. A policeman woke me up at four a.m. Tapping on the window. 'Excuse me, sir, can I ask why you're parked here?'"

"Pissed and lost, as I recall," Imogen said.

"No Google maps back then," I said. "You'd ripped my map up and chucked it out of the window, along with your shoes and my sunglasses."

"That sounds about right."

"I'd been driving around, absolutely bloody lost, for hours. Then you stopped speaking to me. I had to listen to your Genesis cassettes while I went in circles in the countryside."

"Christ, I don't remember that. Genesis…" She laughed. "Christ. I must really have wanted to punish you that day."

"I remember the policeman going to look at you on the back seat in a sleeping bag, then he came back to study me."

"Maybe he thought you'd kidnapped me."

"You never looked that innocent, Imogen," I said.

"He didn't move us on though, did he?"

"No, but what I didn't tell you that night was what he told me."

"What did he say?"

"We were parked on a lonely little country lane. Nothing for miles around. Do you remember? That's what *I* thought anyway. He leaned in close to the window and said, 'You might want to lock your doors, son. There's a lunatic asylum on the other side of that hedge and sometimes the patients go walkabout.'"

"Oh, Noah, and you *believed* him?"

"The way he delivered that line he could have won a BAFTA."

"No wonder you tried to get into my sleeping bag after that," Imogen said, with a playful smile.

"Yeah, that was *absolutely* the reason…"

The light had faded from the day. All I could see was a rectangle of the last of the afternoon framed in the doorway. Imogen had noticed the night closing in, and her mood gradually changed. She hurried us out of there. She locked up quickly, gathered Lily up into her arms and led us back to the car. She tried to cover it up but being there after dark was clearly a source of anxiety. I wondered what it was she'd seen here that could unnerve her in such a manner.

We got in the car and drove away.

Six

Out of the blue, Julian called Oliver in the April of 1984. He hadn't spoken to the artist in several years. It was seven in the morning.

"Oliver," he said, "it's about Malcolm. I'm afraid it's bad news."

Malcolm had asked for him, Julian said, and could he come down to London to see him?

"Of course I will," Oliver said, his mind suddenly quite blank. The world had fallen away from him. He was standing in the kitchen with the phone in his hand, dragging mud in from the fields on his boots, but he was adrift, lost in space. He'd often feel this way when he was down in the bunker, running through procedures. Imagining a vast silenced world beyond the hatch. A flash of light and it would all be gone.

He rifled through the drawers to find the train timetable and then packed quickly, trying not to think too deeply about what was waiting for him in London. He called Jenny to alert her of his impending absence. She and Imogen had been gone for almost eight years. Even now, after a hard day's toil in the fields, he'd return, part of him still expecting them to be here, lighting up the rooms with the comfort of their presence. Jenny at the kitchen table, trying to balance their books, growing increasingly frustrated; Imogen watching TV or working on homework in her bedroom. He'd taken it for granted all those years, that things would never change, that he could be wilfully ignorant of Jenny's feelings and coast all the way to the end of their lives, but that was not the case. If he'd allowed himself to change, then why should he ever have expected her to stay the same? He came home in the late afternoon, and he made his dinner for one and read a book as the evening arrived. He'd called *Radio Rentals* and arranged for them to take the TV back; it only depressed him now. It seemed to him that the eighties was a shallow decade thus far, but he supposed that was simply his age; you got to a certain point in your life where you felt like the rug had been pulled from beneath your feet; you looked around and suddenly nothing was familiar or comforting anymore. He did the pools each week and hoped that a windfall might change his life in some way. He didn't know how.

Oliver didn't say why he was going down to London, but Jenny knew that if it wasn't work – and it hadn't been work since 1976 – then it was probably Malcolm again, for the first time since 1979. She didn't enquire any further; she never had in all those years, and she'd never asked why it had ended so suddenly either after that holiday in the South of France. Theirs had never been that kind of marriage, and perhaps that was why it had foundered. He simply told her he'd be away for an indefinite period of time and that he wouldn't be around to see Imogen, who would be back from university this weekend. She had grown up so fast.

Jenny hadn't gone far when she and Imogen had moved out. She'd found a small flat above the bank in Lethebury. It wasn't much to look at. Oliver had volunteered to help move their things to the new place.

It was a strange, muted detente that set the template for the next few years. Their lives unexamined and left to go stale. They'd never discussed divorce. Neither of them could contend with being with someone else. But they knew they could not be together.

Nonetheless, every weekend for the last couple of years they had sat down for Sunday dinner together and talked about the weather, about work. Jenny had gone back to working part-time for the insurance company, and Oliver had started labouring for a local farmer, often toiling in the fields from an outrageously early hour until late in the afternoon. It was back-breaking work, and at 41, he was probably too old for it at this point. But what to do with the rest of his life? He'd considered this for years now and never managed to come up with a satisfactory answer. The only time he felt like himself was down in the bunker, usually when he was alone (he wasn't overly enamoured by Nigel and Clive, the other volunteers. If he had to spend his remaining days with the two of them after the bomb had dropped, then he'd hoped they'd perish quickly from radiation poisoning.) In the dim light of that poky little room underground, he could consider the malaise of his personal life and rearrange it accordingly, make the narrative work in a way that made everyone content with their lot. His imagination had always been his greatest ally. It was just a shame that the BBC and the British audience hadn't seen it in quite the same way.

With his case packed, he put on his best suit. Malcolm had bought it for him before their holiday to Birdy's chateau. The jacket was a bit tight beneath the armpits now but it would pass muster for the week. He wanted Malcolm to see he'd made the effort, that he remembered this among all his many benevolent gestures. The train left at ten a.m. It was mostly empty and it didn't stop at all the little stations along the way, so they reached Paddington before one in the afternoon. There was no one waiting for him this time. In the past it had always been Malcolm, looking elegant and refined on a bench among the crowds of people. *Ordinary people*, like Oliver. Malcolm was anything but ordinary. Always presented in a perfectly cut and tailored suit and brogues, cleanly shaven and with beautifully coiffured blond hair. Oliver had felt like an unmade bed beside him when they'd first met, but Malcolm had never judged. He'd insisted he saw the artist in Oliver long before Oliver had. Hearing himself referred to as an artist made him deeply uncomfortable. *Julian* was an artist. There was a hard streak of conservative pragmatism in Oliver that denied and decried that creative urge in him. But Malcolm's belief in him had been the engine that had driven those projects for the BBC, even if the journey had taken them nowhere.

Oliver hadn't seen or heard from Malcolm since that holiday in the South of France. After the parting Oliver had returned home to Lethebury and simply got on with things. Some small part of him quietly expected a letter or perhaps a call one winter evening, when he found himself feeling particularly low. Kenneth wrote once or twice, but he didn't address the events that had led to the parting of ways. He simply wrote about life in London, his diminishing cache, his dwindling finances.

Julian is back in Blighty, he'd written once. *He sounds like a bleeding yank now! Malcolm and I went to his exhibition at the Royal Academy. Lots of paintings of men by pools with their wedding tackle out. Well, really!* It was the only time he'd mentioned Malcolm.

Oliver hadn't felt the loss as keenly as he had with Jenny. He'd simply accepted what was and put it behind him, moved on. He'd never really paused to consider the depth of his feelings for Malcolm. Perhaps if he had, it might have broken him sooner.

Oliver took the Circle Line from Paddington to Westminster. From there it was a ten-minute walk across Westminster Bridge to St. Thomas' Hospital. He stood waiting at reception for five minutes with his case at his feet and his jacket folded over his arm. By the time he asked for directions to the ward where Malcolm was being treated, a cold sweat had broken out across his forehead. Now he was close to whatever was waiting for him in this hospital, he wasn't sure he was prepared. Perhaps you never could be in these situations.

He wandered for almost fifteen minutes, stopping to ask nurses for directions. The further he went, the less sure he was of his destination. He'd left the wards behind and now the corridors were piled up with boxes and rusty filing cabinets, the detritus of years of treatments. He passed empty offices and arrived at intersections with no one around. Just as he was about to give up and retrace his steps he heard the sounds of people nearby. He turned a corner and arrived at what looked like a makeshift reception in a Victorian section that seemed as if it had avoided progress in the intervening 130 years or so.

"I'm here to see Malcolm Church," he told the severe looking woman at the reception desk.

"Are you a relative?"

"No," he said. "I'm a friend."

She seemed to appraise him for a moment, and then tucked a stray hair behind her ear. "Do you want gloves and a surgical mask?"

Oliver bit his lip, glanced through the heavy doors at the ward, at the beds filled with men. He felt a sudden tumult of emotion in his chest that he could barely contain. "No," he said. "I do not."

"Sign this," she said and passed him a clipboard with a form. He scanned it briefly and then signed it, passed it back to her. "He's in the last bed on the right-hand side," she said.

Oliver glanced with mounting horror at the other men as he passed their beds. Some of them were asleep, some of them accompanied by other men or a family member, some of them alone, staring with sunken eyes at him. Machines bleeping, drips, clean white sheets, books and cards and drinks on bedside cabinets, half-eaten fruit, wilted flowers. He took in these little details, seeing but not seeing because the entire picture would reduce him terribly before he even reached Malcolm.

It was Julian he recognised first. He was more soberly dressed than Oliver had ever seen him. Part of his persona had been those colourful spectacles and braces and the Picasso pullovers. But he was wearing a creased white shirt and black trousers, a black tie, the knot loosened. He looked exhausted. He embraced Oliver, kissed his cheek. The two men relinquished each other but Julian continued to grip his arms. His face was hard, his eyes swimming. Words weren't sufficient, so he said nothing.

"Hello Oliver." The voice from behind Julian was small, and sufficiently familiar. But the man in the bed couldn't be Malcolm. *His* Malcolm was an elegant, healthy specimen. A man of refinement, well-read and well-spoken, but with the occasional lapse that allowed in that Rochdale accent. *His* Malcolm had thick blond hair and strong arms. Oliver remembered those arms around him, remembered floating in the sea beside him, staring up into the impossible blue. Once he could have fallen into Malcolm's strong arms and forgotten that the world didn't fit him properly. In those arms he could have forgotten that everything he perceived as wrong was in fact perfectly correct.

But this was his Malcolm now. A skull with thin, papery skin stretched across it. The hair was almost gone. Just soft blond wisps of it left. Oliver could see the hollow of his collarbone, the pronounced knobs of his elbows and wrist bones. The violet-coloured lesions decorating his neck and chest. Malcolm raised a hand towards Oliver and tried to smile, let the limb fall to the bed again. There was too much effort involved in that simple gesture now.

"Oh, Malcolm, *no*... No." The words dried up in Oliver's throat. The world was falling away from him again. Away from the two of them. This colourless man in this colourless ward in this colourless hospital in this frequently carelessly cruel and colourless world. He felt tears spring from his eyes and roll down his cheeks. "You don't have to touch me," Malcolm said. "Not if you don't want to."

Oliver exhaled and it became a sob that wracked his entire body. He took Malcolm's hand and held it to his face. Julian pulled the chair up to the bed and sat Oliver's quavering body down in it. "Thank you," Oliver said, absently. Julian suddenly seemed very far away. He was aware that he was holding Malcolm's hand too tightly. The bones felt like kindling to him. There was something about how terribly *reduced* he was, how far away from the man he used to be that clutched at Oliver's heart. One of Malcolm's pyjama buttons had come loose. The fine wisps of hair across his skull made him seem naked. Little details that suddenly seemed huge.

"Malcolm," Oliver said finally, his voice hoarse. "Why didn't you call me?" He turned to Julian. "Why did you wait until now?"

"I didn't want you to see me like this," Malcolm said. "I made Julian promise not to call you." He smiled. "I thought perhaps I'd get better. Actually, thanks to PoppyHarp I *did* get better for a while, but now, well…" He tailed off and the smile left his face. He suddenly looked terribly lost.

"*PoppyHarp?*" Oliver said.

Malcolm waved the comment away. "Ignore me, I'm delirious."

Oliver reached across and did up the loosened button on Malcolm's pyjamas, because it was bothering him. Malcolm's eyes followed his movements. Finally he closed a hand over Oliver's and tried to squeeze it. His skin was papery and cold.

"I'm sorry," Oliver said. "I'm *so* bloody sorry."

"Whatever for?"

"For how I left. For how I dealt with things. That holiday…"

"There's nothing to apologise for, Oliver." Malcolm smiled. "It's forgotten. All that matters is… well, that you're here now. That…"

"I insisted that I call you," Julian said. "I wanted you to have a chance to see him…"

No one could finish their sentences anymore.

"You just missed my mother," Malcolm said. "That *did* happen, didn't it?" he asked Julian. "I didn't hallucinate that?" And then to Oliver: "The drugs they're pumping me full of… they haven't got a bloody clue. I'm all over the place."

Julian smiled softly. "No. No, that happened. She arrived with her surgical mask and gloves," he said to Oliver. "Sat where you are now, holding her handbag stiffly in between them, just in case Malcolm lunged at her, or something."

"She was scared," Malcolm said. "She didn't understand. All she knows is what she's read in *The Sun* or the *Mail*. 'Gay plague'… fucking bastards." He laughed bitterly, and then began to cough, closed his eyes afterwards. "She wouldn't touch me, not even with her gloves on," he said, after a moment. "No goodbye kiss."

"She'll come back," Julian said.

"No, she won't." Malcolm glanced away, his eyes glassy.

"What can I do?" Oliver asked. "Now I'm here?"

Malcolm opened his eyes and looked at him. Tried to squeeze his hand again. "This is enough," he said. "Just this."

———

Later, after Malcolm had fallen asleep, Julian took Oliver to a cafe in the hospital where they sat at a Formica table beside a window and sipped at bad coffee. Outside it was raining. On the street people were beginning to make their way home, hurrying towards the Tube, crowding on buses, sheltering in pubs until the rain abated. It felt to Oliver as if they were in two separate worlds. Neither could exist in harmony with the other, so here they were, sealed away, in stasis while the rest of the world continued to revolve.

"He was taken ill over Christmas," Julian said. "He was diagnosed with Pneumocystis. It's a form of pneumonia caused by fungus and Kaposi's sarcoma. Those are the lesions on his skin that you can see. He'd been losing weight before that. We knew something was wrong, what with all the reports in the papers and on the news. You can't escape it."

"I've read about it," Oliver said. "I just never thought it would happen to someone I know." He shrugged. "I feel a bit isolated from the real world out there in the Malverns."

"I've been going to more and more funerals this last year or so," Julian said. "First it was friends of friends, then friends, then old flames." He sighed, sipped at his coffee. "This winter has been the worst. It's like a season of goodbyes. From the hospital bed to the graveside. I keep thinking it'll be me next. We're dropping like flies."

"I'll stay," Oliver said. "I'll do whatever I can."

Julian nodded. "I don't think we have much longer if I'm being brutally honest, Oliver." He glanced away, his eyes glazed with tears. "I think he'll be happier with you here."

"We've barely spoken in years," Oliver said.

"He talks about you, you know," Julian said. "Every now and then. You were the one that got away." He smiled. "We all have one of them."

Oliver didn't know how to respond to that. He felt that he'd left that aspect of himself behind when he stopped coming to London. That freedom to be someone else, the man he suspected he'd always been. But he'd made the wrong decisions, long ago, and there was no way to change who he was now. All those roads led nowhere. He was lost in between. "It was too difficult for me," he began, searching for the appropriate words, "to be the man he wanted me to be…"

"He knew that, Oliver. He realised that he'd tried to push you into being someone else. If you weren't comfortable, then you'd never be happy. He only wanted the best for you, but you had to come to it on your own terms."

Oliver nodded, feeling like he'd failed Malcolm by not being brave enough to be the man he imagined he could be. "Is there anyone else?" he asked.

"How do you mean?"

"I mean another man. Someone in his life who'd take umbrage at me being here."

Julian smiled. "There are plenty of *other men*, Oliver. I suppose that's our Malcolm's problem."

"Oh," Oliver said. "I didn't realise."

"Not when you were in the picture," Julian said. "Don't think that. He took a vow of abstinence. Said he was saving himself for you. Not even Hudson Powell."

"So afterwards then."

"I suppose so. It's the business he's in. The lifestyle at the BBC does seem to throw up a lot of opportunities for that sort of thing."

"Does the BBC know?"

"Oh, yes," Julian said. "They fired him in January."

"They *fired* him?"

"When they released him from hospital after Christmas, he went back to work, but they knew what was up. He was obviously, visibly ill, but he thought he could bluster his way through it. You know our Malcolm. That's always how he's done things. Sliding through life on charm and bluster. A few days and they had him in, gave him his marching orders there and then. He'd worked there almost twenty years."

"That's appalling."

"That's Britain, Oliver. It's going to the dogs. Five years of the bloody Conservatives. I met a chap at a party. Freelance journalist, it turned out. He told me that AIDS related stories sold more papers than bingo. It doesn't matter what the impact is on people's lives. It's an 'us and them' mentality now."

Julian stood finally. He'd worked himself up into a livid state. "I'm sorry, Oliver, I need a cigarette. I'll be back in a bit once I've calmed down. I'll see you on the ward."

Afterwards Oliver sat at the table, staring at the rain on the windows. The streets were quieter now. He felt bereft, as if he'd arrived at a play near the end, having missed his cues. Somehow the actors had muddled through without him, but now the story was all wrong. He remembered that conversation he'd had with Julian at his studio on the very first weekend in London. He'd never forgotten his words. *Sometimes you get distracted and you look away from something that's always been there. And by the time you look again, it's become a memory.*

—

That week Oliver stayed at Julian's apartment in Belgravia, a place so new that the furniture was still sealed in plastic, and the carpets were a shade of cream that made Oliver want to take off his shoes before he set foot in the place. The rooms were huge and empty. When he switched the TV on, the sound seemed to carry throughout the rooms, so he turned it off again.

"I bought the place after seeing it once," Julian told him in the hospital on the second day. "I've done bugger all to it. Barely stayed there more than three nights in eight months. I still spend all my time at the studio in Pembroke Gardens. I prefer to sleep there to be honest. Feels more like home."

The place in Belgravia wasn't a home, but Oliver gladly fell into its bed at night after a day at the hospital. Officially they still frowned on people being there out of visiting hours, but there was a community of them now, making sure that these men were not alone in their final months, weeks, days. Oliver and Julian would take it in turns initially, but then find that both of them were there by Malcolm's bedside, or else sitting next to the beds of other men whose families had deserted them, and had no lovers or friends to keep them company.

On the third day, Kenneth Bliss showed his face for the first time. He arrived in the ward with the same mixture of disorientation and alarm that all visitors displayed. He was holding the gloves and the surgical mask in his hand but he hadn't put them on. He came to the bedside and said: "Do I need these or not?"

"I'm more likely to catch something from you to be honest, Kenny," Malcolm said.

"Christ, how sick you look, you dear, dear man."

"Thank you for that. That makes me feel much better."

Bliss pursed his lips and considered Malcolm in the bed, too weak to even lift his arm. For a moment,

Oliver thought that he was giving way to emotion, but he shook his head and resolved himself. "Christ, Malcolm," he said, leaning down to gently place a kiss on Malcolm's cheek. "What are we going to do with you, eh?" He tossed the gloves and mask on the bedside cabinet.

"I'm thinking of having him stuffed," Julian suggested.

"Once a week and twice on a Sunday," Kenneth said.

He embraced Julian and Oliver and then sat down beside Malcolm, took his hand. "It dampens one's spirits to be in places like these."

"One doesn't have much choice in the matter," Malcolm said. "What have you been up to, Kenny? I haven't seen you in months."

Bliss sighed theatrically. "I've been doing Noel Coward at the Queen's Theatre for the last three months."

"Noel must be exhausted," Julian offered.

Bliss glanced at Julian and flared his nostrils. "'A Song at Twilight'. One of his last plays where he abandoned his customary reticence on his homosexuality."

"That must be packing them in at the moment."

"I had high hopes for it. Just as I did for *PoppyHarp*..." Bliss glanced at Oliver and smiled ruefully. "But it's a bit of a damp squib. The producer keeps telling me that I'm too slow, that I should be slicker in this day and age. I told him he probably should have cast someone else if he wanted that. I've rarely encountered such obdurate fucking stupidity. He's a frightful boor of a man for a theatre director."

They all sat in a companionable silence for a while, listening to Malcolm's ragged breaths.

"I don't think I have to worry about this, you know," Bliss said. "This AIDS. I went to the Blood Donor Centre at Margaret Street to give blood. They asked me to fill in a form testifying to abstention from promiscuity." He waited a moment, a practiced beat. "Chance would be a fine thing at my age," he said with a sly smile.

They all laughed. It helped a little bit.

"Hello, Malcolm."

They hadn't noticed her arrive. She was well-dressed, her hair short and grey. She had a briefcase. She'd clearly just arrived from a day's work.

"Anna," Malcolm said. "I never expected to see you here."

Anna glanced at the assembled faces around the bed, clearly aware who they all were. She nodded to them. She had a hard face, and a manner that suggested she didn't suffer fools gladly. "I'm sorry," she said to Malcolm. "I only just heard about all this."

"This is Anna Horne, one of my old BBC colleagues," Malcolm said.

"I'm sorry about all of that in January," Anna said. "I wanted to speak up but it was above my pay-grade in the end."

"Could Anna and I have some time alone?" Malcolm asked them then.

Oliver rose first, feeling oddly anxious about the interloper. He led Kenneth and Julian away, leaving them to it.

———

Anna sought Oliver out half an hour later in the cafeteria. Julian and Kenneth were outside smoking.

"I'm sorry about all that," Anna said. She looked less composed now. Mortality was the great leveller. "I'd like to properly introduce myself. Anna Horne," she said, extending her hand. "I'm the head of the children's television department."

Oliver rose and took her hand, introducing himself.

"I know who you are," Anna said. "Malcolm was quite the champion of your work."

"He's a good fellow," Oliver said. "Too good, in fact. Charitable to a fault."

"The Corporation have treated him abominably," Anna said. "All those years of service, only to be dismissed like that."

"I assumed that was how the BBC had always done business. Casting people aside once they'd had their fill of them."

"They're running scared of the government now," Anna said. "All the values and practices contested at every level. Thatcher thinks that the BBC is part of an establishment that needs to be re-engineered. They think that the BBC spending is profligate, that the plays are too political, standards of taste and decency out of touch with the public." She sighed, glanced away at the corridor, at the end of which lay Malcolm. "He's just the first. There will be others. The BBC is infested with all sorts of immorality."

"Is that how you see homosexuality? As immoral?" Oliver felt irritated suddenly. At the injustice of Malcolm's disease, at the impasse he found himself at, and at his own brief brushes with the corporation which had rolled over him and simply rolled on.

"Of course not," Anna said. "Ask the woman I've lived with for the past six years."

"I apologise."

"That's quite alright, Oliver. I share your frustration. The kind of immorality I'm referring to is… well, it'll all come out one day."

"I think these people know how to protect their own interests," Oliver said. "That's how it always works, as I understand it."

"When I met Malcolm in 1971, I was a researcher for *Play School*. I thought he was just like the rest of them, you know, that vulgar boy's club mentality that's always existed at the BBC in one shape or another. But then he came to me about a young chap he'd met from the Malverns. He invited me for dinner one night and proceeded to talk about you all evening. He thought you were a rough diamond. He told me the premise of *The Adventures of Imogen and Florian*. Then he told me about your cowshed. That fabled cowshed. By the end of 1972, I think everyone at Television Centre had heard about that bloody cowshed of yours."

Anna smiled and paused, a softness arriving to set out its stall in her eyes, her face. She glanced around at her surroundings – wondering, Oliver supposed, how she'd arrived here. He knew how she felt.

"He felt a very real sense of obligation to you, Oliver. He very much wanted for your work to find an audience. He took it very badly when he failed."

"It was never his duty to make my work a success," Oliver said. "I never asked for that."

"I've known Malcolm for almost thirteen years now," Anna said. "We've worked on countless projects, but he never cared as deeply about any of them as he did yours." She leaned forward, stretched a hand across the table that fell short of Oliver's. "He never cared about *anyone* in the way that he cared about you," she said. "No one ever came close."

Oliver nodded. He couldn't look at Anna. He felt unaccustomed to the tears brimming in his eyes.

"Oh, Oliver, I didn't wish to upset you."

Oliver shook his head. "I'm quite all right."

She studied him for a moment and then nodded. "Well, look, I discussed this with Malcolm, and he agreed that it was something I should bring to you. There's this young chap I know, Freddie Steadman. He shows immense promise, I think. Well, anyway, he's been contracted by the Central Office of Information to produce a series of Public Information films."

Oliver nodded. "Well, what has that got to do with me?"

"He's a young man. Twenty-something. He asked me about *The Adventures of Imogen and Florian*. He has quite fond memories of your programme. He would have been about twelve or thirteen when they were transmitted. Obviously he never saw them again, but he heard that I might know something about them." Anna leaned forward, as if offering him a gift – which, in retrospect, Oliver supposed she was. "He requested your involvement in these films, if you're interested."

"Aren't they just short things, warning children about rabies and road safety?"

"Well, yes…" Anna said, her brow creasing. It was as if he'd passed the gift back, unopened. "But there's an awful lot of leeway for creativity. And education, of course. An entire generation of children would see these films."

Oliver nodded, pressed his fingertips to his eyes. He nodded again, to compose himself. "This is really not the time, is it?" he said finally. "I'm not sure about going back into the lion's den again. It's never really gotten me anywhere. *And* I think I need to be close to Malcolm at the moment."

"I quite understand your reticence, Oliver," Anna said. She took a card from her bag and slid it across the table. "It'd be a couple of hours of your time while you're down here. If you find you are available, call me. I can arrange a meeting with Freddie."

Oliver nodded, stared at the card on the table between them with what must have looked like unbridled skepticism.

"It won't bite," Anna said, smiling.

"Oh, it might," Oliver said.

"*Do* think about it, Oliver," Anna said as she rose from her seat. She shook his hand again before she strode away. Oliver stared at the card until he saw Bliss and Julian returning. He slid it off the table and slipped it into his pocket.

———

Oliver met Freddie Steadman in a nondescript office building in Soho that proved to be a private production studio. It was currently in use with sets for house interiors, a cyclorama, and a back screen which could be decorated to give the impression of depth. It was a sit-com of some kind. Something modern, a bit anarchic. Oliver felt out of place with the youthful energy of the people there. When he spoke to them, they proved to be Oxbridge-educated and courteous enough, but it made him feel old, a little bit past it.

Freddie Steadman was a brash, energetic man. He sat opposite Oliver in a bare office that reminded him of a room he might visit to get a doctor's examination. Steadman wouldn't sit still. He was like an eager puppy. His eyes were huge and watery, a remnant of the child he'd been just a few years ago. He'd exhausted Oliver within minutes.

"I can still vividly remember sitting down and watching *The Adventures of Imogen and Florian*," Steadman had told him from the outset of their meeting. "I was *far* too old for it at that point, I suppose. Just into my teens, but my younger sister was watching it, and I spent a fair portion of my youth looking after her. No choice really. My father left when we were young and my mother had to work to keep us afloat. She was an actress – *Z-Cars*, *On the Buses*, *Upstairs, Downstairs*… I was the lad who didn't get to go off with my friends on our bikes. Bit of a sheltered upbringing. But you know, my sister is at university now, and she's the most independent woman I know. It didn't do us any harm.

"But anyway, yes, *Imogen and Florian* scared her senseless. She wouldn't watch it after the first episode. But I did. In *secret*." He laughed. "There was something hypnotic and sort of vaguely endearing about it, about that slightly crude quality to the characters and the animation."

"I'm sorry that you think it was crude," Oliver said, stung by the casual slight. "I put a lot of effort into those shows."

"Oh, I didn't mean to offend you, Oliver. When I say crude, I mean it as a bloody compliment. That slightly, I don't know, *rustic* quality, which you simply wouldn't have achieved if there had been a whole retinue of animators working in a studio in Broadcasting House. When I discussed it with Anna, she told me that you worked out of a converted cowshed in your backyard."

"Yes, that's true. Homemade equipment. I taught myself how to do everything."

"You see that's bloody marvellous, Oliver. *That's* what made *The Adventures of Imogen and Florian* so unique and strange." Steadman sat back, ran his fingers through the thick tangle of curls on his head. "I'd assumed that you must have been on copious amounts of drugs to come up with some of the stuff in that show."

Oliver smiled. "Sorry to disappoint you. I barely even drink. I suppose I just have a fertile imagination."

"Well, it's an absolute fucking *crime* that it wasn't shown again. We're depriving new generations of children from seeing it."

It didn't matter how welcome these observations were, albeit long after the fact... Oliver was having misgivings about this whole thing. He should be at Malcolm's side. What if something happened while he was here? How would anyone get in touch with him? But it had been Malcolm who'd insisted he come here to talk to Steadman. Anna seemed to have faith in his abilities, and Malcolm had faith in Anna's instincts. After discussing it with Oliver after Anna had left, he'd asked the nurse for a phone so he could make a call to Steadman personally in order to arrange a meeting. Despite his own misgivings, Oliver could tell that Malcolm was secretly delighted to still be able to pull some strings for his benefit.

"If Freddie Steadman wants you to be involved in some way just because he has some misty romantic memory of your show, then I think you should at least sit down in a room with him and hear him out," he'd said. The determined look on his face had suggested he wouldn't take no for an answer. He'd repeated himself to make himself clear. "*Hear. Him. Out.*"

Oliver had grudgingly acquiesced and finally agreed to the meeting.

"I sat in a room like this in 1972," he said. "Sweating through my shirt, hoping they weren't going to take my one good idea from me." He glanced up, surprised to realise he was talking aloud. Steadman had uncrossed his legs and was leaning forward to listen. "Malcolm championed me, shielded me from all the politics of the bloody place. I just tootled off back to my home, to my cowshed, and made the show I wanted to make without any interference."

"Pardon my French, Oliver, but I've made a point of ignoring the fucking *suits*," Steadman said. "As little interference from them as possible. They're relics from a different age."

"But you see being isolated from all of this was *detrimental* in the end," Oliver said, watching the shadows of the rain crawl down all of the walls. "I didn't know the first thing about what children wanted to see. I was entirely ignorant and that was a mistake. I thought that the ideas in my head would make everyone sit up and notice. And for years – bloody *years* – I laboured under the misapprehension that I wasn't the one at fault. That it was the *audience* who weren't smart enough to grasp what a bloody misunderstood genius I was."

"But you were right, Oliver," Steadman said. "Absolutely fucking spot-on with your instincts. I think truly meaningful or 'pure' art, if you will, is created *solely* for the purpose of expression. It shouldn't be tainted by *any* outside force. That idea that you have to produce something that appeals to a mass audience *instantly* dilutes its purpose.

"They left you to your own devices and you produced something that I personally believe will stand the test of time, whether it gets shown again or not. People have long memories, Oliver. If you'd produced *Imogen and Florian* at the BBC with other people polluting your vision, with endless fucking *middle-men* coming in, throwing their tuppence-worth in, it wouldn't be remembered half as fondly."

"But that's just it," Oliver said. "It was forgotten anyway. It didn't matter if it was meaningful or not. I put a year's worth of my life into that show and it went out into the world and nothing came back. *Nothing* came of it. And it ruined my life, my marriage, my relationship with my daughter. Everything that was actually meaningful to me. And I didn't see any of that coming at the time."

Oliver chanced a look at the young man, aware that he'd allowed a stranger too much of an insight into his life. He had a grudging admiration for Steadman's ideals about art over commerce. But he suspected he'd be ground down by this whole process too, just as Oliver had. There was no room in this business for misplaced aspirations. They gave you just enough rope to hang you with.

"What do you want from me anyway?" he asked finally. The question sounded despondent when it left his mouth. "These... Public Information Films. I don't really grasp what I have to offer you."

"Look, you understand the purpose of these things, don't you?" Steadman said. "Public Information Films are usually aimed at children. When the local ITV station reaches a point in a break where they haven't managed to sell their quota of advertising space, they'll stick one of these little films on. Usually something to do with road safety or electricity pylons, or rabies or going off with strangers. They're like a collective smack on the legs if you do them properly. You really need to *scare* the little buggers."

"I must have caught some of them here and there, I'm sure," Oliver admitted. "Imogen must have seen them after school. I seem to recall one animated film with a child and his cat."

"Yes, the *Charley Says* films," Steadman said. "Richard Taylor Cartoons. Paper cut-out animation techniques. Again, crude but very effective. A seven-year-old and his ginger tom, Charley, voiced by Kenny Everett. The dangers of stoves and strangers and water."

"Is that what you want?" Oliver said. "For me to animate these films for you?"

"Not exactly. I've completed six scripts for these Public Information Films," Steadman said, leaning forward in his seat. "I realised after watching some of the old films from the seventies that the things that stick in your head are their bluntness and lack of subtlety. They're generally exempt from classification due to their educational nature anyway. This is why we had things like *Apaches* by John McKenzie, who went on to make *The Long Good Friday*. Children being killed by various dangers on the farm. *The Spirit of Dark and Lonely Water* by Jeff Grant. Pretty dark stuff generally."

Steadman reached into a bag beside his chair and produced a sheaf of papers, spreading them out across the table for Oliver to look at. "I have these ideas and sketches," he said. "Admittedly they're pretty rough, but I know what I want. What's in my head."

Oliver stood so that he could look at the drawings. Steadman stood beside him, arranging the papers to could map it all out. He caught the gist of it: a wise old owl called Butterworth, a dim mole called Montgomery, and a reckless sheep called Farley, watching over the familiar situations – road safety, the dangers of train tracks, vandalism, fireworks – and warning children of their dangers. Oliver tried to focus on Steadman's words but they began to swim away from him. It all seemed a little bit inconsequential to him. A small part of him had anticipated the prospect of a new road to travel down, an opportunity to rectify old wrongs; something that built upon his small body of work and introduced it to a new generation. But these films, they seemed like a cul-de-sac, a new low in his career, such as it was. Was he now in the future that they'd promised in the seventies? A future of diminishing returns?

"So where do I fit into all of this?" he asked.

"I'd very much like for you to go back to that cowshed of yours and create Butterworth, Montgomery and Farley for me."

Oliver glanced down at the rough sketches Steadman had made, his creative curiosity piqued, despite himself. That old familiar itch. Could he bring these characters to life the way he used to? "I've never really collaborated as such before…"

He sensed Steadman stiffen at what he realised was a gross misunderstanding.

"Oh, well, this isn't a collaboration as such, Oliver. I won't require you to actually *work* on the films in any sense. What I want from you is your keen eye for character design. I don't want something slick. I want characters that wouldn't be out of place living in that doll's house in *The Adventures of Imogen and Florian.*"

Oliver nodded and sat back down. He felt like an old fool. Even after all this time, a small part of him had thought this might be the opportunity he tried to delude himself that he didn't crave on an almost daily basis. He wanted to believe that those years hadn't been wasted, that they were a stepping stone to something bigger and better.

Steadman gathered up his sketches and notes quietly, into a folder. There had been a shift in the atmosphere in the room. But Steadman was too ambitious to be embarrassed. "Look, I'm sorry that you seem to have got the wrong end of the stick, Oliver. To be quite honest I could get this done far quicker without you, but I'd personally prefer to see you create these characters. I'd like a whole new generation to be exposed to your imagination."

He opened the door for Oliver, indicating that the meeting was over. He shook his hand and said, "The money is good too, if that's any kind of inducement..."

———

Oliver returned to Julian's place in Belgravia and there the two men convened, outside of visiting hours, waiting for the inevitable call from the hospital. Malcolm was deteriorating rapidly. They were gradually learning how to mourn someone before they were gone. One morning Julian took Oliver to the studios in Pembroke Gardens to show him his current work in progress. A series of small flower etchings: one for each friend Julian had lost. Oriental hellebores, irises, lilies and sunflowers.

"It's a paltry offering, I know," Julian said. "No substitute for what their lives represented in any way. But I came back after the first funeral and that was what came out of me. They feel like memories. Nothing specific, just an impression of the men I knew and the feelings they inspired in me. You can't really define what it is in literal terms. I don't think you really remember the things you do and see. You just remember a memory of a memory. And I think we rewrite memory much the way history is rewritten."

"They're beautiful," Oliver said. There was a bare, bereft quality to each of the etchings. They left him feeling brittle, close to tears.

"I read yesterday that people were afraid that gay plumbers might infect a cistern," Julian said. "That they think you can catch AIDS from communion wine. Or the fucking swimming baths."

"That's the press for you," Oliver said. "All these inflammatory articles. Until I came back here, I had no idea how it had affected your community." He paused, hearing it finally. "*Our* community," he said, and reached out to squeeze Julian's hand.

The phone began to ring.

———

Malcolm died that day.

When they arrived, a man who'd been at Malcolm's bedside was just leaving. Oliver didn't take much notice of him. Plenty of men came and went, most of them strangers. But when Oliver passed him he heard several keening musical notes in his head that quickly resolved into a harmony so sweet and familiar that he had to smile at it. Then his ears popped. Oliver watched the man leave the ward, hoping for him to turn and show his face, just once. *Just once*. He didn't. He felt a keen sense of loss that lingered for the rest of the morning.

Later, Oliver was dozing in his chair. Someone had covered him with an eiderdown. There were crumbs on his shirt from a packet of biscuits that Bliss had passed around earlier. He'd been dreaming on and off about Malcolm. A day they'd spent together while they filmed *PoppyHarp*. A memory that he treasured above all others. That long hot summer of 1976, before life had turned so sour. Not even the slightest whisper of a breeze anywhere. Clothes plastered to the skin as soon as you stepped outside. They'd gone up through the Malverns for the day, hiked one of Cleobury Mortimer's routes, which offered panoramic rural views of the South Shropshire countryside and the river Rea. It had been a mistake in the heat, but the memory of the day lingered in Oliver's mind. They'd stopped at the river and sat on the banks, their bare feet in the cool water. They'd brought a picnic of sandwiches and some beer that was almost undrinkable as it was so warm. They caught sight of a kingfisher on the other side of the bank. It hovered above the water, its brightly coloured plumage making it stand out against the low hanging branches and hills beyond the river. Malcolm talked about his childhood, growing up in Rochdale and then abroad. His father was a pilot in the RAF and Malcolm and his mother followed him to numerous postings around the world. He talked about Kenya and Rhodesia, boats taking them to ports filled with colours and sounds and sights so magnificent he could scarcely contain them all in his memory. For a while his childhood had been thrilling, but then his father had died when his aircraft crashed. He was posthumously awarded the Distinguished Flying Cross. Malcolm and his mother had visited Buckingham Palace to collect it from the Queen. There were no words to describe a day like that, the emotions contained within it. It was a time capsule, buried deep inside him.

Malcolm had kissed Oliver then. Their feet were still in the river. Oliver had resisted momentarily, then all of that diffidence fell away and he ran his fingers through Malcolm's hair and kissed him back. They embraced and for a moment the world seemed to stop and he remembered it all quite perfectly: the smell of the river and the shade of the trees hanging above them, the heat on their browning skin, the kingfisher hovering above the water, the taste of warm beer and cheese and ham, the sensation of Malcolm's mouth on his. Like racing toward a cliff without wings, secure in the knowledge that he would know how to build them on the way down. It was an exquisite reminiscence. Not even floating in the sea together in the South of France could touch it. The memory of a memory that was so sweet that it followed him out of sleep.

Malcolm was still there, a jarring shadow of the man in his dream. Oliver caught him just as he left. There were no final words. He didn't even wake. One minute he was breathing softly, and then he was not. It was as if he'd slipped quietly from the ward while they sat beside him. Oliver hesitated for a moment, suspended in the place between the life he'd had and not grasped and the one he was left with. Then he roused Julian and they called for a nurse and stood aside, allowing Malcolm to slip away from them entirely.

———

It was another funeral for Julian to attend, and another etching to complete. It wouldn't be his last. Three years later he would follow his twenty-six friends to an early grave. But before that they buried Malcolm and then said their goodbyes at Paddington Station. Oliver took a train home and would only return to London for funerals. There was no reason to return anymore. The city was a closed book to him now.

Upon arriving at the station in Lethebury he made his way to Jenny's door and wept in her arms for almost an hour. They didn't talk much. To Jenny, Malcolm was the man who'd ruined their marriage. She made Oliver dinner and they watched the TV in companionable silence. She'd always known what he needed. He stayed the night, as Imogen was back at university. He lay in her room, surrounded by her things. He barely slept. His mind kept returning to that day with Malcolm, their feet in the river. He studied the memory from all angles, rewinding it like videotape, back to the start again and again. The memory of a memory. He was afraid that if he kept looking at it, it might degrade. But he wanted to exist *inside* it somehow, and be away from the grey world he'd been left with. In the morning he rose early and let himself out, acutely embarrassed at the fool he'd made of himself with Jenny, and made his way home.

That day he started work on the characters for Freddie Steadman's Public Information Films.

Seven

Imogen still had an old VCR, so we settled Lily down in front of the TV to watch some of Oliver's tapes of *The Adventures of Imogen and Florian*. We sat in the conservatory, where I could see the town of Lethebury spread out below us, its details evaporating beneath a fresh bombardment of snow. From here I could also watch some of Oliver Frayling's strange little show, lighting up Lily's face as she sat cross-legged in front of the TV, her colouring books scattered around her on the carpet. I couldn't hear it, but it was all so familiar, so hypnotic. I had to keep dragging my attention away from it whenever Imogen spoke. My eyes moving from her nine-year-old self to the 55-year-old in front of me. It allowed me to fall into a surreal, almost hypnagogic state, aided by the bottle of wine that we had opened over dinner.

"You have my books," I said. I'd noticed them on a shelf in the front room. "The history of my life in what is loosely termed 'literature.'"

A Brief History of English Magic ran to six novels. It featured a huge cast of characters, both real and imagined: William Blake, Dr John Dee, William Shakespeare, Aleister Crowley, Gerald Gardner, Merlin, Spring Heeled Jack, Herne the Hunter... I'd attempted to weave them into a tapestry of tales set against England's magical past: from Arthur's Camelot to the witches of Pendle Hill; from the construction of Stonehenge to the formation of the Hermetic Order of the Golden Dawn. I'd assumed I'd get to the second volume and someone from Harper Collins would call to tell me that the first book had only sold twelve copies, and would I please cease and desist. But that call didn't happen, so I kept calm and carried on. I'd spent almost ten years researching and writing. By the time I began my final pass on book six of *A Brief History of English Magic*, I was also writing a completely different kind of book, *The Separation of Things*. It was a strange, slim volume, more like magical realism than anything else. On the back of my name, it sold moderately well. But then my next book grew wings and became a New York Times bestseller. *A Year of Miracles and Floods* was written while I accompanied Abigail Walker across America during her band's farewell tour. Something of her peripatetic life and the country where she was born was absorbed into the story I was writing: a road journey about an immortal woman in pursuit of a secret society that has its roots in American history, and which is preparing for the end of days. We conceived Lily in the insalubrious surroundings of a cheap motel in Rapid City, South Dakota. After the tour we came back to England, married, and started a new life with a child. Abigail embarked on a solo career. Things were good. After the success of *A Year of Miracles and Floods* I took some time off to be a father, but I was already making notes for my series of children's novels called *London is Dreaming*. I wanted to write something that I could read to Lily when she was old enough.

And so it went for another few years. We made each other laugh. We inspired each other to creative highs. We travelled and we talked constantly. And then she left me.

"She gave no indication that she was unhappy?" Imogen said, uncorking another bottle of wine after Lily had fallen asleep in front of the TV.

"Maybe? I don't know anymore, to be honest. I've looked at it from so many different angles at this point that I think it might send me mad," I said. "You tell yourself not to keep going down that road but then it's three a.m. and you're lying in bed trying to piece the final days together, looking for an errant look or something one of us said."

"That way madness lies," Imogen agreed.

"I suppose we were polar opposites. In fact, I *know* we were, but after eight or nine years, you assume that those differences don't matter anymore."

"How was she different?"

"Abigail didn't know how to be in a room by herself. She was born to perform in some way. Her folks had encouraged her to get up and sing and play the piano from an early age. Classic American hippie parents. She ran around half-naked and barefoot on Martha's Vineyard, and then the family spent the next thirteen years moving around the country in pursuit of themselves. By the time she was 21 she was talking to her therapist about boundary issues. I, on the other hand, am, as you know, an only child from a broken family, who spent most of his childhood in a home. And I'm *perfectly* happy being in a room alone. In fact, it's a requisite for a writer."

"How did she cope with Lily and the autism?"

I shook my head. "I thought she handled it fine. She was good at being Lily's mum, you know? It took her a while to get acclimatised to it. After all those years of being in a band, she was used to other people telling her where she was supposed to be, bringing her coffee, making arrangements. When it was just us, I could sometimes see her getting cabin fever. She was there but she wasn't there. She couldn't really cope with sitting still.

"Again," I said, "sitting still is kind of in the job description for being a writer."

We drifted from one subject to another as the evening wore on. We began to rediscover all of our old rhythms, recalled old jokes that only we understood. I thought we only passed this way once, but I started to wonder if I was wrong about that. This was the third time around for us now. Almost as if circumstance was continually bringing us back together. I checked on Lily, who we'd carried, fast asleep, to one of the guest rooms, nestled under the eaves of the house. She was sleeping soundly.

Imogen talked about Jeffrey. I could tell it was still difficult for her. The stories still had sharp edges. "We were on holiday. This was six years ago. We'd saved for a couple of years to go to the Caribbean. One of those once-in-a-lifetime kinds of holidays. We were staying in Antigua for a few days and we'd hired a boat to go out to Bird Island. We anchored and went snorkeling the reef nearby. I lost track of Jeffrey at some point but it didn't seem to matter; I knew he was nearby. I think they refer to it as one of those 'life moments'."

"Bucket list experiences."

"Yes. Absolutely. I felt very aware of myself and my place in the world. I didn't want it to end. There was something in that silence and the beauty of the coral reef that seemed to be filling me to the absolute brim. It's almost indescribable, that feeling. "

Imogen's face clouded as the memory soured on her. "When I surfaced, I found that the weather had changed and a storm had rolled in. The sky was black. I mean, *bible black*, Noah. There were these *huge* waves rolling in. Obviously, I started to panic. All of that calm, shattered in an instant. Jeffrey wasn't there. Neither was the boat. I couldn't see any sign of it, but I knew I couldn't have swum out that far."

"Christ, that must have been terrifying."

"It felt like a bad dream. I started to make my way towards the shore, but the waves were just sucking me further and further out to sea. At that point I *really* started to panic. I wasn't strong enough to get back. I was certain that I was going to drown. Alone. But then, after I'd gone under several times, a boat appeared out of nowhere. It was this old fishing boat, coming home for the day. Two positively *ancient* men with skin like leather. They plucked me out of the water within ten minutes. I was lucky. *Exceedingly* lucky. But I was still out of my mind with panic. I thought Jeffrey was under the water somewhere. I had a sudden horrifying notion of flying home without him and facing the rest of my life with that awful memory.

"But then when we got to shore, there he was. He'd surfaced before me and got back in the boat, sailed back to the harbour without me."

"I don't understand," I said.

"He'd *forgotten* me. Just for twenty minutes or so. Like a door had closed in his mind. Then the cloud lifted and he cottoned on to the situation again. He was about to go back out to search for me." Imogen exhaled, drained the last of the wine.

"Was that the first time that it had happened?"

"No, it had been happening before that. Little lapses in memory that he laughed about. Losing things, forgetting names, places, faces. He'd travelled down to London on business one time and forgotten which train to get home. Absolutely *no* idea of the station or the times. He'd finally called me, appalled at the lapse. But we didn't think that it might be dementia. Not then. He seemed far too young for us to think that."

We ate supper and then sat on the couch in the lounge while the snow fell lazily beyond the windows. Imogen kicked off her shoes and put her bare feet on my lap. I stared at her painted toenails longer than was necessary. We listened to some music, talked about my books. She told me about the text from her friend when she'd bumped into me in London, and the three-word description she'd sent back. We laughed a lot about the old days. She was quick to temper then. We tried to count how many times she'd thrown a drink in my face just for disagreeing about a book or a song. We discussed anything save for the one thing we should have been talking about.

And then finally, once the wine had loosened my tongue enough, I said: "Are we going to talk about that old rabbit of yours?"

For a moment, nothing. The light of the flames from the fire danced across Imogen's face. I was about to speak, but then she said, "Of course. There isn't long to wait now."

At midnight Imogen took my hand and pulled me away from the sofa. We were both a little tipsy, but there was a hard look to her eyes that changed the energy in the room. After seeing the rabbit last night, I had no idea what else to expect. I still had Florian's buttons in my pocket. I kept putting my hand in there to knead them through my fingers, to remind myself of the reality of what I'd seen.

We needed our coats and boots. After we'd pulled them on Imogen led me out to the conservatory again, then opened the door and we stepped out into the thick mounds of snow. After the warmth of the lounge the cold took my breath away. The snow was still falling, slow and hypnotic. The silence seemed vast; just that ambient hum of life happening elsewhere, miles away. I trudged after Imogen to the edge of the property. Beyond the perimeter the land fell away into the valley where Oliver's house squatted, old and alone. A huge landscape of unspoiled countryside, dry-stone walls, trees and houses, buried beneath a weeks' worth of snow. You could see for miles. The sky was pale, luminous, breathtaking.

"Look," Imogen said, "down there."

She was pointing down towards the town of Lethebury. I could make out the road that snaked through it, the black and white timber-framed structures along the high street, the Market House, raised on its sixteen pillars.

I didn't see it at first. When I did, it took a moment for me to comprehend.

It was after midnight but the town was teeming with life. It looked like the townspeople were awake and going about business usually reserved for the daytime. But then my brain engaged and I noticed how jerky their movements were. That cognitive dissonance of seeing something that the brain doesn't have enough information to adequately process. They weren't real. I couldn't see them with any real clarity, but every one of them was moving like marionettes on strings. They were missing frames. Somewhere Oliver was getting the 3/4 second exposure, and then moving them again, one tiny increment at a time until it gave the impression of life. They stumbled through the streets in quick, stiff wooden movements, repeating the process like automatons.

I'd gripped Imogen's arm unconsciously. "Christ," I said finally. "What the *fuck* is happening here, Imogen?"

"I don't know," she said.

"They aren't *real people*, are they?"

"No, I don't think so."

"How long has this been going on?"

"Six months? Maybe a little longer. I'm not entirely sure."

"This is Oliver's doing, isn't it?"

"I suppose it has to be. I've seen Florian too, some of the other animals." Imogen took my hand. We were both shaking, partially from the cold, but the sight of those things, moving spasmodically around the town was shocking. I wanted to look away, but I couldn't.

"The first time, I woke up to find Florian on my bed, staring at me," Imogen said. "This was a few weeks after Jeffrey had passed. I thought I was losing my mind. I knew it wasn't a dream. He stared at me for quite a long time, as if he was trying to place me. He *recognised* me, Noah. Even after all these years. He knew who I was, as if it all actually happened to us. After a while he clambered off the bed and disappeared behind the wardrobe.

"My first concern was my mind. The apple doesn't fall far from the tree, does it? My mother had suffered from bipolar disorder. I was worried that the strain of the past few years had taken some awful toll on me, might have brought out whatever was latent in me. Dad had gone missing and then there were years of watching Jeffrey's personality disappear until he was taken from me. But what do you say? It's not like I could visit my GP and tell him I was seeing this rabbit I spent a year of my childhood travelling with in an obscure little TV show."

"No," I said. "They'd lock you up and throw away the key."

"After a while it sort of sunk in that it wasn't some figment of my imagination. He brought friends with him, one night. Antoine, who was the rat in a fez, and Fizbatch, the monkey with cymbals. I woke up with them all staring at me. It felt like Florian had told them about me and they'd all come to decide if I was who they thought I was. I got up and sat on the edge of the bed beside them. They were a bit reticent at first, but eventually they came close enough for me to touch. After all these years they were a little worse for wear. At some point all the fear I was harbouring fell away and I felt this extraordinary *fondness* for them.

"It was just a little TV show that Dad made one year in his cowshed and the house. You know? And I was bloody *bored* most of the time. Sitting around until he asked me to *stand there* and *say this. Look surprised. Look scared.* But I suppose because I was young, when I saw the finished episodes, it almost felt as if I'd really gone on all of those adventures that Dad made up. Visiting all those children's homes. It was as if I had to *become* the girl he'd created in the show.

"I think seeing Florian and his friends there on my bed made me feel closer to Dad, even though he was long gone. There are so many things that I can't let go of. Not yet. But they helped."

"But if Oliver is responsible, then where is he?"

Imogen looked at me. "It's been almost twelve years, Noah," she said. "If he's still alive somewhere, why wouldn't he contact me?"

———

We'd drunk a lot of wine. At the end of the evening, we sat on the edge of Imogen's bed, a little bit flushed with alcohol, a little bit bewildered by what we'd seen. We were hesitant with our hands, unsure what to say, flustered by the extent of our feelings. I suppose it was too soon for both of us. Finally, she rested her head on my shoulder and we stared at nothing, slightly bemused. We were aware of each other in a way that recalled the past. The past made it easy to make another mistake.

"We don't have to do anything," she said finally.

"I know," I said. "You know I don't expect that."

"I think I'd forgotten about myself. All I cared about for so long was Jeffrey's well-being. It was my duty to love him until the bitter end."

"You can't reinvent the wheel overnight, Imogen," I said. "This will all take time."

"But that's just it, Noah. I'm 55. I don't *want* to waste any more time. Dad squandered *his* life, hiding away from his true nature. I don't want to end up like that. Everywhere I look I see Jeffrey. This place, it's filled with events and memories that I wouldn't want to let go of. But it feels like it's holding me in place now, stopping me moving forward."

"That will change," I said. "You've got plenty of good years in you yet. We both have."

"Abigail was wrong," she sighed in my ear after a moment. "Why would anyone leave you?" she said.

I laughed. "I know, right? I'm a real bloody catch."

"Noah," she said. "You're such a big comforting *bear* of a man."

"Thank you, I think."

"No, *really*. I remember seeing all those people waiting for you in the line for your autograph. I think that's what Dad wanted. To give them something and then just feel some of that love reflected back at him. You should be able to put something out into the world with the certainty that it *will* come back to you one day."

Imogen began to touch me. "I'd forgotten the comfort that you brought with you. With your hands," she said, touching my fingers. "Your face." She traced a finger against the stubble on my jaw. "Your belly." She placed her hand flat against my stomach and I laughed again. Softly. I was a little bit breathless at that moment. Finally, Imogen ran her hand up my ribcage and let it rest on my chest. "Your heart. Your big, big heart."

"But look at me," I said. "Beard. Grey. Sad."

She took my face in her hands. "Noah, I haven't seen sad in you since you got here."

So instead of making a mistake we lay on the bed in our clothes and waited for Florian to come to Imogen's room, but then Imogen fell asleep beside me, and the rabbit didn't show anyway. Sleep wouldn't come for me, so I went to check on Lily, then ventured downstairs and found myself sitting down with Oliver's journals, which he'd kept from the late sixties until his disappearance. They were intermittent, but there was an honesty to them that startled me. With the benefit of seeing a life in such an abridged form, it was easy to see what meant the most to him. And although it was clear how devoted he was to Jenny and Imogen, they seemed like quite minor characters in his life. Meeting Malcolm was a seismic event; it changed him incrementally into the man he hadn't realised he was.

I found myself longing to be in a room with Oliver, Malcolm, Julian and Kenneth. I think I could have happily sat talking to them all day long. I felt a profound ache in my soul that all of these men were long gone from the world.

I kept expecting Florian to make an appearance, leaving a trail of buttons in his wake, but that night he kept his distance.

From me, at least.

Part Three

The Man Who
Cast No Shadow

One

It was an unremarkable concrete structure with flaking green paint and a rusty metal hatch. All that could be seen of the Royal Observer Corps monitoring post from above ground was some weathered concrete and steel.

Between 1956 and 1965, the UK government ordered the construction of 1,563 monitoring posts at a distance of about 15 miles apart. 31 larger HQ and control centres were also built.

The ROC was very well organised. The volunteers met every week. They were trained for their duties, which were to be carried out during the launch of a nuclear attack and were to continue to operate as the missiles fell and exploded, and then for up to three weeks after an attack. Underground Observers would ready their instruments to monitor the destruction. There was a Bomb Power Indicator to measure the blast wave, and a meter to detect radiation levels. Both were connected to the world above by pipes, meaning Observers could obtain readings from the 'safety' of their bunker, but the Ground Zero Indicator, a pinhole camera set up to capture the location of the nuclear burst, was above ground; one unlucky Observer had the task of going outside, sixty seconds after the blast, to obtain the scorched photographic paper inside it. This would have been the first glimpse of a post-nuclear Britain and a visual assessment of the mushroom cloud.

Reports from these tiny bunkers would be communicated via secure phone lines to civil servants in subterranean regional outposts, who'd create a picture of the country, determining which areas were safe and which were annihilated and, using weather forecasts, where radiation was likely to descend. This would allow the authorities to see which transport routes were accessible in order to gain aid. It would also allow fallout warnings to be issued.

Oliver had practiced these nuclear war games with Nigel and Clive, the other two ROC volunteers in the bunker, which had been built into a hill in the same year as the Bay of Pigs invasion and the construction of the Berlin Wall began. Oliver volunteered at the age of eighteen. It was less than a mile away from his home. He made the walk every weekend without fail, save for the rare occasions he had been in London attending to business with Malcolm. They went through the various training exercises, learning how to properly use the equipment, simulate anticipated situations, and cope with life spent underground. There was an annual medical review. By the late eighties, it was just Oliver making the trek each weekend. But as the Cold War came to an end in 1991, the ROC was stood down. The vast majority of the posts were demolished, left to fall into disrepair, or vandalised and flooded with rainwater. About seventy of the sites were preserved by private individuals, trusts or heritage agencies.

Oliver continued to visit the bunker in the months after its closure. He kept it maintained and secure from vandals. He'd served 'down the hole' for thirty years. Although it could scarcely have been described as homely, Oliver treasured his days spent in the bunker. It calmed his mind. It always had. He'd put up with the witless banter that spewed from Nigel and Clive. After they'd gone, he'd remain down there, increasingly reluctant to return to the real world. Sometimes he imagined the bombs exploding, the country and its population reduced to ashes. Regardless of the realities of the situation (he was well aware he'd be without fresh water within six days, and be dead not long after that), he often entertained extended fantasies of being the last man standing in Britain, walking the irradiated heaths and highways, a final witness before the sickness began.

He'd read something the American actor John Barrymore had said: 'A man is not old until regrets take the place of his dreams'. The words dismayed Oliver. He'd been old for years if that was the case. After some conversations with the authorities, he'd bought the bunker for the sum of £1,000. He'd squirrelled away money here and there for some time. There had been a sizeable cheque from Freddie Steadman upon receipt of the three large puppets Oliver had created for his Public Information Films. It was a quick and painless acquisition for him. He'd been committed to this bunker for more than half of his life. He couldn't let it go.

He continued to trek across the fields and up the hill to his bunker. He would unlock the heavy metal hatch to reveal a narrow shaft and a steel ladder which descended 25 feet underground. The bunker was small, designed to accommodate only the three volunteers. It was cold and spartan. A tiny room with a chemical toilet and a larger room with a desk and a pair of bunk beds. The equipment remained, along with simulated maps of fallout from nuclear strikes on England. There was no heating, no natural light, just an electric generator with enough diesel in it to last six months.

He brought little treasures down here gradually: a crude crocheted replica of Florian that Imogen had made when she was nine and presented to him, a black and white photo of Jenny at the age of 16 on Morecambe beach, windswept and smiling at him as he took the picture, the delicate flower etching of a poppy that Julian had completed after Malcolm's death and posted to Oliver as a gift, another worn paperback copy of *Alice's Adventures in Wonderland* that still entertained him to this day. There was a photograph secreted within the pages of Malcolm and himself, taken when they were on holiday in the south of France; every time Oliver took it out to look at it, his pulse raced and warmth rushed through his veins. Then, gradually, he returned to normal and he would fall into a great well of sadness that he often thought might finish him off entirely. Eventually he would slip the picture back into the pages of the book and forget for a time quite how sad he was, how old and filled with regret.

———

One day in the summer of 1996, Jenny rang him up. "Oliver, I have something to tell you."

"Oh, yes?" He was somewhat distracted by a morning spent replacing a pipe beneath the kitchen sink. The upkeep on the house was beginning to become almost overwhelming, and his funds were running low. "What's that, then? Should I be sitting down?"

"Well, perhaps," Jenny said.

"Christ," he said. "You're not dying, are you?" He said it lightly, but the tone of her voice had initiated a brittle hysteria in him. People rarely rang with good news at his age. He sat on a kitchen chair, his palms suddenly slick.

"No, Oliver, I am not bloody well dying, you daft bugger."

"Well, what the devil is it then?"

"You remember Charles?" Jenny said. "You met him last Christmas."

"Oh, yes. *Charles.*" A sour little man who ran a haulage firm out of Hereford. He'd lost a lot of weight due to an illness of some kind, and subsequently all of his clothes positively *hung* off him. Why the silly little fool couldn't buy new ones was beyond him. Perhaps, Oliver mused, he was expecting to put all the weight back on. "Lovely chap," he offered.

"Yes, well. Charles offered to marry me over dinner at the *Sixpence and Stars* a week ago and I said, why not."

Oliver began to speak but his voice had deserted him momentarily.

"Oliver?"

After a moment he put the phone down and sat staring into space for half an hour. Then, remembering himself, he resumed his work on the sink.

A little later, Jenny arrived at the house. She still had a key so she let herself in. Oliver was still beneath the sink. When he glanced up, there she was, standing over him with her hands on her hips.

"*Jesus Christ*, woman!" he shouted. "At least make a sound when you come in. You could give a man bloody heart failure."

"Oliver," she said in a tone that he knew all too well, although he hadn't heard it in some years. "Get up off the floor and talk to me."

She was older now of course, but when he sat opposite her as he did most Sundays for dinner, he only saw the girl he'd met when they were both sixteen, both of them too young to know how many ways the world could wound them. Her bipolar was being treated with better medication now. She was focused and independent again, no longer subject to the whims and vicissitudes of poor mental health. She was the woman he'd known before Malcolm had come along. They'd finally divorced last year. It was a painless process. It didn't seem real. Just papers on the kitchen table that he'd had to sign. He still wore his wedding band. He didn't think he'd be able to get it off his finger anymore. He didn't like the way she looked at him now, in this moment. Pity. It rankled him.

"So, when's the joyous day?"

She looked at him, looked away. Her eyes were glassy with tears. She thumped the table softly and extended a hand to him. He took it, stared at it. The same slender hand that she'd placed on his brow when they were young, that she'd run across his ribs, that had pleasured him on occasion. "Oliver, don't make this difficult. Please. I've sat on this news for a week, because I knew you'd react like this."

"Sorry I'm so bloody predictable,"

She smiled. "You couldn't be predictable if you tried."

"What did Imogen say?"

Their daughter had just completed her post-graduate teacher training in Leeds, and intended to move back to Lethebury, where she'd been offered a post at the local comprehensive school. Imogen had become a fiery but pragmatic woman, so much more her mother than her father. She visited him when she came back for a weekend to stay with her mother. No more than an hour, both of them ending up feeling deeply uncomfortable, unable to broach what it was that had divided their family. After she had gone, Oliver would sit alone at this very table, imagining being able to explain what it was within him, and his reasons for this division. The words might flow across paper but they only ever stalled on his tongue.

"Imogen asked if I'd thought it through before I said yes."

"Have you?"

"Well, of course, Oliver. I'm not going to make such a huge decision at this point in my life without weighing up the pros and cons." She sighed. "But I'm not exactly a spring-chicken either. I accepted his proposal a couple of days ago."

"I'm happy for you."

"Oh, Oliver *do* give over."

"What have you told him about me?"

"Oh, nothing he hadn't already gathered from our conversations, Oliver. I'd already told him we were singing from different prayer books."

He had to laugh at that.

"I suppose that'll be an end to our Sunday dinners." Even as he said it, he was aware that it was a petty remark, designed only to make her feel guilty.

"I'll be moving to Hereford," Jenny said. "I'm sorry, Oliver."

Oliver presented a stiff smile to her, and relinquished her hand, although she was reluctant to let it go. "That's quite all right," he said. He rose. "Look, I really need to be getting on with this bloody sink if I'm going to be finished before teatime…"

Jenny studied him for a moment across the kitchen table. She glanced around then, at the room she'd lived in for all those years, as if saying goodbye to it finally.

Then she got up and left without another word.

———

In the winter of 1996, he heard from Freddie Steadman again. After Malcolm had died in 1984, Oliver had cleaned off the dust in the cowshed and constructed the characters Freddie had requested for the Public Information Films. He'd gone back to the slightly crude techniques he'd utilised when he'd made the characters for *Imogen and Florian*. For the wise old owl, Butterworth, the dim mole, Montgomery and the reckless sheep, Farley, Oliver had sourced some taxidermied animals from a man in Hereford, then fitted them with wires and replaced arms and legs using foam and felt, thread and glue. He was quite satisfied with the results. They seemed to him to confer the requisite character that Steadman had requested. By the time he was finished with them, Oliver was loathe to let them go. He'd gotten attached to them. A part of his creative mind, which had lain fallow for years, was sparked into life by the notion of these farmyard animals. He'd grown pig-headed in his dotage; a part of him was feeling the need to compete with what he thought would be inferior ideas. But he had to let them go. Steadman had made it clear that he didn't require anything more from Oliver.

From what he'd gathered the films had been transmitted widely around the regions, and had garnered quite the cult following. Steadman had sent Oliver tapes of the finished films, but he no longer owned a TV, let alone a video recorder. He set them aside and tried to forget about the whole affair. Steadman had paid him a reasonable enough fee for his services. He told himself it was sufficient.

But that wasn't the end of the matter. Steadman had spent the last twelve years trying to sell the concept of his farmyard characters expanded into a children's TV show. Finally, the BBC had seen the potential of the format. Steadman contacted Oliver and asked if he'd be interested in creating a couple more characters from his designs to expand the roster for the show. Oliver was initially reluctant, but the fee that Steadman had offered was too good to refuse. Twelve years after closing the door on his cowshed, he unlocked it to work on Steadman's sketches and create new characters. He constructed them and sent them off, refusing to get attached, to assign histories to these animals, to compose stories that no one wanted to hear.

The show was a huge commercial success in Britain and abroad. Even without a TV, Oliver couldn't escape it. It won multiple BAFTA awards throughout its run. Shortly after its debut, Butterworth, Montgomery and Farley dolls were available internationally, and were the top-selling toy in 1997. Costumes and educational video games featuring the characters followed, along with kids' meal tie-ins at fast-food restaurants. Although the programme was aimed at children between the ages of one and four, it generated a substantial cult following with university and college students.

Oliver saw the characters he'd created in his cowshed on magazine covers and in newspapers. There were profiles on Steadman, who appeared in the show as the farmer who had befriended the animals. Back in 1984, Oliver had requested that Steadman remove any mention of his involvement in exchange for an up-front payment. When Steadman had contacted him again in 1996, Oliver had insisted on the same stipulation. His name was not mentioned anywhere in relation to the programme.

Imogen had finally bought him a second-hand TV and video recorder when she'd arrived one evening to find him sitting alone in the dark. Neither she nor her mother knew about his involvement with the show. Steadman had sent more videotapes for him to watch. Finally, Oliver capitulated and sat down one evening to view them. They were better than he'd expected, but fell short of what he'd imagined when he'd built the characters in his cowshed. It stung him a little, the fame and adulation Freddie Steadman had achieved for the show, but he knew he had to relinquish it. He told himself success was not something he hankered after anymore.

Kenneth Bliss died in 2002. The cause of death was an overdose of barbiturates, but an inquest recorded an open verdict as it wasn't possible to establish whether his death was a suicide or an accident. They'd corresponded off and on since Malcolm's death. He'd been a lonely man in his final years, despite a network of friends and acquaintances built up from years in show business. But after Malcolm and Julian had died, he'd confided to feeling increasingly adrift. They had understood him better than most, accepted his various foibles and eccentricities. He hadn't worked in years, save for doing the rounds on the chat-show circuit. He often reminisced about the summer of 1976, when they'd filmed *PoppyHarp*, although Oliver only really recalled Bliss complaining bitterly about the intolerable heat and the shortcomings of the script.

Oliver had attended the funeral service at East Finchley and found himself glancing around, as if expecting Malcolm or Julian to arrive and whisk him away into the city for an unpredictable evening. But there was no one he recognised. Everything was the same, and different at the same time. He paid his respects and caught the train home. He was back before dark.

That evening Oliver braved the rain and made his way through the fields to the bunker. He unlocked the heavy metal hatch and clambered down the steel ladder. He lit some candles and sat on the edge of the bunk bed, picked up his copy of *Alice's Adventures in Wonderland*, and fished out the photograph of Malcolm. He seemed to feel his loss more keenly that night. He closed his eyes and filled his head with fond memories.

Malcolm, looking like a rare butterfly amongst the chaos of his cowshed. His beautiful pin-stripe suit already getting dusty from all those old toys and furniture and boxes and notebooks and parts. Smiling, placing a hand on Oliver's knee.

That delicious excitement as the train rolled into Paddington Station, Malcolm greeting him with open arms. At first it had only made Oliver uncomfortable, but as the years wore on, it felt like a sloughing off of the chains he inflicted on himself on a daily basis. Those days spent in London were an exercise in learning how to be himself after a lifetime of denial.

Malcolm's forehead against his during the power cut in Julian's studio, their hands entwined in the darkness. The sound of London traffic drifting in through the open windows of his flat in Pimlico. One door being opened that led to another door, and another, deeper into a house he didn't know the dimensions of.

And then they were kissing with their feet in the cool river, the heat of a seemingly endless summer on their skin, the Malverns spread out before them. There was only the holiday at Birdy's chateau after that, a memory spoiled by how it had all ended. And then there was the full-stop of an emaciated man in a hospital bed, beyond help. He wouldn't visit that memory. It was the end of everything, really. The death of possibility.

Oliver had fallen asleep on the bed. A peculiar noise woke him. The candles were guttering in the dishes, stealing away the last of the light they offered. There was a warping sound to the air around him. It trailed the last vestiges of a dream filled with the sweet memory of Malcolm and Julian and Kenneth, and those days, the edges smoothed away to reveal a perfection he longed for constantly. He rose from the bed, hearing the sound of a note moving from dissonance to consonance, to resolution. He remembered the sound.

The atmosphere changed in the room. And then his ears popped.

Oliver's hands were shaking as he fumbled in the dark for his matches. He could sense the presence of someone else in the small room, now palpably close. He dropped three matches before he could get one lit. He dropped that too when he saw the face, bobbing up out of the darkness opposite.

"Hello, Oliver," it said, the sound of the voice seeming to warp in and out of his ears.

Oliver sat, trembling on the bed for a moment before the other man took the matches from his hand and lit the candle.

Oliver gripped the bed, his heart racing, sending a name up from his belly, into his throat and onto his tongue. "PoppyHarp?" he said.

Two

Imogen and I rose early the next morning to visit Oliver's bunker. Lily was still asleep, so we left her in bed. We wouldn't be away too long.

The day was beautiful. If the snow hadn't been lying so thick on the ground, you'd have been forgiven for thinking it was a summer day. The sky was blue, the air cold and crisp. When we stepped outside, the stillness in the draws and drops of the land, the rounded hills and empty valleys seemed vast and wide. Nothing but the steady crunch of our boots as we tramped through the snow, across two fields and towards a hill that stood between Imogen's house and Oliver's old place. It took twenty minutes before we crested the hill, long overgrown with barren trees and brambles. From its peak we could see for miles. Although lines of tracks curved away across the fields, the only other signs of life were a couple of goldfinches with their unmistakable red masks. They burst from the trees above us, dancing across branches frilled with snow. They came to rest and stared down at us, their heads cocked, as if waiting for us to make the next move. We had to tug a knot of hawthorn branches aside and dust away the snow to reveal the rusted hatch. Imogen had a key for the padlock. When she wrenched the hatch open it revealed a narrow shaft leading down into pitch darkness. Imogen had brought a torch with her; I used the one on my phone. She swung her leg over onto the rungs of the steel ladder, gripped the torch in her teeth and descended into the dark. I followed her down.

The access shaft was narrower than I'd imagined. I had a surge of claustrophobia when I felt myself scuffing against the sides. I discovered that there was a shallow pool of water on the ground when I reached the bottom. The bunker was nothing more than a room and a poky cupboard which contained a chemical toilet. It smelled of earth and damp and at least ten years' worth of neglect. It was cramped and bitterly cold. There were polystyrene tiles on the walls and ceiling, many of which had peeled away and rotted. Two rusted iron bunk-beds, long stripped of their mattresses and bedding; a desk with several archaic looking meters and gauges.

"The notion of clambering down here, thinking that the nuclear bombs were about to land in England..." I said. "Christ, it doesn't bear thinking about."

"Dad liked to imagine it on a weekly basis," Imogen said. She'd found a candle and lit it. The glow flickered around the room, illuminating a cupboard and some tea making facilities, a couple of plastic chairs, some shelving with books and boxes of tea bags, a first aid kit, some tools and log books. "I found it all a bit morbid, to be honest," she said, sitting on the edge of one of the bunk beds.

"Did he bring you down here when you were a little girl?" I asked.

"A couple of times, although he considered it a breach of protocol. He kept telling me not to touch anything. He was the same with Nigel and Clive, the other volunteers. I think they quietly hated him. They stopped turning up eventually."

"Did you understand the purpose of it?"

"Sort of. I was dimly aware that Dad took it very, *very* seriously. Every weekend, running through procedures he knew like the back of his hand. Mum thought it was nonsense. But she thought that about most of his interests. She thought they were all grand follies. That was why when she remarried, it was to a pragmatic man with a steady business. A head on his shoulders. That sort of chap." She smiled. "I think once I was old enough to understand the reasons for this bunker, I found it terrifying. I would have terrible anxiety dreams about the bomb going off. Dad would be in his little bunker with Nigel and Clive, and me and Mum would be outside, hammering on the hatch while a mushroom cloud bloomed on the horizon."

"Do you think he would have taken you down into the bunker?" I asked. "If it had happened."

"Probably not. He loved us, but *rules were rules.*"

"It doesn't really strike me as providing much in the way of safety."

"Oh, I don't think it would have. Dad was realistic. I think I knew that they wouldn't survive a nuclear attack, no matter how well-prepared they were. They only had enough water to last six days, at any rate. And the ventilation system wasn't exactly state-of-the-art. The air coming down from the outside wasn't filtered."

I noticed a book on the shelves behind the door. *Alice's Adventures in Wonderland*. It looked almost identical to the one of Imogen's that he'd left behind for me at the children's home. "I read Oliver's journals while you were asleep," I said.

"Then you know him as well as I did."

I took the book down, riffled though the pages. I knew exactly what I was looking for. There were pictures of Jenny and Imogen on a cork board near the control panel, browning and curling with age. But this was the picture Oliver could never bring himself to show the world.

Malcolm was a little like I'd expected him to look, but at the same time, utterly different. A flinty gaze, softened somewhat by very gentle eyes that twinkled with mischief. A clearly fastidious nature, evidenced by his immaculate blond hair and a perfectly smooth, yet weak chin. A cravat, of all things, dated this photo to the seventies. He carried it as well as anyone could carry a cravat. Suddenly Oliver's story *came to life* for me.

"Have you seen this?" I said, offering the photo to Imogen.

"Oh, yes. Malcolm," she said. "Hidden away, as usual."

"It must have been difficult for Oliver," I offered. "Living with his homosexuality. It's a parochial little place, Lethebury."

"But that's the thing. He didn't *live* with it at all," Imogen said. She handed the photo back. She'd barely glanced at it. "Dad was never happy. Not really. None of his creative ventures worked out, and he couldn't accept who he was, not even when there was no reason to hide it. I would have respected him more if he'd just gone and lived, you know? Properly *lived* his life. But he just lingered on all those years. He was like a ghost."

There was something else behind the books that I had to tug away from the wall. It broke my heart a little to see it. It was the etching of a poppy that Julian had completed after Malcolm's death. He'd sent it to Oliver before he died. Once it would have been worth a small fortune. An original Julian Grayson etching. Now it was spoiled by a line of rainwater that had flowed down the wall and inside the frame. I stared at it for a moment. All of these things, a little bit ruined by Oliver's inability to go forward or back.

"Who was PoppyHarp?" I asked finally.

"It was the Play for Today, wasn't it?" Imogen said.

"No. The last thing in Oliver's journals in 2002," I said. "Oliver falls asleep in here and when he wakes up there's someone with him. He calls him PoppyHarp."

"I don't know," Imogen said. "I think he probably embroidered the truth here and there. That's what you writers do, isn't it?"

"Maybe," I said. But it seemed like such a curious note to end the journals on.

I was about to return the photograph of Malcolm to its rightful place in between the page of *Alice's Adventures in Wonderland* when something else slid from the back of the book. It almost landed in the water at my feet, but I caught it.

"What is it?" Imogen said.

"It's a letter." It was spread across a couple of pages in small handwriting. I couldn't read it in this light without my glasses.

"Bring it with you," Imogen said, rising from the bed. "We should be getting back before Lily wakes up."

———

Dear Oliver,

I trust that Julian will deliver this to you after I am gone. Don't worry; this is not one of those awful sentimental farewell letters. I cannot abide them! If you're reading this, then I'm dead and gone and that's the end of the matter. I lived a good life, Oliver. Probably too good for my own health, but that's neither here nor there.

I want to explain about PoppyHarp.

I think when we started writing our Play for Today, I told you a little about my childhood and where PoppyHarp came from. I wasn't being entirely truthful with you at the time, Oliver. Had I told you the unvarnished truth of things, you'd have thought me potty, I'm sure. PoppyHarp was, as I said, my only childhood friend. My imaginary friend. Why did I name him PoppyHarp? Well, my father was an RAF pilot and we followed him all over the world until he died in an air crash in Myanmar. His plane was recovered by the Burmese authorities in a two-acre field of opium poppies. And my mother played the harp as a young woman in a local orchestra. When she met my father she put it away in a spare room, forgot that she had ever played it. But then, after my dad passed, I would hear her playing it after I'd gone to bed. Her abandoned instrument. I think the sound of it lifted her spirits, away from the sadness of her life. The sound of it would lull me to sleep and suggest the threshold between this world and another. So PoppyHarp was a little piece of him and a little piece of her.

After Father died, Mother and I moved back to Rochdale and lived in a two-up, two-down in rather reduced circumstances. Mother worked in a factory that produced rubber. I spent much of my childhood alone. I just didn't fit in with the other lads at school. Rochdale wasn't a place for a fairy like me in the late 50's.

I remember the night he arrived quite clearly. I was twelve. I had just discovered the joy of masturbating. What a turning point in any young adolescent's life! When I came that very first time, I heard a sound in my head, like several notes unifying. Then my ears popped and there he was at the foot of the bed, staring at me with my limp little cock in my hand.

PoppyHarp.

He was there for me throughout my lonely adolescence. Of course, no one else could see him. I used to whisper when I was in bed, lying next to him. I was at an age when my mother would have been concerned about her boy still talking to his imaginary friend. He would walk with me to school in the mornings and then be there waiting for me at the gates, every afternoon. I wasn't entirely sure how real he was. I assumed perhaps that when I couldn't see him, he ceased to exist.

I always knew that I wasn't like the other lads at school. At that point, all they talked about was catching a glimpse of a girl's tits, or about finding pornographic magazines in the woods. I felt no such inclinations towards any of the girls at school. And none of them displayed any interest in me either. I think when I was a lad, I looked a bit furtive for them. And I couldn't do much about my teeth or my ears at that age. Luckily, I grew into myself by the time I hit my twenties.

PoppyHarp understood who I was, long before I did. He never pushed the matter, of course. He simply listened to my woes and offered advice as he saw fit. I never once wondered how he knew what he did, where all his wise words and bon mots came from. They certainly couldn't have come from me at that age!

We slept in the same bed for years. We'd cuddle, nothing more. But as time went on, I gradually became aware that I found him curiously attractive. Eventually my arousal at times was difficult to disguise. And so at the age of fifteen I lost my virginity to PoppyHarp. He was gentle, knew exactly what I needed. After that we had sex whenever and wherever we could, much like any teenagers in the first flush of amorous activity. I couldn't have asked for a better initiation. He made me content to be who I was.

But of course, these things cannot last forever.

At eighteen, I decided to move away from Rochdale and go to London to seek my fortune. Even then I intended to work at the BBC. PoppyHarp came with me, of course. I rented a little flat in Wood Lane near Shepherd's Bush. I worked my way up the ladder, starting out as an assistant to the Prop Store Manager. I fell in love with the place, I admit. I never really fell out of love with it. I made friends quickly there, and I discovered that life was far more bohemian in London than it was in Rochdale. The first time I brought a man back to my poky little flat, PoppyHarp excused himself. I felt awful, as if I was betraying him, but by this time, I was starting to question what I was doing with an imaginary friend. Of course, I'd realised that he wasn't imaginary, not really. He could simply make himself invisible to others as he wished. He also had the ability to perform what I consider minor miracles. Nothing grand. They were brittle little things, as delicate as gossamer. Houses of cards, easily toppled but while they stood, they were beautiful, fragile little things.

Eventually PoppyHarp was aware that his services were no longer required. One day when I returned home, he was gone. He'd left a note telling me that someone else would need him more than I, but should I ever require his presence again, I only had to imagine him and he would return.

And so we went our separate ways and I lived my life. A full life. A wonderful life in many ways. It was so much more special having loved you, Oliver. I've often wished that we could have had a more fulfilling relationship than we did, but do not feel that is in any way a slight. We had what we had and it was special.

PoppyHarp returned to me a few months ago when I was first hospitalised. I dreamed of him and then as I woke I heard those notes unifying and the pressure building in my ears. And then POP! There he was beside the bed, older, but essentially unchanged. I asked for one of his miracles and he did what he could. He gave me a couple of extra months. It was all he could offer me. I asked if he'd lived a good life. He told me it had been filled with lovers and friends and happiness. I sensed that he was simply being kind. Sometimes I think he has lived many lives, solely in service of others for as long as they need him, and then he moves on. Sometimes I wonder if he never really left me and simply lingered in the shadows of my life. I suspect now that my whole life – and yours – has been touched with his gentle enchantments. Either way I suspect it's a sad kind of existence for him.

He intends to visit me today. I shall ask for one final kindness. I'm sure he'll do what he can. It is my fondest wish that he comes to you one day, Oliver. I hope he'll make you happy in some way.
All of my love,
Malcolm.

———

After we returned from the bunker, we took Lily out for the day. We found ourselves hiking a short route from St. Mary's Church in Cleobury Mortimer and through the River Rea Valley. The snow-covered footpaths were hard to follow and I had to carry Lily on my shoulders for much of the way as we crossed over stiles and followed the path along the fast-flowing river. Mid-way we paused to appreciate the beautiful view over Cleobury, and then found a bench where we could sit and eat some sandwiches we'd made for lunch.

"This is where they came isn't it?" I said after a while. "Malcolm and Oliver, while they were making *PoppyHarp*."

Imogen pretended she hadn't heard. I reached across and placed a hand over hers. Lily glanced up into my face and then at Imogen's, aware that something peculiar and adult had passed between us that she could not decode. Imogen was staring at the river. "As close as I can guess," she said.

"It sounded like he was happy here that day." Oliver and Malcolm had trekked out here in that long hot summer of 1976 and sat on the bank, their feet in the river. *Like racing toward a cliff without wings, secure in the knowledge that he would know how to build them on the way down.*

She nodded. "Malcolm could have made him happy. Who knows? If Dad had gone to live in London with him, things might have been different. They might both still be alive. They could have been together all these years. Just *living*."

"It must have been difficult for Oliver. His background, this area."

"It's a shame he didn't have PoppyHarp earlier."

"Do you think what Malcolm wrote is true?"

She shrugged. "After seeing Florian come to my bedroom to stare at me, I'm starting to accept that there are 'more things in heaven and earth, Horatio.'"

"*I* saw Florian last night," Lily said while she bit into an apple segment. "And his friends, Antoine and Fizbatch."

"Did you?" I said, stroking her hair, glancing at Imogen. "While you were in bed?"

"I was waiting for them. I knew they'd come. Florian wanted me to go with them, through the door."

Those words made my heart flutter with anxiety. "What did you say, sweetheart?"

"I couldn't fit," Lily said. "I'm too *big*, Daddy. The door's too *small*."

It made me think of Alice, following the white rabbit, swallowing the potions to change her size. "What did they say, when they realised that you couldn't go with them?"

Lily shrugged. Glanced at me from the corner of her eye. "They went away." She screwed up her face. "I want to go with them, Daddy. I just want to see what it's like. *Just once.*"

"I understand, sweetheart, but we don't know where they come from. Who knows? It could be dangerous."

"Florian said he'd come back tonight. He said there was another path to where he came from, and I could go with him." Lily wouldn't look me in the eye anymore. She scratched at the picnic table with a fingernail. "But he said I mustn't tell you about it."

I scooped her up then and found myself clinging to her, staring at Imogen in disbelief. She took my hand and squeezed it and we lapsed into silence. All I could think was how I had to protect the last of my family. I couldn't lose my daughter. She was all I had left; she was all that had held me together this past year after Abigail had left us.

We packed up our things and went back to Lethebury.

Three

That night, against my better judgement, we put Lily to bed and waited for Florian and his friends to return. We didn't speak to Lily about it. As far as I could tell there was very little chance of my daughter coming to harm. I didn't actually think that there was any real malice in Florian's intentions, but that didn't mean he would be aware of the myriad dangers that could befall a young autistic child. He was, after all, make-believe, and I supposed, only blessed with the most basic of cognitive functions. Perhaps he harboured quiet intentions of making my daughter his new adventuring companion.

Imogen and I had discussed it for a couple of hours after returning from our hike and it seemed like the only real option if we were going to get to the bottom of things. Whatever was happening was labouring behind a veil that required something that we hadn't the tools or the perception to lift.

So we put Lily to bed, then after half an hour we slipped into the room where she slept and hid in the ensuite bathroom. I began to feel absurd, crouched in the darkness beside Imogen, peering through the gap in the slightly open door. Lily snored quietly, the tears rolling down her face. I'd hoped that the anticipation of Florian's arrival might act as a balm to her subconscious in some way. What eight-year-old wouldn't want a rabbit, a rat and a monkey to be their secret companions, promising night-time adventures while the adults slept? A part of me envied her that sense of wonder, but most of me was glad that she had something that brought some light into her eyes. I didn't wish to take it away from her.

We waited, and an hour or more passed. Sometimes we whispered to each other but mostly we sat, Imogen leaning against me, just like we did when we were young, stoned on her Persian rug in that flat in Worcester, listening to Nick Drake or The Incredible String Band. Then, just as I felt my legs would never straighten out ever again, I spotted the light from the hall spilling across the bedroom floor, and three shadows moved clumsily into view. I still didn't have a handle on it. A little fragment of my childhood that had sprung from its fixed moorings, from the weight and certainty of this lonely little part of the world and spun it off its axis, quietly and gently, leading to someplace else, to something that refused to have its wings pinned back and be defined.

Antoine and Fizbatch loitered by the door while Florian clambered up onto the bed in strange flickering movements that made me feel like I was blinking a lot. I could see the fine pink veins in his stiff little ears. Frames missing from the scene as he hesitated beside my daughter's face, his pinched muzzle twitching, his eyes softening beneath his tatty little top hat. I almost missed it from my position in the en-suite. With his white gloves he touched away the teardrops on Lily's face. They turned to shining pearls which he gathered up into a handkerchief. Before I could consider the ramifications of that gesture, he gently rested a paw on Lily's face, waking her immediately.

Lily sat up and smiled at the three of them. A smile of unabashed delight. It almost broke me to see it. But then all I felt was an extraordinary affection and gratitude for them, for what they represented in my life and Imogen's, and now my daughter's. I wanted to step out and lift them up then, offer them a place in my heart for the rest of my days. But I could feel Imogen with her hands on me, holding me in check. She'd seen what Florian had done too, gathered the enormity of the gesture. She pressed her face to mine.

Florian led Lily out of the room with Antoine and Fizbatch following them. Antoine's fez slipped from his head and he stopped, gathered it up, glanced back at us, *directly at us*, still hiding in the en-suite. He smiled and winked knowingly, then scampered away.

After a moment we emerged from the room and pursued them. It wasn't difficult. Florian was duty bound by his creator to leave a trail of buttons in his wake. He led us out of the house and into the freshly fallen snow. I'd left Lily's coat and wellington boots beside the door, so that she wouldn't forget to put them on. We followed the buttons and Lily's boot prints beside the tiny impressions which the animal's paws left in the snow. It was a clear night. A full moon, illuminating everything. I could hear Lily talking to them every now and then. Her voice carried across the lonely valley. But I couldn't hear Florian's response, even when it was quite clear that he was answering her questions. Perhaps I was too old to hear him.

Imogen and I tramped across the fields in pursuit of Lily and her companions until I realised where Florian was leading her. The hill where Oliver's bunker sat looked like a film set in the extraordinary way the moon illuminated everything. I kept catching glimpses of them in the distance. A sleepy eight-year-old, holding the paw of a shabby rabbit, while his friends stumbled behind them in jerky stop-motion. A line of buttons and footprints in the snow. As they clambered up the hill, it looked like an illustration from a treasured childhood book. I suppose that was only natural. We were about to follow a white rabbit down a hole in the ground.

"Look at you," Imogen said, while we held back at the foot of the hill.

"What do you mean?" I said, but I knew. My heart was beating fast. The cold was freezing my fingertips, my nose, my ears. As fearful as I was for my daughter's safety, I felt alive; a sense that these days in Lethebury with Imogen were bringing me back to life. I'd been clinging to the wreckage of my marriage with Abigail, waiting for resolution, hoping she'd swim my way again so I could allow her back in; and in doing so losing sight of the man I'd been before her, forgetting what I did to make sense of my life. It was *this*. This gentle madness of creation, of imagination, of allowing yourself to let go.

"I haven't seen *sad* once, Noah Bailey," Imogen said. "Not once."

Florian had his own set of keys to the bunker. He sorted through a mass of them on a huge rusted ring that he'd fished from his waistcoat pocket. I saw his eyes narrowing as he scrutinized them. When he found the right one, Fizbatch clapped his cymbals together in delight. The sound of it resounded around the valley. Florian gave the monkey a sour look and shook his head in disappointment. Fizbatch looked crestfallen until Lily reached across and stroked his head. His face lit up at the simple gesture of affection.

PoppyHarp

Florian lifted the hatch and clambered up over
its lip and down onto the ladder. Lily followed him
in, and I felt a sudden surge of parental anxiety now
that she was out of sight. I lurched up the hill in
pursuit of them, eager to catch sight of my daughter
again, desperate to know where the rabbit would lead
us next. By the time I reached the top of the hill I
was out of breath. Imogen caught up with me and
we stood, bent over, our hands on our knees, gasping
for breath. Antoine was the last one in, and he had
tugged the hatch back in place after him. I didn't wait
to see if they'd made it all the way down the ladder. I
flung the hatch back and peered in, but the moonlight
didn't offer sufficient illumination. I fumbled with my
phone and activated the torch, swept the beam down
into the gloom, hoping for a glimpse of my daughter's
face staring back up at me.

Nothing. Not a sign of any of them. I could feel my
heart seizing up in my chest, squeezing the last of my
breath out of me. "Lily!" I called out. "Daddy's here.
Shout if you can hear me."

I didn't wait for a reply and clambered into the
narrow hatch and squeezed myself down the ladder,
Imogen hurrying after me. I splashed down into the
inch or so of water underfoot and cast the beam of
light from my phone around the little cupboard that
contained the chemical toilet, and then the main room
itself. It picked out the maps on the wall, and the dials
and meters, the shelves, the rusted iron bunk-beds.
But Lily was gone.

"Noah," Imogen said as I fell to my knees in the
water and peered beneath the beds, the desk, behind
the chemical toilet. But I wouldn't listen to her. I could
barely breathe. I'd *allowed* this to happen.

"There *has* to be a door," I was frantic now. "Big enough for Lily to get through."

But I knew, even as I exhausted myself with my labours, that this was not the case.

"Noah," Imogen said finally, when there were no more places to look in this tiny little space. "*Sit* down," she said, with the gently scolding tone of a school teacher to a child. "*Please.*" I had a fleeting memory of Imogen sitting next to me in the children's home, asking me questions, showing me her book. Everything she ever was existed in her grey eyes.

I gave in, slumped down beside her, the springs complaining sharply in the silence. I could feel the water soaking into my boots, freezing my feet, the fluttering panic dissipating into something vast and wide and empty. I thought of Lily, perhaps already far away with Florian and his friends from the dollhouse, lost like Oliver in Elsewhere.

"What if we never find her?" I said, shivering in the gloom. "What if I just allowed her to get away from me?"

Imogen clasped my hand tightly. "This is where it begins," she said.

"What, are we supposed to fall asleep and hope PoppyHarp comes to lead us there?"

"I don't think we need him."

"I don't think we can just click our heels and hope magic shit happens, Imogen."

"If there's no door down here, how do you think Lily left?"

I considered the darkness for a moment, the solemn weight of the hill around us. I cast the light from my phone around the room, picked out Julian's ruined etching of the poppy, and then the battered copy of *Alice's Adventures in Wonderland* on the shelf, with Malcolm's photograph hidden within its pages. I felt like that. Hidden within pages of text that was my life.

I caught the ember of a revelation within that notion but it was slippery, gone again, lost in the shadows. "Take me Elsewhere," I said. "Isn't that how it works?"

"Turn off the light, dummy," Imogen said.

I didn't want to. It felt like abandoning my daughter entirely. She didn't like the dark. I wanted to reach into it to pluck her back from where they'd taken her. But I couldn't, so I switched off my phone and sat in the silence, allowing the darkness to encompass us. Imogen was still holding my hand.

We sat for some time down there in that hole in the ground. Holding onto each other. Gradually I let my anxiety go. I realised it was only holding me back. Then I let myself drift away too; the sense of who I was, the man I'd been, of what I felt had been expected of me in that part of my life with Abigail, that keen sense of failure and of the irresolution of it all. I let go of the uncertainty of Lily's autism; if I got her back, I would muddle through. I could only steer her through this uncertain part of her life with pure intentions and hope that it would be enough. I let that go. I let the writing go too. That would return to me. I had no doubt about it.

And all that was left was Imogen and the memories of our life, almost thirty years ago, and even further back than that. A succession of untainted memories. Time smoothing away the creases, all the little absurdities of youth that don't really mean much with half a lifetime dragging at your heels. I'd thought that we only pass this way once in a lifetime. And now here we were. Third time around.

I let that go too and I drifted up into the darkness, allowing my essence to go free.

"I think it's time," I heard Imogen say, from somewhere in the distance.

I followed her, my feet heavy in the cold water. My eyes had adjusted enough to see the iron rungs of the ladder. Imogen went first. Beyond her I could see the glimmer of the stars in the sky. It didn't look like anything had changed.

But everything had.

Four

I'd like to tell you that we emerged into another, better place. An Elsewhere dappled with the sunlight of half-recalled summers, birds in the trees and low-hanging fruit on the vine. Your own little plot of Eden for the twilight years of your life, where the days and nights were filled with wine and song and beautiful boys and girls, running through the trees. That very English urge for an unchanging Arcadian idyll.

I think perhaps there might have been aspects of that utopia here once, possibly in those first few years that Oliver spent building it with PoppyHarp's assistance. Given the tools of a raw untrammelled kind of magic, how could you not be seduced into making everything you'd ever wished for, flesh, blood and real?

In the years since we left that place behind, I've thought about it often. How could I not? It's in my nature to dream about impossible things and get them down on paper before the ink is dry in my mind's eye. You don't encounter much in this world that's touched or tainted by magic. You're aware of the astounding aspects of science and the natural world, but your years on Earth have denuded the raw wonder of those things: the spellbinding marvels of diving the Great Barrier Reef; or coming into land over Tokyo at night; or pausing to consider the journey of Voyager 1, forty years and 21 billion miles from the Earth; the daily miracle of the internet; consciousness; love...

But this was something else. I'd read magic referred to in its earliest descriptions as 'the art'. I think that this can be seen quite literally. That magic is art in whatever form you consider it, be that writing, music, painting. Art is the science of manipulating symbols, words or images to achieve a change in consciousness. To cast a spell is simply to spell, to manipulate words to render this change in consciousness. Oliver had been constructing this place in his mind ever since the first day he'd sat down with the idea of *The Adventures of Imogen and Florian* in his head. Casting that spell by writing it down, and dreaming it into being, making the animals with his own bare hands, filming them, editing them together into a story. And even if the thing that he had sent out into the world hadn't come back for him in the way he'd envisioned, it had arrived in the form of Malcolm, a little earthquake he'd been feeling for all the years of his life. I wondered, as Malcolm had, if PoppyHarp had been the architect of that, long before either of them had met. Perhaps there was a little of PoppyHarp in every aspect of both Malcolm's and Oliver's lives. In mine and Imogen's too.

This private universe was the map back to Oliver's forfeited past. But a map is not the reality of the world, but rather what the mapmaker and his map are telling us is real. It was Oliver's way back into the world and *away* from the world. His imagination, stretching the limits of PoppyHarp's skills of enchantment.

From the hill, the sky was the first thing to strike you. Once it must have been quite something to behold. A late-period Turner, perhaps: all shimmering, barely recognisable elements, lost in a maelstrom of hues and violent brush strokes. Sudden ecstatic washes of colour, like the sun coming out on a rainy day. But now, looking closely, the sky seemed too immediate and without dimension. It looked like old paint flaking off board to reveal the pale, ordinary world beneath. All along that journey into Oliver's Elsewhere was the sense of the world I knew, so close it was palpable, the walls so slender as to be almost diaphanous. It took a while to define what it was that contributed to the sense of artificiality to the surroundings. It came to me incrementally. There was no breeze riffling through the trees and no birds chirruping in the branches. The river was still. There were no signs of life anywhere.

Oliver hadn't needed his imagination for the house he'd built for himself in Elsewhere. It was, brick for brick, the grand old Victorian house, looming large in the valley, surrounded by the rolling hills and fields and woodland.

"I hadn't expected that," I said to Imogen.

"He lived in this house all of his life," she said. "It was all he knew. I suppose it was where he felt most safe."

It had pointed him from youth to every truth he'd told himself to believe in, even when circumstances had suggested otherwise. His parents' values constricting him like a narrow room without windows.

The house was as fragile as a spider web. It looked like a jigsaw with pieces of the picture missing. Beyond it the scenery was false, no more than a competently rendered image, washed in the colours of summer. Although everything in that world that Oliver had made with PoppyHarp was embroidered with as much detail as he could supply it with, it still carried the artificial quality of a set from a movie from the thirties or forties.

We didn't hesitate to enter. I had hoped to find Lily waiting here with Florian and his friends, but there was no sign of them outside. Sound carried with a strange echo while we travelled through Elsewhere, as if we were inside a large aircraft hangar. But I didn't hear my daughter's voice, so I kept moving at a furious pace, Imogen hurrying to keep up. I was acutely aware of her reticence about what we might find inside the house. But I simply wanted my child back, safe and sound. I took Imogen's hand and held it tightly. We would provide strength for each other, whatever we discovered in there.

The hallway beyond the front door was identical to the one we'd visited the other day. An open space with chequered tiles, and a staircase leading to a galleried landing. I could hear the steady sound of a ticking grandfather clock. The heartbeat of *The Adventures of Imogen and Florian*.

We would have moved faster but what was waiting for us downstairs kept derailing us.

Oliver's mother and father were in the drawing room. I felt Imogen clutch at me when we crossed the threshold and found them there. Grandparents whom she only recognised from photographs, both of them dead before she was even born.

"Christ," she said, unwilling to approach them. "Are they real?"

"I honestly don't know what's real and what's not anymore."

Their movements were so slow that it chilled my blood to look at them for too long. Clearly Oliver had constructed a scene here from his memories of childhood. His father in the armchair, clutching a stiff copy of the Times. His mother almost frozen in the act of ironing her husband's trousers. A little slice of domestic idyll, the like of which we take for granted as a child, when your parents seem immortal. I was seven when I lost my mother. I still dreamed of her sometimes, but her face is all but lost to me, save for a handful of photographs.

Once we were certain that they were almost immobile, Imogen and I approached, reached out and touched them. There were tiny hairline cracks in their faces, as if they were made of fine old porcelain. They'd slowed to a frame a minute, so that it was more like a *tableau vivant*, a frozen moment in time.

"Mum and Dad," I said. "Always there for you in the front room. Never getting old, never dying."

"This is just…" Words failed Imogen then.

"A little bit sad, and a little bit creepy," I offered.

"I suppose that sums up my dad's imagination fairly concisely," Imogen said. She pressed the back of a hand to her grandfather's face. "It's cold," she said. "It's not much of an illusion. You couldn't fool yourself for long with it."

The kitchen proved more disturbing for Imogen. Another scene, frozen in time. Another moment of domestic bliss that Oliver had decided to construct so that he could visit and revisit it when he desired their company. His wife Jenny, standing at the stove, stirring something long congealed that had probably once bubbled for effect, and Imogen at the age of seven or eight, seated at the kitchen table, intent on the day's homework. There was a patina of dust on them.

"Mum?" Imogen said. She hesitated at the kitchen door. I could tell she wanted to go to her mother and put her arms around her. But that would have made no sense. Instead, she ventured across the room and, after a moment of indecision, she simply rested her face against her mother's back and inhaled the fabric of her dress. Her eyes welled with tears. She fought so that they remained unshed. Jenny had suffered a stroke not long after remarrying. She recovered, but died a while later, in the winter of 2005. By that time, Oliver was already going missing for days, constructing this little bubble of a world. He'd missed her death, her funeral. Imogen had struggled to recover any kind of goodwill she'd harboured for him after that. He was away for months at a time, and no one noticed. It was only when he'd gone for good in 2009 that anyone noticed his absence.

"This would have been from around the time he started to work on *The Adventures of Imogen and Florian*, wouldn't it?" I said.

Imogen nodded. She looked reluctant to relinquish her mother, but eventually she stepped away. "I think so. We were happy enough then, I suppose. He was making his little show and Mum was showing the first signs of mania and depression. She was starting to realise that something was wrong in the marriage. I don't think Dad had really noticed the cracks, to be honest. He was too wrapped up in working on the show to really see it."

"But he must have loved you both to do this," I offered.

"*This* isn't how you show love."

"Maybe it was all he thought he had. The only way he could express it."

"That's just an excuse, Noah."

I nodded. I suppose it was. Making little worlds, preserved in aspic that you could visit without shame or guilt, was no justification for not being present in your life when it mattered. His only excuse was being unable to exist in the world he wanted and feeling burdened by the one he was left with.

But this was no way to live. A world where time has no real existence. A place where the past was never dead. I could only really feel pity for a man granted a wish and who'd decided to haunt his life for the rest of his days.

We kept moving. I was starting to worry that I wouldn't find my daughter here. But I couldn't allow myself to consider the alternatives just yet. The notion of losing her made my heart flutter so much my head spun.

We found what we took to be a replica of Malcolm Church's 1976 Pimlico flat in one of the larger rooms upstairs. There was a record on the gramophone, the needle caught on the run-out groove; an expensive leather couch built into something white and plastic that resembled an art installation; some huge, crazy painted graphics in primary colours on the wall around the fireplace, and a plush sheepskin rug laid out before it.

The words wouldn't form in my mouth. All of this was simply too odd and sad to frame in the mind. And I could see the effect this was having on Imogen. How could her fractured history with her father hope to be recovered by discovering this place, this shrine to a failed life? She stalled at the threshold to this room when she saw Malcolm, there on the couch, meticulously recreated by Oliver and PoppyHarp.

Simon Avery

Malcolm would always be the place where Imogen's tolerance ran out. Not because of Oliver's sexual proclivities, but because he was the man who'd come between Oliver and her mother. How could she ever hope to fully accept the man who'd taken her father away from her?

Here, Malcolm was the young and vital man that Oliver had first encountered in the seventies, immaculate in a black corduroy blazer with wide lapels. The top button of his shirt unbuttoned. His legs were crossed. One arm was flung out across the back of the couch, a tumbler of scotch in his hand. Those gentle eyes were his selling point. A perfect Paul Newman blue. He had an easy smile on his face, a little bit of a come-hither edge to it. Here was everything that Oliver had long kept in abeyance, out in the open finally. But a layer of dust had settled on him; a fine gossamer of cobweb ran from his nose to the tumbler.

I sat down beside him, touched his hand. Cold as porcelain. This close I could see all the fine hairline cracks in his face. Too much pressure from my hand and he'd crumble to dust, much like everything else in here. After a minute he blinked and I flinched, but that was the limit to his enchantment now. A clock winding down to stillness.

Imogen had gone to stand on the balcony. I'd realised that I could hear the ambient sound of London traffic out there; perhaps one of those curious tricks that the mind puts in place to convince you of the illusion. But when I joined her, I realised that the sound was a recording. The view was false too, nothing more than a passable matte painting of the faded elegance of St George's Square.

"What did Malcolm call them in his letter?" Imogen said. "PoppyHarp's bag of tricks – 'Brittle little things. Houses of cards that are easily toppled.'"

We found everything we were looking for in the attic. Of course we did. Where else did all the old things, lost things and forgotten things go?

Much of the roof was gone. It hadn't caved in or blown away, it was simply absent, as if the house was gradually erasing itself. I realised that the stars that we could see as we climbed the narrow staircase to the attic were *our* stars. Oliver's attempt at the fantastic puzzle of a tempestuous Turner sky had crumbled away to reveal the real world. It was just a hair's breadth away from this one, a simple step to one side. I assumed that there were other fissures elsewhere, as well as entry points that only Florian and his friends knew about. Every now and then they fell through the cracks; all of these stop-motion enchantments, creeping into Lethebury after darkness fell. From here you could see Oliver's attempt at the town in the distance, with its shadowy stop-motion people, giving the impression of life, happening elsewhere. These were the limits of Oliver's imagination and PoppyHarp's enchantments, like the constraints of a low-budget studio sit-com.

"*Daddy!*"

And then there was my daughter. Lily ran into my arms and a relief as pure and beautiful as anything I'd ever felt enveloped me. I clung to her for a moment.

Imogen embraced us both, stroked Lily's golden hair, letting out a long exhalation. "Oh, good God almighty, young lady, you gave us a scare," she said after a moment. We both laughed. By that time, I think we were both slightly hysterical. It seemed to be the only response to what we'd found there.

"What are you doing up here, sweetheart?" I asked, studying her face for any scrapes or bruises. But she was unharmed. Smiling. Thrillingly engaged.

"Florian and Antoine and Fizbatch brought me up here," she said, breathlessly. "This is where their Daddy is. But he doesn't talk to them anymore and it makes them sad."

They were seated in a semi-circle around Oliver. He had made his way up here, to find his seat in front of Imogen's dollhouse. There was a window here too that offered a view of the riverbank where he'd picnicked with Malcolm in that long, hot summer of 1976.

Imogen approached him first. He had been gone twelve years. All that time without resolution. Threads that refused to be tied. Stories that remained unfinished. I knew all about that. It prevents you from closing the book and moving on. There were all kinds of issues between them, but they were also father and daughter. And for a moment at least, it diminished all of those problems, all of that distance that had built up.

"Oh, Dad…" she began. She tried to push the tears back into her eyes, but they were already rolling down her face. "Look at you, up here. Alone." She touched his face to be sure he was real, and then kneeled on the floor and pressed her face into his neck. She sobbed quietly.

I let her sit like that for a while. Florian and his friends were staring at Oliver with the kind of devotion that you only see in dogs. Their enchantment showed no sign of fading. They all sat cross-legged in front of him, bewildered by these events. I felt that flush of love for them again. They were just lost animals now. I think in their limited capacity for thought they recognised Imogen. She had, after all, been Florian's travelling companion all those years ago. They had history together. Perhaps Florian couldn't understand how the little girl had gotten so old when he'd barely changed at all. They would work it out between them.

Oliver looked like he'd fallen asleep. But he'd been dead for some time, some months probably. I supposed that now he was gone, the world was decaying in his absence. Flaking away, like dandelion clocks in a breeze. One day soon, it would all crumble, with no trace of it. The funfair was being dismantled.

There was no sign of PoppyHarp. I investigated the other rooms and asked Lily if she had seen another man, although I had no way to describe him to her. She hadn't. Perhaps after the six years or so that it had taken for them to build this place, he was surplus to requirements again. I supposed that he had moved on, gone wherever he was needed. It was his vocation. It was what he'd done for years, decades, centuries perhaps. Or maybe he hadn't gone far at all.

Finding this place was its undoing. It was what made the clocks stop ticking. Our incursion began to hasten the decay that was already underway. Soon there was little left of the attic. I picked Oliver up and carried him away from there. Imogen took Lily, and Florian, Antoine and Fizbatch followed us. It took me some time to realise that their movements were no longer marred by that jerky quality that disturbed the eye and the brain. The frames were no longer missing. They were real now. Real enough.

Oliver didn't seem to weigh anything. He was just an old man, a bag of bones. But he was a father and he'd been loved. He'd created something and offered it to the world for everyone to see, but no one had really taken notice. Sometimes the wheel doesn't keep turning for us. Part of me understood why he'd seen no other option but to run away from his life and towards this abstraction of one. He'd been living forever in the wake of the past, doomed never to be able to reach it again. This was just the memory of a memory.

By the time we reached the hill and looked back, it was almost gone.

Epilogue

Something That's Always Been There

One

When Lily and I returned home a week or so later, Abigail was waiting for us.

At first, I didn't want to hear any of her excuses or apologies. I was angry. It was the wrong time for this to happen. It wasn't fair for her to turn up in our lives again after abandoning us. But I wouldn't turn her away from her daughter. I made her a bed and let her back in. She slept in the spare room, got up in the morning and prepared Lily's breakfast; subtly inveigled herself back into our routines. We talked a little bit about why she'd left us. I *wanted* to understand. The ice that had formed across the surface of our failed marriage gently thawed, a day at a time. She was Lily's mother, and I'd never once attempted to malign her in my daughter's presence, regardless of my feelings. Eventually Lily would grow up to form her own opinions.

I didn't ask her to leave. The home that we'd made for each other in Brighton had become alien to me without her in it. Filled with memories and events that had gone sour on me. Every room had a story to tell us and it only ever began with Abigail dancing through a doorway, or snoring in the tub, or playing the piano in the backroom. Gradually as the weeks went by the thaw continued. After a couple of months, she moved back into the bedroom and we began to move forward, hesitant of what the future held for us. Trust can take years to be rebuilt.

After six months we moved to Paris. We decided we needed a new start and Paris was where we'd honeymooned. We'd adored the place from afar for years.

Despite – or perhaps because of – everything that had happened, the new book that I'd promised my publishers after returning from Lethebury eluded me. Several times I sat down to write Oliver's story and stalled, unsure how to proceed with it. Although much of it was simply the story of a man who had cast no shadow, whose whole life story was one of stifled ambition and repressed emotion, there was still that subtle madness beneath it all that needed to be addressed in order for readers to see the whole picture.

Imogen had given me her blessing to write Oliver's story in any way I saw fit, but it constantly stymied me. There was the matter of my relationship with Imogen to address too. There had been that vague promise of a tentative long-distance relationship between us while she continued to work on selling the properties in Lethebury, and I returned to our home in Brighton. A little part of me had wanted to ask her to come and stay with us and let the chips fall where they may, but I suppose we were both too old to take that kind of risk with our lives, or to even float the idea between us. But then Abigail happened, and any kind of idea of a budding romance went out of the window. Imogen didn't judge me about my decisions with Abigail. Eventually our relationship diminished to a phone call, then to an email or a text here and there. We had to quietly let the possibility of something go, which caused me great regret. It also allowed me to conveniently abandon the idea of telling Oliver's story. It felt like it belonged to me less and less. The only thing that remained in my mind was the mystery of PoppyHarp. The constant stranger in all the rooms of that particular story.

Abigail and I had friends in Paris who had an apartment in Rue des Abesses that we could rent for a summer while we felt our way forward. The ancient hilltop neighbourhood of Montmartre, in Paris's 18th arrondissement, was once the playground for artists such as Renoir, Toulouse-Lautrec, Van Gogh and Degas, and a popular haunt for bohemians and creative types since the 19th century. Gentrification has meant many of the artists have moved out and the moneyed have moved in, and local authorities have chased away the pimps and prostitutes from Pigalle, but it still retains its allure. For the first few months I walked around in a curious daze as Paris gradually seduced me. We ate with old friends in restaurants, practised halting French on the locals, people-watched over breakfast in the cafes, made new friends with everyone, from the man who baked delicious pastries in the shop below our apartment, to Albert, the ageing drag-queen who lived upstairs from us. After six months, I felt settled here. Abigail was different now, contrite, I suppose. Aware that the division she'd caused in our family would be difficult to mend. We didn't really properly address what had happened between us, which in retrospect left us with a pretty brittle structure to hang our future on. But it was Lily I was thinking of. She was doing well in Paris. She was being home-schooled by a young man trained in educating children with autism. He was from Aldershot, but had ended up in Paris in much the same way as us. That gentle way of persuasion the city had with you. One day you woke up and it was four years later and your kid was speaking French more fluently that you.

Four years. And then Abigail left us again.

Two

I returned to our apartment one day to find her possessions – her clothes, her instruments, her records and books – all gone again. I found a note on the mantelpiece that read:

Dear Noah,

I'm sorry that I have done this to you and Lily again. I have no excuse to offer. I've realised that I'm simply not happy being in one place for too long. I love you both dearly but this life in Paris – as beautiful as it is – is simply something I cannot continue with. I'm returning to America.

I'm so sorry.

All my love,

Abigail x

She hadn't even said goodbye to Lily.

And so, we moved on without her. In those four years I'd written one book, a half-hearted novel that raked over old themes from *A Brief History of English Magic*. It sold well enough, but I kept on thinking about Oliver and Malcolm. And PoppyHarp. PoppyHarp especially. I couldn't let any of it go. And why? Because after Abigail left, some of that magic decided to return to us.

The night after Abigail ran away again, I was trying to settle Lily, who'd gone into the melt-down of all melt-downs. She was twelve, and this hadn't happened since the early days in Paris. Nothing would settle her, not her still-beloved colouring books, nor the stories she'd become accustomed to me telling her at bedtime. She wanted her absent mother. I'd started to suspect that Paris had been a grand folly, and now that Abigail was gone, I started wondering if I should book us flights back to England, even though we had nowhere to live there anymore.

I'd left Lily alone for a moment to make us something to eat. The histrionics had subsided, so I knew the worst of it was over. But after a few minutes in the kitchen, I realised that the bedroom had fallen silent, which unnerved me enough to drop what I was doing and rush back to Lily.

I found her sat cross-legged on the bed, smiling at me. The melt-down was over, because she had company. Somehow Florian, Antoine and Fizbatch had made their way across the channel to visit us. They'd followed us to Paris, travelling on a peculiar sliver of enchantment that seemed entirely theirs, long after PoppyHarp's magic had faded away. They'd simply been waiting for Abigail to leave. I found the doorway behind Lily's wardrobe the following day. I didn't understand it. I still don't.

I'd reluctantly allowed them to stay the night with my little girl, although I was concerned about indulging her in such an insular world that she would not be allowed to share with anyone other than me, and the impact it might have on her social skills later down the line. But in the subsequent weeks, they seemed strangely aware of the necessity to keep their nature secret, and made themselves scarce whenever we had company. Even if Lily spoke of them, people assumed they were a component of the secret world she would retreat to when the real one was too much for her.

Three

Another couple of years passed.

By the time Lily was 14, I noticed that Florian and his friends appeared less frequently. I'd enrolled my little girl in a school that specialised in English-speaking children with special educational needs. And although she continued to struggle with various situations, social cues and divergences from routine, she made a few good friends who came around to play music and eat dinner at our table.

One night I found Florian, Antoine and Fizbatch at the back of Lily's closet. At some point they'd returned to their original taxidermied state. The last vestige of their enchantment had run out with the gradual maturing of my daughter. She had left those childhood things behind. I'd felt a sharp stab of sadness at the sorry sight of them, abandoned with the shoes and the games and the books. I took them out, one by one, and stroked their fur, taken aback at the extent of my feelings for them. It felt like the unexpected final chapter of a book I wasn't ready to close yet. It was clear that I missed them more than Lily did. By the time we realise what it is we miss about childhood the most, our years there are long gone. That little sliver of enchantment that had begun with Oliver and Malcolm and PoppyHarp had fallen between the cracks of our lives and I began to quietly grieve for it.

I'd struggled to write anything of worth. Deadlines came and went. My agent stopped calling. I'd attempted to research PoppyHarp, but how do you even begin to unravel the mystery of something like that? There were so few clues. I didn't believe that an imaginary friend was all he was, although he was certainly that to Malcolm, and more. I gathered from his final letter to Oliver that he suspected that PoppyHarp must be more than human, and perhaps he'd lived a much longer life than most. I knew nothing of his appearance. Neither Malcolm nor Oliver had described him. So instead, I considered the matter of PoppyHarp's enchantments – *brittle little things, as delicate as gossamer.* Magic that would eventually blow away in the breeze. He seemed to come to people to offer them their heart's desires. Within reason. PoppyHarp couldn't change the world, but he could change *their* worlds.

This made me think of the genie in the bottle, which derived from the *jinn*, from Arabic and Islamic mythology and theology. Although the more I read, the clearer it was that there was little evidence surrounding the jinn that suggested them serving man. That particular idea of a genie offering wishes in exchange for freedom originated in the story, 'The Fisherman and the Jinni' in *One Thousand and One Nights.*

Perhaps PoppyHarp was part of that mythology. Or maybe he was something else entirely. I had no frame of reference. I scoured the internet for mentions of imaginary friends and genies and magical beings that served humanity. Very soon I realised the folly of my search for PoppyHarp. He was one of these things, or else none of them. Reluctantly I let it go. I floundered. I felt lost, aimless. The city's charms had lost their lustre now I was a single parent again. I had no idea how to move forward.

And then one day, six years after that winter in Lethebury, there was Imogen.

Four

It was summer in Paris. One of those eternal, golden days in late July. I'd been to lunch with a couple of friends from England. Afterwards I'd killed an hour in *Shakespeare and Co*, browsing the books. By the time I was making my way home, the last golden wisps of the sun were curling around the edges of the ancient architecture like flames taking hold of a treasured photograph. There was a sudden rain shower that chased all but the most determined Parisians and tourists indoors. No one would be dining on the terraces for a while.

And then, there she was, on the opposite side of the road, sheltering under an umbrella. I would have recognised her anywhere. That sudden jolt of time, unseating you momentarily, sending you back almost forty years and home again without the slightest click of the heels. I called her name, beginning to doubt myself. Small details flooded my senses. The light glimmering through the trees. The automobiles moving slowly on the Quai de Montebello. A million points of light on the Seine. The pungent smell of ozone in the air, prefacing a summer storm. Imogen glanced up and recognised me immediately. A huge, sudden smile on her face. Her hair was longer now, and completely grey, like mine. Those soft, grey eyes that knew me like no one else really knew me. She was wearing a red dress. I crossed the road, weaving through the traffic to get to her.

And my life began again.

That evening, while Albert our upstairs neighbour looked after Lily, Imogen and I went out to eat at a restaurant off the Rue de Bac. It didn't take long to find each other's rhythms again.

"The BFI screened the first two episodes of *The Adventures of Imogen and Florian* when they released the complete series on DVD," Imogen told me. "Later on, there was a screening of *PoppyHarp* too."

"I'm sorry I missed that," I said. "I got the invitation but it was too difficult to get back for one evening."

Imogen closed a hand over mine. "The place was absolutely packed. All of those people who seemed to suddenly know all about Dad and the show. I even had to sign some photographs of me as a child with Florian."

"Nostalgia for children's TV is big business these days," I said. "All those fifty-something's, hankering after their lost childhoods. Playing with Lego and pretending it's for their kids."

"I wondered how Dad would have reacted to that kind of thing," Imogen said. "He didn't like a fuss, but I think he would have been so delighted to finally be recognised for his abilities."

"I think that's all he wanted," I agreed. "To feel validated. That all that work wasn't in vain."

Imogen nodded. "Standing there I half-imagined Dad to turn up with Malcolm and Kenneth and Julian. I've read his journals a couple of times over the years. I think I've started to understand him better now. I can let all the rest of it go."

I told Imogen about our life here in Paris, about Abigail's return and departure, the progress that Lily had made over the years. We didn't address the matter of Abigail then. We simply talked about old times. She'd moved away from Lethebury to an apartment in London after selling the properties. She'd enjoyed life there, but she admitted to spells of loneliness.

"You can surround yourself with friends and colleagues, but when you close the door, that silence is just *deafening*," she said. "I didn't realise how difficult it was to move on from all those years with Jeffrey." She smiled. "I think he came with me. I suppose it was inevitable. Selling a house is one thing, but divesting yourself of twenty years of marriage is something else entirely. I'm worried he'll haunt every house I live in." She took my hand again. She kept doing it. I couldn't tell if it was to assure herself that I was real, or to hold onto me in case I bolted. I had no intention of doing that. I was overjoyed to see her. I hadn't realised how much I'd missed her. Despite my floundering career my time in Paris had been busy enough, but I felt a similar pang of emptiness in the evenings during these last two years. Once I'd closed the book on Lily's bedtime story (something that I knew would soon come to an end now she was almost 15, but I'd cling to it until the bitter end, damn it), the rooms in my apartment seemed vast and empty. I hadn't really accepted it until setting eyes on Imogen. Suddenly I craved her in my life again.

"Why are you here, Imogen?" I asked finally, when the dessert and the coffee was done with. Beyond the window, the city was lit up. All around us, the sound of life happening, right here, right now.

She smiled softly and folded her napkin, folded it again. "Because of you," she said.

It was exactly what I wanted to hear.

Five

Imogen's vacation became something more permanent. She rented out her London apartment and moved into mine. Lily adored her, and the feeling was mutual. Things seemed to fall into place. Imogen took a post teaching part-time in the school Lily was enrolled in. My little girl seemed to grow up quickly with another woman in the apartment. We felt the transformation over the subsequent months. A gradual sense of our lives shifting to make room for changed relationships, changed routines and perspectives. The gentle alchemy of old friends, old lovers becoming something else again. I couldn't put a name to it. These rooms had been lived in shadows without us recognising it. Now they were filled with light and life. At some point I stopped seeing our past when I looked at Imogen. I only saw our future.

Then one day when Lily and Imogen were at school, I found the buttons. I followed the trail and they led me to the bedroom. Florian was studying his top hat, blowing the dust off it, his nose twitching. Antoine and Fizbatch were more nervous, eager to please me. They ran around my legs and jumped up when I sat down on the bed next to Florian. I gave each of them some attention, feeling a surge of emotion, a gentle knot in my stomach, a tightness in my throat. For a while I couldn't speak. Florian took out a discoloured handkerchief and offered it to me with a stiff outstretched paw. Some tiny pearls tumbled out of it onto the bed. I thought of him taking away my daughter's tears six years ago.

"I've missed you," I said finally.

He just smiled at me.

And so our lives went for a while. Imogen and Lily and Florian, Antoine and Fizbatch, living like the strangest of families. The three animals would come and watch TV with us in the evening, or sit beside Lily while she did her homework. It didn't seem so odd to me. I was glad for a little of that old enchantment in our lives.

I thought it was me. After Imogen came back, I began to write again; about Oliver and Malcolm and PoppyHarp. And Imogen and Lily and myself. The story of our lives. I saw it clearly now from the correct angle, and I wanted to get it all down on paper while I could. I thought that by reviving it in my mind I had reignited that curious magic again.

But it wasn't that.

One day I came home and heard Imogen talking to someone in the kitchen. I thought perhaps it was Lily or the animals. But when I crossed the threshold, I realised that she was alone. She didn't have her phone with her either.

"Imogen," I said. "What's going on?"

I didn't know the look on her face. It unnerved me. She looked like a cornered animal, but I hadn't intended there to be any kind of note of accusation in my voice. Finally, she crossed the room and took my hands. She glanced behind her, but there was no one there. "It's time, I think," she said.

"Time for what?"

"Sit down, Noah."

I sat.

"My Dad left me all of the things he owned," she began. "The house and everything in it. All the memories and all the regrets. He left me something else too. *Someone* else."

I knew what was coming. I could feel a pressure in my head. My heart was beating very fast. I could hear notes quivering in the air.

"He came when I needed him. That was Dad's final request. After all the magic and everything else. He wanted me to be happy. I tried to do that, to put Jeffrey and all those years behind me enough to think about the future, but I couldn't make it work. I suppose I could have been content, living out my last twenty or thirty years like that. Going to shows and restaurants with friends, maybe the occasional little fling. But that wasn't what I wanted. I wanted to be delirious again, I wanted to live in rooms filled with laughter and creativity and love."

Imogen glanced behind her again and I could feel his naked gaze, even though I couldn't see him. "And so, he came. Just like that. And I asked him what there was to be done about the situation. But the enchantment had already begun. He'd been moving our lives around all this time, carrying us to London, to Paris, setting the stage as it were. Waiting until we were in the right place so that this could happen."

"The two of us meeting on the Quai de Montebello – that was manufactured by him?"

"As much as anything is, yes."

"Abigail coming and going. That was him too?"

"I think so. People need time to arrive at their proper destination," she said. "A little nudging here and there. There are all kinds of stops and diversions along the way."

"'Sometimes you get distracted and you look away from something that's always been there," I said. "And by the time you look away again, it's become a memory.'"

"Neither of us wanted that, did we?" Imogen said. "If we did, we never learned anything from Dad's life."

"So, what is he?" I said after a while. "A genie?"

"He's much more than that, Noah. He was created by God out of a smokeless fire. He roamed the Earth before Adam."

"He's an angel," I said. "*Our* guardian angel?"

"I suppose he is. He belongs to us now, for as long as we need him. That was what Dad wanted."

My final question sounded like the breath going out of me, because it did. "Can I see him?"

Imogen smiled. "Of course."

She turned and said his name.

The atmosphere changed in the room then. I heard the sound of a note moving from dissonance to consonance, to resolution. It was all a matter of seeing, and letting go.

And then my ears popped.

Many years ago, while driving through a little village called Shipston-on-Stour in the Cotswolds, I spotted a window display of faded old puppets and marionettes. I had to pull the car over and take some pictures. There was something very creepy about the setting and how faded everything seemed on that winter day, and it settled in my brain until it gradually gave birth to the story you have just read.

Several books aided in my research for *PoppyHarp*.

Seeing Things, a memoir by Oliver Postgate was essential - Postgate co-created *Bagpuss*, *The Clangers* and *Noggin the Nog*, all TV staples for kids growing up in the UK in the 70s, and he was who I modelled my Oliver on. It's a fascinating memoir for those of us of a certain age.

The Kenneth Williams Diaries by Russell Davies is a searingly honest, very funny, and extremely sad insight into the mind of one of the UK's most beloved actor/ entertainers. He was an extraordinarily larger than life figure who I've always remembered fondly from his heyday, and my Kenneth is hopefully as multifaceted in this novel. He was an absolute joy to write.

I found Christopher Simon Sykes' biography of David Hockney useful for elements of Julian's character and elements of the London culture during the 70s. David Hendy's *The BBC: A People's History* was also immensely insightful.

I'd like to thank Steve Shaw for publishing not just this novel, but also *Sorrowmouth* and *A Box Full of Darkness*. One of these days I'll make it to a convention and I'll owe you a beer or two!

Thanks to Andy Cox, a tireless supporter of my work since the early 90s; I'm hugely indebted to him.

Thanks also to Gary McMahon, Priya Sharma, Stephen Volk, Nicholas Royle, Julie C. Day, Andrew Hook, John Linwood Grant, Dave Brzeski and Ted E. Grau – all exceptional writers and incredibly kind folk who've helped me over the years. Thank you for your support.

Thanks to old friends who've been there for me over the years – Adrian Jones, Brian Baker, Joe Hegarty, Steve Lowe, Peter Brown, Alan Harper, Colin Clynes and Man-Dick Tam. We may not always be in touch but I still think about you all.

I will never forget the friendship of Joel Lane and Chris Monk, who we lost far too soon. I have such fond memories from our time spent together. Even now I still write with Joel in mind as my first reader.

My love to Mum and Gavin; and to my Dad – you will always remain in my thoughts.

To Daisy, who makes me smile every day, even when that seems like a very difficult thing. You're a very good girl.

And to Amanda, who listens to me read these books as I write them. You have the patience of a saint and I count myself extremely lucky to have met you. I love you very much.

For almost thirty years, Simon Avery's fiction has been published in a variety of magazines and anthologies, including *Black Static*, *Occult Detective Quarterly*, *Great British Horror 4: Dark and Stormy Nights* and *The Year's Best Dark Fantasy and Horror*. His novella *The Teardrop Method* was short-listed for the World Fantasy Award. A collection, *A Box Full of Darkness*, and a novella, *Sorrowmouth*, are also available from Black Shuck Books.

Milton Keynes UK
Ingram Content Group UK Ltd.
UKHW030148051224
452010UK00001B/46